Fractured Heart

THE REDEMPTION SERIES
BOOK ONE

KRYSTLE LEWALLEN

ISBN 13: 978-0615928333
ISBN 10: 0615928331

Second Edition
November 2013

Contact the Author
http://krystlelewallen.com/
https://www.facebook.com/krystlelewallenwrites
https://twitter.com/KrystleLewallen
krystlelewallenbooks@gmail.com

Photographer
Pam Bell Photography, Inc.

Cover Model
Makaela Hall

Cover Designed by Krystle Lewallen

Table of Contents

Dedication

For my grandma:
Life was better with you in it. But I know that you are at
peace as you rest easily in the arms of Jesus.

*"And God shall wipe away all tears from their eyes; and
there shall be no more death, neither sorrow, nor crying,
neither shall there be any more pain: for the former things
are passed away."*

Revelation 21:4

Epigraph

It is because we love them so much that we lay our heart in
their hands. So when they do not treat it delicately,
instead choosing to squeeze the life out of it, it becomes
fractured. A fractured heart, almost impossible to heal the
pain etched into that
tiny little organ.

But there is mercy...

Chapter One

I haven't been here before, this place that is as dark as a bottomless hole, where time and pain does not matter, but I welcome the escape. The emptiness that I feel inside has hollowed out my existence. Every action seems manufactured and every sound is wordless.

I don't know how long I have been lying here—minutes, hours, days? I can hear the soft chatter of people outside of my room. There are sounds of footsteps across the wooden floors, doors opening and closing, cars arriving and leaving. Familiar faces peek in through a crack in the door, but quickly, they close it.

Then, there is silence. No more cars or soft chatter. No one peeks in through the crack in the door, but I don't care. All of my needs have gone, and all of my ambitions—washed away. There is nothing but the burn in my chest when I think about her. And then the dark consumes me again.

~~~

My bedroom door opens, and I stare blankly as my aunt walks toward me. Her lips move, but I don't understand the words. She looks worried, sad. Kneeling in front of me, she places her elbows on my bed, steeples her hands together, and closes her eyes. Placing her forehead on her joined fingertips, there is complete silence.

Standing up, she looks at me and moves my hair away from my wet cheek. She says something else, but again, they are wordless sounds. And then, she turns and walks out of the room, closing the door behind her.

It grows dark, so I close my eyes in an attempt to sleep. When they open, the room is full of light again—unlike me.

There is a tray of food on my night stand, but I can't seem to move. Then, I think about her being gone, and hot tears start to roll down my cheeks, my pillow absorbing every drop. The pain returns, so I curl into a ball and sob quietly into my blanket. After a few hours of quietly sobbing, my tears desert me. Finding a speck on the wall, I stare at it, feeling numb inside.

I hear footsteps and the turn of the doorknob outside my room. But the door doesn't open, and the doorknob snaps back into its resting place. There is silence, a sigh, and then, the sound of footsteps fading away. I rise off my bed in search of the bathroom, but every move feels distant. Once I am finished, I lay back down in my bed staring at the food on my night stand. I don't feel like eating. My stomach growls in anticipation, but I am too gone to care about my body's basic needs beyond the involuntary. I could care less if I wasted away from hunger. It doesn't matter anymore. None of it matters. Life is meaningless without her in it.

My bedroom door opens again, but I don't need to look to see who it is. I know it's Faye. She sits in a chair in the corner of my room. Pulling out a book, she opens it and starts to read.

Faye has always been a great friend. She is always there when I need her, but it doesn't seem to matter right now. Nothing seems to matter. I should probably say something to her. Something like, "Hi." or "What are you doing?" or "Go away." That last one seems the most likely to come out of my mouth right now, but I can't even work up the energy to speak at all.

I fall asleep again, waking a little while later to the sound of Faye reading. She is reading from our favorite book, *Divergent*. We have read it together so many times, that I can repeat every line verbatim. Her attempt to comfort me with the familiarity is void.

I sit up feeling a little light headed. Faye stops reading

mid sentence and is frozen, as if she is afraid that one little movement from her will cause a relapse in my actions. I rise out of bed and repeat the mechanical-like movement of going to the bathroom. When I come out, she is lying on my bed with the book hovering above her face, staring intently at it.

Walking over to the bed, I pull the covers back and slip under them. After a few moments, I turn toward Faye. Her eyes lock with mine. A sudden burst of emotion explodes from me. "Why" is all I can manage to croak out before I start crying all over again, the force of it shaking my whole body.

Faye gathers me in her arms, and I bury my face in her shoulder. She strokes my hair and holds me tight—just like Grandma would do. It makes me miss her even more and adds fuel to the fire.

"We'll never know," Faye says quietly. "But there has to be a reason. There's always a reason," she whispers into my hair. "You have to go on."

What possible reason could there be for this much tragedy to strike one person's life, all before the age of eighteen? This wasn't the first tragedy that I have had to endure. My life was a never-ending mass of tragedies.

I lost my father to cancer when I was six. I watched him become pale and weak. His eyes became sunken and his skin loose and leathery. This man who had once been so strong, who used to run around and chase me in the backyard, couldn't even lift his arms to hug me. He died while I was at school, making it impossible for me to say goodbye.

My dad's death broke my mom. Choosing a life of utter freedom for herself, she disregarded the children that she had. Drugs and alcohol became a constant in her life. But, where did that leave me and my brother? She never gave us a thought. My brother and I spent many nights alone, having to feed ourselves. Collin was twelve at the time and didn't know how to do much cooking. We got by on a lot of microwavable food. When there was nothing left to eat, we would ask our neighbor for food. She was kind and would come over to cook for us at times. If it hadn't been for her, we probably would have starved.

After missing too much school, Child Services was called. When they came to investigate our condition, my mom was passed out on the couch. Empty liquor containers littered the coffee table, and a bottle of pills sat next to her cigarettes. They hauled her off to jail and took me and my brother to a temporary foster home where we lived for six months.

Our grandmother picked us up one day. I had never met her or any other family on my mom's side. My mom had closed herself off from them. Why? I didn't know.

All of our bags were packed and loaded into her tiny car. She had light brown skin and long black hair. She was short; just a little taller than Collin was. When she smiled, the crinkles around her eyes made her look pretty. She walked over to the steps we were sitting on, leaned down, and stuck her hand out.

Collin did not hesitate, he placed his hand in hers and shook it vigorously.

"Hi," she said, smiling widely. "I'm Susan, your grandmother." I could tell Collin took an instant liking to her. "Wow, that's some powerful handshake you got there. Do you play baseball?"

"No, but I like baseball." His voice rose just a little, and his eyes widened as the corners of his lips turned up.

"You're in luck. I know a little league coach who would love to have you on his team; especially with an arm like that." She looked over at me, but I didn't feel the instant connection like Collin obviously had. "Katy, that dress is gorgeous." I was wearing a pink and purple sundress. It was my best, and I wanted to look nice for her.

"Thank you," I said shyly.

Standing up, her gaze moved between Collin and I. "How would you guys like to come live with me?" she asked. I didn't think we had a choice, since she had already taken so much effort cramming all of our bags into that tiny car she had.

Collin stood quickly. "Really?" He was excited about the prospect of living with our new grandma. I wasn't sure, so I just sat there.

She smiles at him, and her eyes twinkle brightly as she looks over at me. "Katy, how about you? I have a dog at home named Pixie, and she loves kids. I am certain she would love to have some company, besides me."

I loved dogs. Although, we could never have one. Mom always said they were too much responsibility, and she was not going to add to her list of things that she was already responsible for. Dad always rallied for us, but Mom always won the arguments. It wasn't even a thought after Dad died.

I liked the idea of having a dog, more than I would admit, so I went with the most logical answer to her question.

"Well you did already pack the car," I reasoned. She smiled widely as I placed my hand in her outstretched one.

When we got into the car, she let me and Collin pick the music. We got to take turns, and I was happy for the first time in a long time. With Mom, I felt like we were never allowed to do anything—not even talk.

It didn't take long for me to grow attached to Grandma. She taught me so much and encouraged me to do good things with my life. Most of all, she loved me unconditionally. It seemed that's what was missing with Mom. It was the extra ingredient that made life much sweeter and more livable. Grandma was truly a breath of fresh air.

We were close and talked about everything—including boys. I watched as she would sing while cooking. She made us laugh, hugged us often, helped us with homework, and grounded us when we got in trouble. She very quickly became special to me. I was thankful God had put her in my life.

I loved her, and she loved us. But now, she was gone. I would never get to hear her sweet voice or feel her embrace again. I'd never get to watch as she cooked and sang.

My dad was gone, my mom was gone, and now my grandma was gone. Her passing was the worst of all, because she had raised and loved me.

It wasn't fair to have every person ripped out of my life. I found myself shouting at God 'Why'. What was the point of taking every person on this earth who loved me away? Now, I felt like there was no one. *I was alone,* was my last thought as pain glided over me.

I let myself slide back into that dark place just so the pain would stop. I cried for a while longer, then slipped into what I hoped was a deep sleep from which I would not wake.

Chapter Two

I do wake up. Faye is gone, and the sun is shining through the window pane, bouncing off the mirror above my dresser. Everything looks illuminated and too bright, so I squint until my eyes can adjust, realizing that someone had already been in to open my curtains.

I can hear the birds chirping their beautiful song outside, like a tiny symphony had taken up residence in the trees.

Trying to move my body was difficult. It was stiff from the inactivity, and my mouth felt like it had been stuffed with cotton and set on fire. There was a new tray on my nightstand with a bowl of oatmeal, strawberries, and a glass of water. Knowing exactly what my body needs, I sit up and reach for the water, wincing as my back makes several crunching noises on the way.

Water had never tasted so good. Beautiful, crisp, delicious water. It was perfect as it slid down my throat, cooling the fire. I sigh in relief after finishing off the whole glass. Setting it back on the tray, I notice an orange pill bottle. Curious, I pick it up to examine more closely—antidepressants.

Something I never thought I would have to take. My mother took antidepressants when my dad died. I remember her yelling at Collin 'Get my pills'

At twelve, he was curious so, of course, he handed them to her and asked, "What are these for?"

"Magic pills," she had said bitterly. We were such an inconvenience to her. "So I don't have to deal with everything." That's what she said, she didn't want to deal. I have to admit, that would be the easy way out—taking the pills and dulling the pain. But I was NOTHING like my mom, NOTHING!

The thought of needing something like this made me angry. I didn't want to be like her; a drunk who popped pills and didn't care for her kids. She didn't care if she lived or died, so why would she care about us?

Suddenly, anger rises in me and bubbles out over the surface. Throwing the bottle across the room in my fit of rage, it hits the wall, opens, and scatters all over the floor.

How dare my aunt try to medicate me! It's been two days since my grandma passed away. I am entitled to my grief. I start to wonder if my aunt had been the one to suggest medication to my mom when my dad died. And look how that turned out.

Furious, I get out of bed. My anger fuels me, making it possible to ignore the stiff joints and weakness. I want to tell my aunt exactly how I feel. Before I can get any further then the end of my nightstand; she comes bursting through the door.

"Katy! Are you okay? I heard a loud noise," she says worriedly, walking quickly over to me. She notices the open pills scattered on the floor and her brows furrow. "What happened? I thought you fell." I stand there, fist clenched, trying to put the most vicious look on my face.

"Pills, Aunt Rita. Really?" I say, behind tight lips and closed teeth. She looks shocked by my anger but quickly recovers. The anger feels strangely good. It's better than the pain.

Walking over to the pills that lie on the floor, she starts to scoop them up. "I thought they might help. You were scaring me." There is a hint of frustration in her tone. "You didn't want to come out of your room, didn't want to be bothered, wouldn't talk to anyone, and didn't want to eat." Scooping the last of the pills off the floor she stands, puts them back into the bottle, twists the top back on, and sets them on my desk.

"So you thought the answer was to give me a pill that

would make me forget her?" I knew that didn't make any sense. The pills wouldn't make me forget her, but that's what it felt like to me in this moment. She was trying to make me forget my grandma. I didn't want to forget. I wanted to remember her smile, her laugh, and her hug.

My aunt walks over to me, placing her hands on my shoulders. Quietly, she says, "I would never want you to forget her." I consider apologizing, but my anger outweighs my compassion at the moment. So, I settle for an angry comeback.

Leveling my eyes with hers, I say as cruel as I can, "You may want to forget her, but I never will. You can take those pills and swallow them yourself." Stomping off to the bathroom, I leave her with another shocked look on her face.

Closing the door, I lean up against it as weakness takes hold of me again. Feeling dizzy, I slide down the door and sit there, leaning my head back, closing my eyes. My bare legs sprawled out in front of me on the cold floor.

I know what I said to Aunt Rita was beyond cruel. She must have been in the same pain I was in, it was her mother who died, but she was like a mother to me too—had been for the past eleven years.

Hearing the door to my room close a few minutes later; I stand, my legs wobbly and my head spinning. Barely making my way back to my bed, I sit on the edge. Picking up the oatmeal, I take small, slow bites, not wanting to overdo it. There is nothing worse than shoveling food into your mouth just to have it come back up. I regret the thought immediately, because there is something worse. I just experienced it a couple of days ago.

After a few bites I can't eat anymore. So I set the bowl down and head to the shower. It feels good to be moving again after two days, but my body tells a different story as it aches with every move. After the shower, I get dressed in the most comfortable clothes I can find, then step over to my dresser.

Reaching into my jewelry box, I pull out the necklace Grandma gave me when I first came to live with her. It was a beautiful sapphire—heavy at the bottom, and peaking at the top to resemble a teardrop. Surrounding it was a thin silver band of diamonds, but the band didn't meet at the top. Instead, it opened up and away from the sapphire at its peak. The chain connected to the band of diamonds on each end.

The day Grandma gave it to me, she had just picked Collin and me up from school and took Collin to baseball practice. We sat in the car watching him play in the rain. She pulled out a blue box, opened it, and placed the necklace in my tiny hand.

At six, I hadn't appreciated the beauty, nor had I appreciated the gift as much as I do now. *But it was pretty and shiny,* I remember thinking. Those were the thoughts of a little girl who had never had something so beautiful before.

"I'll always catch your tears," she had said. "Until the good Lord decides that I no longer need to be the person to do that, Katy; I will always be there for you." I knew she was telling the truth, as my heart swelled that day and bloomed with so much love. It was the most precious thing I owned.

Putting it on, I hold the teardrop in my hand for several moments and close my eyes; willing that memory to go away, because the memories caused so much pain in the newness of my grief.

Thinking about what I will have to face when I leave my room is giving me no motivation to actually leave. Taking my time, I throw my sandy blonde hair into a messy ponytail. I push myself out of my room and peer down the hallway only to find the house empty.

I don't hear anyone either. All of the doors in the hallway are closed, so I turn left and make my way out to the living room. The room is empty. Walking over to the window that overlooks the front yard, I see that Aunt Rita's car is not parked in the driveway.

Taking a deep breath, I turn around. Grandma always kept a clean and orderly house. Everything was still in its place, just the way we left it on Tuesday morning as I hurried out the door to go to school and Grandma hurried out the door to visit the doctor. It was kind of ironic that she had to visit the doctor that morning. When my aunt came over that afternoon, she had found her lying on the kitchen floor. She had a stroke, one of many. I had no idea. She never wanted me to worry about anything, so she never told me these things. The doctor said she didn't feel much pain. Instead, the pain was left for us.

The bright yellow calla lilies still sat in a vase on the small table by the front door. They were her favorite. We would go to the market every Sunday and pick them up. They were beautiful, sitting there next to the dish with Grandma's keys in it. The keychain hung out of the bowl with my soccer picture on one side and Collin's baseball picture on the other. Next to that sat the Urn. My stomach twisted.

It's too much. I had to get out of here. Without thinking another thought, I grab my keys sitting next to Grandma's and jet out the door. I jump in my little blue beetle that is parked at the curb and take off. I am not really sure where I am going, so I just drive.

After a good thirty minutes, I end up at a little diner called Mel's. It seems like a good place to be alone. There aren't many cars in the parking lot, so I pull in for a cup of coffee.

Stepping into the diner, the smell of bacon assaults my senses, and my mouth starts to water. That's probably a good sign since I only had a few bites of oatmeal just over two hours ago—which is the only thing I have eaten in the past two days. Taking a seat in an empty booth, I try not to think about my grandma, or anything at all, but it's impossible not to think.

I'll be eighteen in three days, and my plan had been to attend college two states over with Faye. It was important to Grandma that I go to college and do something with my life. My mother never did, and my dad worked a factory job. It was hard work, but he did what he had to so that we had food and clothes.

Mom lived off the two hundred and fifty thousand dollar life insurance that Dad had left her, but it went quick. Spent mostly on booze and drugs, it was gone within three months. Two months later, we were taken from my mom and placed in the foster system.

Grandma always told me she wished she had gone to school to further her education. She wanted something for us to be proud of her for. She wanted something that her kids and grandkids could look back and say that what she had done, inspired us. She wanted to set a good example. But she was a good example on her own, even without that. There was so much I still needed to learn from her.

I didn't know what I would do with the rest of my life. I still want to go to college—I think. But everything else was so uncertain now. I don't even know what I want to major in. With tomorrow being the last day of high school, even though I hadn't been since Tuesday and would not be going back, it would seem more real that I was on my own. Especially with Grandma's absence.

Graduation was coming up on Saturday, and I had been invited to plenty of parties. There was no way I could go now—not that I want to go. I don't even want to be here, now. I opted out of the graduation party myself, because Grandma and I had discussed the possibility of me going to New York for the summer instead. She hadn't agreed to anything yet, and I'll never know what her decision had been. Not that it matters, I don't want to think about New York and strokes. I don't want to think about my uncertain future and the absence my heart feels. I just want to stop thinking all together.

Luckily, the waitress chose that moment to come over. She seems worn out in her beige, buttoned-up, collared shirt. Her black apron is tied around her waist with straws sticking out. She has her order pad and her pencil at the ready.

With a forced smile she asks, "What can I get for you, honey?" She is chewing a piece of gum loudly, and it's annoying. I have a hard time ordering with the constant smacking noise, and it makes me want to reach over and smack her silly.

"I'll have a bacon, egg, and cheese sandwich on toast, and a cup of coffee." She writes it down in her little book continuing to smack her lips. I don't think I have ever wanted to hurt someone more than right now. I quietly contemplate punching her in the mouth and walking out, but she walks away saying 'I'll be right back'.

I have never been a violent person, so the direction of my thoughts this morning has taken me by surprise. It seems I am taking my anger out on anyone who is in my path. I wrap my fingers tightly around the sapphire hanging around my neck, and breathe. When I was a kid, sure, I got into a few fights, but someone else always provoked them. Sitting here, thinking about knocking out the waitress for chewing her gum too loudly, is uncharacteristic for me. I have a suspicion my anger is fueled by grief.

I always try to do the right thing, be a good person and not hit waitresses, but then you get your legs swiped out from under you, not just once, but several times, and it makes you this angry person. How do you get past something as terrible as losing a loved one? I understand better now, than I ever did, what grief did to a person. When my dad died, I wasn't this heartbroken. But as you get older, you understand more and more, and it makes things harder.

Grandma used to always tell me 'Life's not always

sunshine, but if it was, what kind of lesson would that teach you? You have to take the rainy, cloudy days just like you take the sunny ones'.

I don't know what kind of lesson her death is supposed to teach me, but I was quickly realizing that life was made up of a bunch of heartbreaks and disappointments.

The waitress returns with my coffee and sandwich and sits it in front of me. Thankfully, she has lost the gum. I stir cream and sugar into my coffee and bring the cup up to my lips, but it's too hot to drink just yet, so I sit there with it poised and ready.

Putting too much cream and sugar into my coffee had always made Grandma make this funny face. Her nose would scrunch up, and her lips would purse. She would joke with me asking 'Would you like some coffee with that sugar and cream?'

She drank it black, sometimes putting a small teaspoon of sugar into it. I could never drink it that way; I tried to drown out the actual flavor of the coffee, because it tasted like dirt. But I liked to sit down in the mornings and have a cup with her in the sunroom or under the gazebo.

I miss her so much it hurt. Almost every memory was good, but they were also like a punch in the face, because that's all I had left of Grandma—just the memories. Right now, they seem like more of a plague than anything else.

"You look like your grandma," a smooth, deep voice says.

Startled by someone standing so close to me, and even more startled by his statement, I look up quickly. A guy with messy brown hair and bright blue eyes is standing at the end of my table. He's wearing a brown leather jacket and a small smile on his pretty face.

Recovering from the shock, I ask, "Excuse me, what did you say?"

He looks uncertain as he repeats his statement. "You look like you could use a friend." Oh, that's not what I heard. Apparently my mind is playing cruel tricks on me.

"Um, no. I'm fine." What I want to say is 'go away'.

"Well, you don't look fine."

I start to feel the anger claw its way back out. "What makes you say that?" I ask, a little annoyed. *Rightfully so*, I think.

"Let's see," he says, sliding into the booth across from me. "You have been sitting here, with that cup of coffee," he points to my cup, "held up like that for at least ten minutes." He leans forward and says quietly, "And you're getting your sandwich all wet."

Not understanding what he means, I look down at my sandwich. He's right—it's wet, soaked with my tears. Embarrassed, I set the cup down and use the back of my hands to wipe my wet cheeks dry. But, when I look up at him, he doesn't have a sad look on his face like I would expect. He just looks puzzled, like he wants to ask me questions. Only he doesn't. Instead, he just sits there waiting for me to talk.

"I have allergies and this...eye condition," I mumble, continuing to wipe my tears. I don't think he is buying it though. Not to mention, as far as excuses go, it wasn't very original.

That small smile tugs at his lips again as he offers me his hand. "I'm Caleb."

Reaching out to put my hand in his, I think twice. It's still damp from my tears. I hesitate, but before I can completely retract, he pulls my hand into his. He doesn't shake it. He simply squeezes it, and I feel something that I haven't felt in four days—energy. It's like a shock to my dull system. I don't understand it.

"I'm Katy," I finally respond. I wonder why this guy is even here? Then I realize that he has been watching me for at least ten minutes. "You're not some creepy guy who watches girls then stalks them, are you? Because I should warn you, I know Krav Maga."

He chuckles quietly, releases my hand, and sits back in the booth—getting comfortable. "No," he shakes his head, "But, I happen to be very efficient in Aikido. You, Katy, do not scare me," he says, grinning.

"I can be very scary," I insist. "I dressed as Britney Spears for Halloween once. Very scary," I say, horrified. He laughs deeply. I have spent the last two days mostly in silence or surrounded by people crying, upset, or just plain mad. So the laughing seems...foreign. It's contagious, so I smile, a smile, I do not feel.

Picking up my cup of coffee, I take a sip. But it's cold, so I set it back down. "So, Krav Maga, huh?" Caleb asks.

"Yup. I can kick some major posterior. Don't mess with me," I threaten seriously.

He puts his hands up in surrender. "Trust me, I won't. How did you get into that? It's a very intense martial art to learn."

The last thing I want to do is tell this stranger, this story. My grandma was the only reason I started Krav Maga a year ago. She had encouraged me to learn something that I could use to protect myself. She even gave me mace every year for my birthday stating that 'If you ever get attacked, this will disable your attacker so you can run'. Of course, I had to ask, "Then why have I been learning Krav Maga?"

She gave me this stern look and said, "You can never be too careful." Shoving the mace into my hands, she turned and walked into her bedroom, closing the door behind her.

Trying to avoid Caleb's question, I simply say, "Just wanted to. No particular reason why." But his searching eyes can see that there is more. He looks at me suspiciously but moves on.

He waves for the waitress who comes over looking irritated. "Can we get another cup of coffee, please? This one has gotten cold." Caleb hands the cup to the waitress. "I think we need some more cream and sugar as well, these are getting low too." He knows how I like my coffee?

"Certainly, anything else?" the waitress responds, disinterested. Caleb shakes his head and looks at me. The waitress looks my way expectantly.

"No, thank you." She nods once and walks away, returning a few seconds later with another cup of coffee, cream, and sugar. I fix it up how I like it and look back at Caleb. "You *are* a creepy stalker guy. How is it that you know what I like in my coffee?" I tease.

He taps under his right eye. "I pay attention. It's part of my job."

"Sure it is, I say skeptically. "And, do tell, what is it that you do?" I cross my arms over my chest and wait patiently for his answer.

"I'm in private security. Being attentive to my surroundings," he gives me a leveled look, "is part of my job. It's very important. I lose that, and," he slaps his hands together loudly making me jump out of my seat, "bam! Someone dies."

He is obviously very serious about his job, so I don't question it any further. Instead, I make a joke to lighten the mood.

"Who do you secure? The president." He just looks at me intently, but doesn't say anything. Maybe he does secure the president, and he's not supposed to tell me. Maybe I could get in trouble just for asking. Fear starts to creep up my back, and I feel my face heat. Caleb starts laughing; a deep rich sound that's oddly comforting. Then I realize that he is joking with me.

Immediately, I scoff at him. "That is so not funny. My grandma thinks that if you even say something negative about the president, someone will come and get you. Like big brother is always listening. I was seriously nervous," I explain. The thought of my grandma makes the sadness start to seep back in like a dark, murky cloud. I talk about her in the present tense, but she isn't presently here. She is gone from this world; her physical body is nothing but dust that can blow away in the wind.

Caleb must catch on to the sudden shift in my mood, no shocker there, because I feel his warm hand wrap around my shaky one. Looking up, he watches me closely.

"Did your grandmother pass away?" he asks, soothingly. I nod my head, but words don't seem to come out. "You were close to her," he says, seeming to understand. It's more of a statement—a fact, than a question. I don't want him to know this about me or see how broken I am. So I try to bury the feelings under the surface and say as little as possible.

"My grandmother raised me since I was six. Losing her was like losing my heart," I try to explain. There is no sadness in his expression like I thought I would see. There is something about him, something different.

"When did it happen?"

"Tuesday." I pull my hand out of his this time and pick up my cup of coffee. Taking a sip, I find that it is cold again. I sigh inwardly and put the cup back down.

"Do you want to know something about me?" He leans back.

"Please." Blowing out a breath, I am relieved that he is changing the subject to himself.

"When I was twelve, my mother was diagnosed with manic depressive disorder. She had been secretly cutting herself for years." I can feel my eyes widen at his candidness, but he just continues. "It started when she was a teenager, but she supposedly had quit when she met my dad." The look on his face is intense as he recalls the memory.

"The doctors said that she hadn't quit, but it had actually escalated over the years. My dad never knew anything about it; she seemed normal to him. She hid her depression very well, and my dad worked a lot. I noticed, sometimes, that she would lock herself in her room, only coming out when she had to. When I would listen at her door, just to make sure she was okay, I would hear her crying." Stopping for a moment, he clears his throat and looks me in the eyes.

"I told my dad about it, but he said that women just did that, they cried all the time, so that's what I believed. He was my dad, and I didn't question my dad. On a Friday night, my mom had dropped me off at a friend's house. I was going to spend the night and go to my baseball game with them in the morning. My parents were supposed to come, but half-way through the game, when neither of them were there, I started to get upset.

"After the game, I told my friend's parents that I wanted to go home. Instead, they took us for pizza and putt-putt. I was there until the following day when my dad came to get me. He looked like he hadn't slept in days. His face was drawn, and he had dark circles under his eyes. He sat me down on my friend's front porch, but didn't say anything. I asked why he looked so sad.

"He said that my mom had been very depressed, and then asked if I knew what that was. I told him yes. I was twelve; I thought I knew everything, of course. But, that was nothing. What he told me next, I let it define who I was for a very long time because I didn't understand. I still don't understand. My mother had hung herself. Her depression had won in the end. It was the single worst moment of my life." As he finishes, he leans in closer to me. "I will never understand why she did it or why things happen like this, but I accepted it. It took me a very long time, but I did."

I didn't know what to say about that, so I just said the only thing I could think of, "Caleb, I'm so sorry. That's horrible." It was the same thing that people had been saying to me for the past two days.

"Yes, it was," he agrees. "But it happened, and I moved on with my life. I realized that there are bigger plans in life for me. I just had to make the right decisions that would lead me in that direction, and embrace them."

I felt like I should tell him more about my life after that. He had shared a piece of himself with me—this almost stranger. But, I couldn't go there yet. The loss of my grandma was too fresh in my mind.

We stayed at the diner and talked for a couple of hours after that. He told me that he attended a local community college for a little while before he decided it wasn't for him. That was when he opened his own private security business.

I couldn't bring myself to tell him anything else personal about my current situation, but I did tell him about my quirky best friend Faye and my brother Collin. As I talked about them, understanding started to rise up in me. I wasn't alone. A little of what I was going through seemed to slip away. After a while, Caleb looks at his watch and sighs.

"I have to go. Not that I want to. It's been nice talking to you, Katy." He gives me that small smile and my insides flutter.

I didn't want him to go, or maybe I didn't want to go home. But, it was time. I felt better after our talk, and I knew I had to go back at some point.

"You really should stop sulking. It doesn't sit right with you," he teases. Pushing up from the booth, he reaches into his jacket pocket and pulls out a card, handing it to me. "Let me give you my card. I teach a women's self-defense class on Saturdays. You should stop by sometime."

Taking the card, I smile, "Have you forgotten?" I point to myself. "Krav Maga." I don't tell him how awful my teacher was and how little I actually know.

"Yes, well, this is completely different." He smiles crookedly at me. "I think you would like it." Throwing a twenty on the table, he waves once, turns on his heal, and heads out the door. I get up, ready to face the house that I lived in with my grandma that holds all of those memories that I thought would only cause me pain. But maybe, I could use those same memories as a tool to keep going.

I'm ready to apologize to Aunt Rita for acting the way I

have, and I'm ready to act like the adult that I will become in three days. Heading out to my car, I feel a weight lifted off of me. The ache of Grandma's absence will always be there, but I will try to live in her memories and not in her death.

With time, my heartbreak will cease to exist leaving in its place only the good memories.

Chapter Three

When I return home, I find Aunt Rita in the study, sitting at Grandma's desk with a drawer open. She has a stack of papers in her lap and three more stacks sitting in front of her on the desk. Looking deep in thought, she studies a paper in the stack on her lap. Deciding its fate, she places it in the middle pile.

"Aunt Rita," I say, my voice wavering. She glances up at me and then back down at the papers, continuing her perusal.

"Yes, Katy. What is it?" Walking in, I sit in the chair next to the desk. I remember coming in here and watching Grandma type something out on her old typewriter. I would laugh, because no one used those anymore.

She didn't want to get rid of it, though, and she always said, "We do not always have to do what everyone else is doing. Sometimes we just need to be our own unique selves. Besides, there is nothing wrong with my typewriter." Being in here again was strange. I had never seen anyone sit at that desk, but Grandma.

Aunt Rita continues to push through the stack of papers. I take a deep breath.

"I'm so sorry for the way I treated you this morning. You didn't deserve that." She stops fingering through the papers and looks up at me, expectantly. "And I am especially sorry for scaring you. I was being selfish and inconsiderate." She studies me with a hard look on her face. I could see the moment she had forgiveness in her eyes. Her look turned from hard stone to a soft sign of resignation.

"Katy, you're going through a lot right now. Although, it does not give you the right to act the way you did, I accept your apology." Sitting the stack of papers on the desk, she rolls her chair in front of mine. "Losing my mother has been extremely difficult. She was also my best friend. She may not have been taking care of me anymore, but I still loved her very much. She was a big part of my life."

A tear slips down my cheek uninvited, and Aunt Rita reaches forward and wraps her arms around my shoulders. I can feel her shaking from her quiet sobs.

"She's gone, Aunt Rita. She's really gone. What are we going to do without her? I don't know what to do," I plead, letting the tears flow freely now. I throw my arms around her and cry into her shoulder. Making soothing noises, she tries to calm me down, but it only makes me cry harder, until I am gasping for breaths. This is the second time someone has tried to sooth me like a child. I really need to grow up.

"Katy, we have to find a way to accept what has happened, and adjust to life accordingly. My mother was a strong lady—emotionally and physically. She would not want you to be crying like this. I know she loved you and Collin like you were her own children," Aunt Rita reminds me. Pulling away, she grabs a tissue from the pocket in her jeans and begins wiping her tears away. Opening the top drawer in Grandma's desk, she pulls out an envelope and hands it to me. "I found this yesterday. I didn't open it because it was addressed to you. It's a birthday card."

Taking the card from her, I read the front. Scrawled in Grandma's handwriting is my name. Tears are still sliding down my cheeks, landing in puddles on the envelope. I hug Aunt Rita one last time as she tells me that the lawyer will be here to tomorrow.

Not wanting to go back to my bedroom, I walk out back toward the garden, taking the envelope with me. This was always my favorite place to be. I would sit under the gazebo with the smell of lavender and jasmine drifting on the breeze. The wind wrapping around me like a blanket, whipping my hair away from my face. I spent most of my time here, reading or doing homework. Grandma would sit out here by herself a lot, basking in its beauty. Sometimes, I would join her. Laying my head in her lap, she would soothingly brush my hair away from my face and we would talk. Usually, I fell asleep because of the peace that it brought me. Would I ever know peace like that again?

When I first came to live with her, this garden was a blip of an existence with only a red rose bush on each side of the entrance to the gazebo. Collin would always brush up against it and scratch his arm to shreds. I fell into it a couple of times, just from being clumsy. One day, when I came out to play under the gazebo with my Barbie dolls, I noticed the rose bushes were gone. There was a big hole in the dirt. I had always admired those roses that were so beautiful, but could hurt so badly.

Grandma came out to bring me a snack and a glass of water. Noticing my puzzled look she leaned down and whispered to me, "I took them out."

I looked at her and asked the one thing that most six-year-olds ask, "Why?"

"Because dear," she walked into the gazebo and set the plate and glass down, "some flowers may look pretty, but that doesn't mean they are worth keeping. There are four other senses—you cannot simply rely on looks alone when it comes to gardening," she explained.

I crawled up on the bench, sitting my Barbie beside me, like she was going to eat with us. Grandma handed me the glass of water and sat down next to me.

"I think we should create a new garden," she sang, putting her arm across my shoulders and pulling me in tight to her.

That sounded magical to my six-year-old ears. "Can we put a waterfall in?" I asked, my voice rising high with excitement.

"Absolutely! We can pick out the flowers together.

Will you help me?" I nodded my head, yes, and plastered a broad smile across my face.

She did most of the planting when I was little. I would hand her tools and plants and water, everything under her supervision. She started to show me how to plant flowers, shrubs, and bushes, and how to take care of them. By the time I was twelve, I was able to work in the garden alone and knew more than any twelve-year-old did about gardening; as well as most adults. Our garden was a massive beauty with the most vibrant colors.

Red geraniums ran the length of the walkway from the backdoor to the gazebo entrance. Purple lavender surrounded the garden that circled the gazebo. And the sweet floral scent of jasmine drifted from the pedestals at the entrance. Sunflowers grew wildly, curving in a half circle around the gazebo. Tall Emerald Green Arborvitaes stood behind them. And the waterfall—it sat just to the left filled with grey and marble colored stones. In complete silence you could hear the water running over the stones, dropping into a pool of itself in finality. Red, yellow, purple—so many different flowers were surrounding it. My favorite was the Chantilly lace flower. It was simply beautiful the way it resembled actual lace.

Oddly, we never planted yellow calla lilies. We did plant every other flower I could think of. Then it hit me—the garden was for me. My selfless grandma, she planted this garden, labored in it for hours—for me. It was something that we could work on together. I would have to work on it by myself now.

Sitting under the gazebo, I pull my legs up to my chin while holding the birthday card in front of me. Taking one deep breath, I stick my finger under the seal and slide to break it.

The cover of the card only bares two words 'Bon Voyage'. *I know exactly what this card contains.* As I open it, the plane ticket to New York falls into my lap, along with a check for enough money to last on my trip. I inhale sharply. She already rented a flat for me, which I knew cost too much money.

We had looked at this particular flat, and it was stunning. It was small, but every flat that was within our price range was small—that was just New York. This one had been a few hundred dollars over our price range. She rented it for two months. I was supposed to leave in three weeks, but I didn't know if I wanted to go anymore. It had always been a dream of mine. With everything going on, it just seemed wrong to go.

On the inside of the card it says 'Adventure Awaits' followed by a note from her that reads:

Katy,

I am so very proud of the mature adult you have become. You deserve this trip and many, many more. There is so much for you to see in life, so much to be lived. Go enjoy it!

Love,

Grandma

Warm hands on my shoulders pull me away from the emotion the card brings out of me, just in time. When I turn, Collin is standing there looking as if he hasn't slept in weeks. His dark blonde hair is in disarray like he was running his hands through it obsessively. I jump up and throw my arms around him. I can't help the feeling of happiness at seeing my brother. Guilt washes over me for feeling happy so soon after Grandma passed, and my smile fades quickly.

With him living in California, we didn't get to see much of each other. He was up for Christmas, but that was six months ago. This sighting is precious, and although it is under the worst of circumstances, I am happy to see him and glad he is home.

We stand there for several moments, hugging each other. I can hear his quiet cries that break my heart. I have never seen or heard him cry. He has been through so much already that he developed a tough exterior and interior. Very little could get him all choked up. I am not surprised that losing our grandma would do just that.

When our cries quiet down and we take back control, he whispers, "I'm so sorry, Katy. I wish I could have been here sooner."

Pulling away, I look him in the eyes. "It's not your fault your flight was canceled and rescheduled. I'm just glad you got here in one piece."

Sitting down on the bench, he takes the card from my grasp. A ghost of a smile tugs at his lips but fades just as quickly as it arrives.

"Grandma," he says, shaking his head. "It's always about doing for others with her." He looks at me with red, sleep-deprived eyes. "New York, Katy? That's huge. I actually tried to talk Grandma out of it. It's too dangerous there."

"I already discussed this with Grandma. Apparently, she does not have the same thought process as you." I cross my arms over my chest defiantly.

"Why do you even want to go to New York? Out of all the places you could have chosen, why there?"

"You wouldn't understand. It doesn't matter, I'm not going." That seems to satisfy him, so he sets the card on the table.

"I heard you were out of it for a couple of days?" Oh no, he must have talked to Aunt Rita.

"Maybe," I say stubbornly.

We sit there silently for a few minutes, not needing words, letting the smell of jasmine and lavender wrap around us, and listen to the wind whistle.

"Grandma's gone, Katy," he says, breaking the silence.

I look down trying to stop the tears from coming. I have cried so much, and I need to be strong. It helps, but I end up with little puddles sitting atop my bottom lids instead. Glancing up, I see that Collin is looking down at me. He places his arm across my shoulder and pulls me close. Leaning my head on his shoulder, we sit there until night falls; and say nothing at all. Aunt Rita comes out to check on us but doesn't say anything.

We eventually go in for the night. I pull out a sleeping bag and lay it out on Collin's floor. His bedroom is the same as it was when he left for California. I don't want to sleep in my room tonight, or possibly ever again, because I'm afraid that I will sink back into that depression from the last two days. Soon, my thoughts are incoherent, as I drift off to sleep.

I wake several times throughout the night; thoughts of Grandma's absence, and my grief, wake me. I try to muffle my cries by putting my arm over my mouth or burying my face in my pillow, but Collin reaches down and places his hand on my arm. It is reassurance that he is there, and he feels the same way. I know it will take time to let memories of Grandma be for good and not for grief.

Sleep eventually comes, but it seems more like seconds than hours since I drifted off. Blinking my eyes open, the sunlight is practically blinding me. Aunt Rita has a habit of opening the curtains so that we have to wake up at the crack of dawn.

Collin, still fast asleep, is lying with the comforter pulled up to his chin, mouth ajar. When he was still living here, Grandma used to joke that anything could crawl in if you slept with your mouth open. Of course, I couldn't resist proving a point.

When he fell asleep in the living room, I would put cookies in his mouth. As soon as the cookie would touch his lips, he would wake up and chase me around the house. I would giggle as he shouted, "Paybacks Katy. You have to fall asleep at some point."

I love my big brother. We are closer than any other siblings I knew, partly because of our six-year age difference, also because he was so mature for his age. But now, as he slept, he looked young and peaceful. I knew once he woke, that look would turn worrisome and strained.

Careful not to wake him, I slide out of my sleeping bag and tiptoe out of the door. Walking down the hallway, making my way to the living room, I glance out the front window.

Aunt Rita's car is gone. Does she always get up this early, and where could she have gone? There can only be so many places open at seven in the morning. I had not asked too many questions about anything, so I didn't know if she was staying here, with us, or if she had gone back to her place last night and come back this morning.

I walk over to the table with our keys and grab my cell phone. Making my way to the kitchen, I head to the fridge and pour a glass of orange juice. After taking a sip, I set it on the counter. I know Collin will want some coffee when he wakes, so I go through the task of making some.

Trying to be quiet, I opt out of using the stove. Instead, I go for a bowl of cereal, taking it and my juice out to the small sunroom off the kitchen. The glass walls in here let the sun in everywhere. Taking a seat at the small table in the center of the room, I rest my feet on the opposite chair and eat my cereal examining my phone in the process.

I have three missed calls and five text messages. Collin called me twice, and there is one missed call from unknown. I open my text messages and start to read. The first three are from Faye:

Faye: We missed you at school today. Love you.

Faye: Everyone at school is so sad. They loved your grandma so much.

And then this morning.

Faye: I hope you're not still in bed, Katy. I will come over there and pour a bucket of ice on you. Grandma would be upset with your behavior.

She's right, Grandma would be upset with my behavior.

I quickly type out a message letting her know that I am as okay as I can be.

The next two messages are from Josh. He was my boyfriend sophomore and junior year, but I broke it off with him at the end of last year, because everything always seemed so tense and uncertain between us. I didn't do uncertain. I stuck to what was normal for me. I've never been an adventure seeker, and I've never been okay in situations that I could not handle. That's why Josh and I didn't work out.

Josh: Sorry about Grandma, I'm here for you.

Josh: Call me, I'm worried about you.

I type out a quick message to him.

Me: I'm all right for now.

Setting the phone down, I finish my cereal and enjoy the view of the garden from in here.

Thinking about Caleb, I reach in my back pocket and take out the card he gave me yesterday. It's very simple, three lines on the entire card:

Caleb Mathews

Self-Defense Instructor

555-726-5624.

I couldn't believe that Caleb told me something so personal about his life. Talking about it didn't seem to bother him either. He had shown up with his story at just the right moment. It's funny how things happen that way. I was sitting there, feeling sorry for myself, letting the sadness overtake me, and he shows up inviting himself to have a seat at my table.

Not seeming to understand I didn't want to be bothered, he pushed on. I didn't mind, so much, after we started the conversation, because he was nice to talk to, and he took my mind off the hurt that was coursing through my body.

My phone beeps in my hand pulling me from my thoughts. It's Josh.

Josh: Ok. Let me know if you need something.

"Hey." Collin walks in with a hand over his mouth, yawning, the other one is carrying a coffee mug. Removing my feet from the chair in front of me, he pulls it out and sits down. "How long have you been up?"

I shake my head. "Not too long, an hour-and-a-half maybe." Sitting Caleb's card down, I reach for my orange juice and take a sip. "Aunt Rita's gone. I thought maybe she would be staying here, with us," I say. Sitting the glass down, I look at Collin, he is looking at the card on the table.

"No, she went home late last night," he mumbles. Picking up the card, he examines it slowly and asks, "What's this?"

"Oh, I'm thinking of taking some self-defense classes," I say, shrugging non-committal. "I met Caleb at a diner yesterday morning. He gave me his card."

Collin takes a sip of his coffee and sets it down on the table, along with Caleb's card. "Caleb Mathews, huh?"

"What? Do you know him?"

"No. I knew a Dillon Mathews in High School. We never really hung out or anything; he was sort of an outsider. I'm not sure what happened to him. But I don't really stay connected with anyone from high school either." Leaning back in his chair, he runs his fingers through his hair. "I mean I heard a few rumors, but I never put much stock in rumors." He takes a sip of his coffee and sets it down.

"Huh. What did you hear?" I ask, leaning in and perking up.

"You know, the usual stuff: he was in jail, got someone pregnant, moved out of state—like I said, rumors."

I briefly entertain the possibility that Caleb is related to this Dillon. But this is a big city with six different high schools. It's more likely that they are not.

"How's Cali?" I ask. Collin had a good job and a fiancé in California. Chelsea, his fiancé, didn't come around at all. When he came home for Christmas every other year, she wouldn't come with him. I used to tease him about whether or not she was real, but I've talked to her a few times when I would call his house. She sounded nice.

"It's good," he replies. "Chelsea wanted to come, but she wasn't able to get out of work. She said she was looking forward to meeting you." I nod my head in acknowledgment and move on.

"Aunt Rita said the lawyer was going to come over today," I sigh. Collin looks troubled by that, but it's fleeting.

"Yeah, she told me when I came in last night. The whole family is supposed to gather here at about three." He glances at his watch then back at me. "It's nine-thirty now, we have a while. Is there something you want to do?"

Shaking my head no, I quickly reconsider. "Actually, can you help me in the garden today? I need to pull some weeds and trim the Evergreens."

Smiling sadly at me, he says, "No problem, little sis."

We change into more comfortable clothes for working outside on a hot day. The clothes I had on yesterday weren't going to cut it. I also felt sort of scummy, but a shower would be pointless since I was going to get sweaty and filthy again.

Working in the garden will clear my mind and prepare it for the upheaval that is coming when the family gets here. I briefly saw Aunt Nora after the funeral. She hugged me, but I was so numb, I didn't feel it. I just walked into my bedroom, collapsed on my bed, and sank into the dark.

Grandma always said that Aunt Nora was the most like my mom. I didn't know what that meant, because I didn't even know my mom. I hadn't seen her in eleven years. But Aunt Nora did drink a lot. She was that relative at Christmas parties who drank way too much, made a fool of herself, and passed out early. Maybe that's what she meant by their comparison. They both were drinkers.

I felt bad for Aunt Nora's kids. You could tell that her actions embarrassed them. They stopped coming to family functions when they moved out of her house.

John and Henry, my grandma's brothers, will probably be here. I love Uncle John and Uncle Henry. Ever since my grandma's husband, Richard, had passed away, they would make weekly visits to our house. That was right before Grandma got custody of Collin and me.

When I was younger, they would always bring me the most outlandish gifts. Uncle John brought me a sword one year. I was fifteen, he had just come over to visit Grandma, and, smiling mischievously, he placed it in my hands. I looked at it, then at him, quizzically.

"It's called an Epee sword. It's used in fencing. It was mine when I was a teenager," he had said.

I looked at the sword again. It was silver plated with a very intricate design cut into the grip. The guard looked like a complicated weave of hardened silver yarn. The blade had the same design as the grip did, venturing all the way down to a groove on the tip. If I were to stab a marshmallow with it, there would be a heart indent left in the marshmallow.

It was stunning the way the light hit the blade, sending a beam of light across the room, but I didn't know what to do with a sword. Uncle John talked plenty about them, and I could tell that he was excited about passing this down to me; not having any kids of his own, so I gave him a big hug and thanked him, telling him I would put it up in a safe place.

Both of my uncles had taken fencing classes when they were young. My grandma had even learned some self-defense in quiet. It wasn't lady-like back then to do that, but she had two older brothers, they had taught her very well. I always thought that was why she had encouraged me to learn Krav Maga. It kept me in shape, but I had yet to use it. I hope that I never have to. I hadn't been to my class since I lost Grandma and wondered just how 'in shape' I would be if I decided to go back.

Walking out to the garden, I go to the little shed on the

side of the house. Grabbing the garden fork and trowel off of the wall, I put them in a bucket that is used to put the pulled weeds in. Grabbing two pairs of work gloves off of the shelf, I walk out and close the door. Collin is already standing in the garden wearing a pair of jogging pants and a white t-shirt. When he sees me he slaps his hands together and rubs them back and forth.

"I'm ready," he says. Grinning at him, I hand over his gloves.

"We'll start over by the waterfall." We both turn and head that way.

We spend the next three hours pulling weeds and trimming the Evergreens. By the time we came in from the heat, it was almost two o'clock. We were sopping wet from sweat and starving. We both went to take a shower and change quickly so we could eat lunch before people started to arrive.

I made grilled cheese sandwiches with ham for us, and we sat at the kitchen island to eat. I was just finishing my sandwich when Aunt Rita walks through the front door. She is carrying two small suitcases. Thinking they are hers, and she had changed her mind about moving in, I started to get up and help her.

But a woman trailed behind her. She had enormous sunglasses on that covered half of her face and a bright orange top that was cut entirely too low to be considered decent. Her white Capri's practically blind me, illuminated by the sunlight outside.

This couldn't be. There was no way, but then again, this would be perfect timing for her. I just stood there with my mouth hanging open, unable to speak. I realize in that moment, that I would never forget her face. Collin, breaking the silence, stood and without any hesitation walked over to Aunt Rita—who was standing between him and our mother.

Chapter Four

"*What* is she doing here?" Collin hisses.

"Now, Collin," Aunt Rita starts, trying to be the voice of reason already, "this is not the time. Your mother-"

"My mother?" he asks, interrupting Aunt Rita. His words are full of angry humor. "She hasn't been my mother in eleven years. She wasn't even my mother before that. My mother...is gone. This woman," he points to our mom standing behind Aunt Rita, "is just someone on this earth who is eating up space." He grabs his keys from the dish and turns, walking out the back door in a fit of pure rage.

Why is it, that the people we love the most will be the first to hurt us? My dad hurt me when he died. I knew it wasn't his choice, but his existence had already left a mark on my heart. His death hurt Mom. She made decisions that ultimately led to hurting herself, although I don't think she cared. In return, those decisions hurt Collin and me; that *was* by choice.

Grandma tore my heart when she passed away. And now, as I stand here, Collin has hurt me. Walking out, leaving me here to deal with all of this alone. We have always dealt with things together, but not today. Without a glance in my direction, he just walked out and left me.

Me, I was rendered completely incapable of movement due to the appearance of my mother—who has been absent from my life for eleven years, not even concerned with my well being. I even thought she hated me at times.

She looked older then her forty-four years. When she took off her sunglasses, I notice the wrinkles on her face. It was clear that she had not taken care of herself.

I hated myself for wanting to know where she had been, what she had been up to, and why she hadn't called or stopped by to see me.

Aunt Rita continued forward, dropping my mom's bags in the living room. Mom walks in, right past me, mumbling something about a long drive and having to pee.

When she is out of the room, I walk up to Aunt Rita to say something, anything intelligible, but the door opens and Uncle Henry walks in.

"There's my favorite girl," he exclaims sadly. He walks over and places his arms around me. For a moment, I forget the woman in the bathroom.

"Hi Uncle Henry," I say muffled. Wrapping my arms around his midsection, I squeeze taking in the scent of cigars and menthol.

"How have you been? I'm glad to see you out of bed." I start to answer his question when Aunt Nora comes through the door followed by Uncle John. Aunt Nora comes over and puts her hand on my cheek then turns and walks away. She has always been a woman of little words.

Uncle John gives me one of his grizzly hugs. Everyone looks sleep deprived and worn out. There are sour faces all around the room. Then my mom comes out of the bathroom.

She doesn't look tired and worn. In fact, it looks as if she went in there and applied makeup and fixed her hair. With her so close, I can see her green eyes, the same ones that have looked back at me in the mirror for the past seventeen years. Her bleach blonde hair is styled neatly, twisted, and pinned up.

It's so quiet in the room until Mom says, "Well isn't this nice, us, all together again after so long." She clasps her hands together in front of her. "It's like a family reunion." She looks at everyone, but skips right past me. I can't help but feel hurt by it.

Uncle Henry is the first to reply. "Julie, what are you doing here?" Authority rings loud and clear in his voice from years of being a judge.

"My mother died," she say a matter-of-factly "Why

wouldn't I be here?" She plasters a fake smile on her face. Who would smile after saying their mother died?

Aunt Nora steps forward. "Let's just get through this the best we can. For Mother's sake." A knock at the door halts any more conversation. It's the lawyer, the one I had seen Grandma meet with on several occasions.

"Are you all ready?" he says when Uncle Henry opens the door. No 'Hi how are you.' just 'Are you ready?' None of us were, well except for Mom maybe.

But we walked into the study anyways; all of us except Collin. One by one we prepared for what most of us didn't want to hear. This was so final—she really was gone.

The lawyer took a seat at Grandma's desk. He pulled out a stack of papers and started rearranging them. The rest of us gathered around finding seats where ever we could. I sat on the floor in front of Uncle John, as far away from my mom as possible.

"I would like to start by saying, that reading a Will is only going to provide you with information." He pushes his glasses up on his nose. "It will take time for the paperwork to be finalized to make this officially legal. It is imperative that you are patient." He takes a look around, making sure that everyone understands. Clearing his throat, he begins reading Grandma's will.

"This is The Last Will and Testament of Susan Laudin;"

"I, Susan Laudin, being of sound and disposing mind, memory and understanding, do herby publish and declare this to be my last will and testament." He pauses for a moment to glance up, at me, then continues.

"First: I hereby leave all of my property and assets to my grandchildren, Katy Laudin and Collin Laudin, in equal shares. This includes, but is not limited to, my estate, any financial accounts that are opened in my name at the time of my death, and the vehicle that I so own."

Looking over at Aunt Rita, she doesn't look surprised.

In fact no one looks surprised—but my mom. She is seething. I can see that this is going to end badly when she stands.

"That can't be right," she protests loudly, throwing her hands in the air, interrupting the lawyer. "She is *my* mother—not theirs," she continues, pointing a sharp finger at herself. "Why would she leave everything to them?" The tone in her voice is accusing, but her words hurt me more than her tone. The amount of hostility this one person has is alarming.

"Julie, this is not the time or the place to voice your opinions. Please, let the lawyer finish." Uncle John puts a soothing hand on my shoulder, but I'm strung so tight it does nothing for me.

This woman who brought me into this world, who was supposed to love me, unconditionally—despises me. But there was nothing I could do about Grandma's wishes.

After my mom rolled her eyes and made some other immature noises, the lawyer continued.

Aunt Rita was named Executor of the Estate, and Grandma left my mother and my aunt part of her life insurance policy. Leaving each of us twenty thousand dollars. Again, my mother made some obscene noises. The whole thing was sickening.

After the lawyer finished reading the will, I stood and walked out of the study and into my room, trying to escape from the people. As soon as I closed the door, it opens again. Turning to see who it was, I immediately retreat.

"You little brat." My mom walks in closing the door behind her. Her face is contorted in anger. It scares me.

"I don't know how you talked my mother into leaving everything to you," she moves toward me, slowly with her fists clenched. Her words are dripping with hate. "I will make sure you don't get any of it." I feel queasy and start to retreat more, but the back of my knees hit the bed. I know there is a look of terror on my face. A part of me knows that she is enjoying that look. Standing in front of me now, my mother raises her hand; I'm too stunned to move. She swings. and slaps me across my face.

It stings, and in a reflexive move I put my hand over my cheek, completely shocked. Then, as anger takes hold and shock is tossed out of the window, I push her out of my way. She stumbles backwards, clearly not expecting me to stand up to her.For a moment, and only a moment, I can see the hurt in her eyes, and I feel a little guilty, but I push it aside.

"You don't know anything about me or Grandma. You have been gone for eleven years. You don't get to walk in here and come at me like that," I say angrily. I start for the door, but her words bring me up short.

"I know more then you can comprehend, little girl. *My* mother has been keeping me well informed of you for the past eleven years. Sending me pictures, letters, report cards. Oh," she almost sings, "I know everything there is to know. How you played soccer and Collin played baseball. I've got pictures of every dance, every game, and every milestone."

That can't be right. Grandma would have never let her be a part of my life from a distance. If she wanted to know what was going on in my life, she should have visited.

But, I highly doubt that she even cared; which is another reason why I knew she wasn't telling the truth. With that final thought I walk out of the room and directly across the hall to Grandma's room.

Stepping inside, I could smell the lavender from the garden. The window was open; the window was always open. Grandma loved to fall asleep to the smell of the garden, listening to the hoot of the owls and the chirp of the crickets.

Her queen size bed was half made. She didn't really toss and turn at night, so only the side of the bed where she had pulled back the blankets was unmade. That was a rule in this house—don't ever waste your time making your bed when you're just going to get in it, and mess it up again. I remember her telling me that when we first moved in. I could almost hear her yelling it through the house. But it was a ghost of a memory.

Best. Rule. Ever. The thought made me smile. Good memories; I had to draw on good memories. But then the pain started to uncoil inside of me, and I thought; *nope too soon.* The memories still caused pain.

Walking over to her bed, I lay down where she would normally lay; wanting to feel closer to her. I could smell her shampoo on the pillow. It made my chest ache knowing that the smell would wear off at some point. Inhaling, I try to trap the scent in my memory. Would I forget her? Someday, when I am older, with a husband and kids, or when I am in college even, would I forget her? I didn't want to. But maybe the truth of it was—I would.

How do you hold on to something that's not tangible, like memories? And once those are gone what would I have left? Pictures! No, I couldn't forget her. There are too many memories, eleven years of them, trapped on pieces of paper all over the house. Stuffed in corners, and buried deep in boxes and dressers. All waiting for moments like these.

I could probably live in this house with my kids some day. She did leave Collin and me the house, and everything in it. But Collin was happy in California. I knew he wouldn't move back. Did I want to stay here? I guess time would tell.

After laying in Grandma's bed for a while, I decide it's time to face my situation, and find out if Mom was here for good or temporarily. I get up and head out the door toward the living room. Everyone is sitting there, including Collin. He doesn't look entirely pleased.

"What's going on?" I ask.

Collin glances up at me quickly, but whips his head back in my direction with a concerned look on his face.

Sitting up straight, he asks, "Katy, what happened to

your face?" I had forgotten about Mom's threat. I touch it without thinking.

"Nothing to worry about." I say it like it doesn't even matter that my mother slapped me. But I didn't want to be the reason this momentary peace would crash and burn. "So, what's going on?" I repeat. Collin doesn't look convinced, but he moves on anyways. I'm sure there will be a discussion about this later.

"We are discussing where Julie will stay." He says her name like it is a bad taste in his mouth. Mom rolls her eyes.

"This is *my* mother's house I will stay here," she says, leaving no room for discussion. My heart lurches.

"No," Collin says, shaking his head. "Grandma left the house to Katy and me. You will not be staying here." Mom does that eye roll thing, that teenagers do, again.

"You don't understand dear boy. That Will does not go into effect until legal documents are signed. Therefore, this house belongs to her next of kin, and that," she says crossing her legs and looking smug, "would include me."

"Julie, can you stay at a hotel? I will pay for it," Uncle Henry says. But Mom doesn't budge. I think she wants to make me mad or push me over the edge, because when she looks at me and smiles; it curls my toes and bile rises in my throat.

"I want to get to know my daughter." It's a joke. Can she really be this awful? My grandma just died, her mother, and I can see in her eyes that she wants nothing more than to hurt me.

What exactly is she expecting me to do? Cry, fight, argue? I don't really know. But I do know, that I don't want to be anything like this woman. So, I do the one thing that I know Collin will not like—but my mom will not expect.

"She can stay," I say with finality. Everyone looks at me with wide eyes. Collin is already shaking his head no. I walk over and grab my purse and keys, turn to head out the door—but stop. There is something I need to say first.

Walking back through the living room; I walk straight over to Mom, lean down, and look her in the eyes. The same eyes that are mine.

"Thank you," I say. She looks confused, but her confusion turns to disdain when I whisper, "For setting such a great example of the very person I don't want to be."

With that, I turn and walk out of the door. When I get in my car, I drive a few blocks down and pull over. Closing my eyes, I lay my head back on the seat and take a deep breath. Just because I told Mom to stay, did not mean that I would. Does that mean I am homeless?

Before I let uncertainty strangle me, I take my cell phone out of my purse and call Faye.

"Katy Ann Laudin! I have been worried sick." Her voice is stern. I smile, because she is trying to do her best impression of Grandma.

"Okay, Grandma," I retort.

"Well, someone has to keep you in line, and Grandma's not here to do that anymore. She would definitely expect me to do it." There is a hint of sadness in her voice. She loved Grandma like she was her grandma too. I hadn't thought about the affect this had on her. Between my selfishness and the distance I had put between us the last couple of days, I don't know why she is still talking to me.

"So you thought you were qualified for the job?"

"Well, no one else has applied. I mean, you're a handful," she exaggerates.

"Are you talking to yourself again?" I say. She laughs, and the sound makes me feel better already. I haven't heard her laugh in so long. I let out a long breath.

"I need to talk to you, and...I need to ask for a favor."

"I was just getting ready to head out and meet Micah, but I'll wait for you. You know how you come first in my life," she says sweetly.

"I'm on my way." We hang up, and I head over there.

I feel bad for taking her away from Micah. They have

been dating for almost four years. They met our freshmen year of high school. But he was a sophomore, so last year he went off to college, seven hours away. He finished finals two weeks ago and is home for the summer, but he has to go back in a couple of months. Then, they won't see each other until Christmas. I always thought long distance relationships would never work. I'm surprised that they have lasted as long as they have. It's nice to see her happy, though.

It takes three minutes to get to Faye's house. I don't even knock, I just walk right in; it's always been that comfortable for me here. Her mom is sitting on the couch in the living room.

"Hey Katy." She puts down the mail she is going through and comes over to me with that sad look in her eyes that I have seen way too much of lately. But she doesn't say sorry like I had expected. Instead, she hugs me tightly and asks me if I want a beer.

"Um, no thank you," I say confused by this question. Is this a test?

"Are you sure?" she says. "Because when my mother died, I needed a whole lot of beer." She emphasizes the 'whole lot' part by waving her hand in a slow half circle.

"No, I'm good. But...thank you?" Faye's mom has always liked to drink. She was a little loose on the discipline too, but she was always there. Coming from that visit with my mom after eleven years of nothing from her, I felt a pang of jealousy. I didn't want to feel that way.

Faye's mom didn't drink a lot, just sometimes. I guess you would call that an occasional drunk, because when she did drink, she would drink way too much.

I never understood people who drank that much. Why would anyone want to drink enough to be incoherent and lose their memory? Anything could happen to you, and you wouldn't even know. That just wasn't for me.

Faye has had a couple of drunk spells this last year. I

would just keep an eye on her. But, I don't ever want to act that way. It's like all of your voluntary actions become involuntary.

Faye's mom shrugs and walks away as Faye comes down the stairs.

"Hey, you want to come up or go out?" I don't want to talk to her about this in public, so I simply say 'up', and we head upstairs.

We both flop down on the bed on our backs and lay there for several seconds. I am trying to work up the nerve to repeat my day all over again, verbally, without crying like a baby. I take a deep breath and look at Faye.

I plan to tell her about my mom and Grandma's will, but instead, I say, "I'm going to New York."

I didn't even know I had made that decision, until I just said it out loud to her. But I can't stay. Not with Mom here. There is too much going on, and I just want to be as far away from it as possible.

Her eyes widen as she sits up. "What? When?"

"Three weeks. It was Grandma's graduation *and* birthday gift to me. We talked about it, but I didn't think we could really afford it." I sit up and she looks at me with concern on her face.

"What happened?" she says with a sigh.

"What do you mean, 'What happened?'" She always knows when something is up.

"You're running, Katy. I've seen you do this before, last year. Things got tough with Josh, and you ran. You didn't even want to put forth any effort with him. You just broke it off and didn't talk to him for a long time; after you told me repeatedly that he didn't do anything wrong." She knows me too well.

I was definitely looking to escape when Josh and I broke up. Our friends where moving forward in thier relationships, and I didn't want to be put in a situation where I felt pressured into the same.

I didn't entirely trust my body's hormonal urges. So, I told Josh that I needed some space. He didn't understand, but neither did I. He wasn't rude about the break up; I think he was just hurt. We were still friends. But the truth was; when I saw him with other girls, starting to date again, I was genuinely happy for him.

Faye and I never keep things from each other. That is what has kept our friendship so strong. I don't want to ruin that, so I tell her what I can.

"My mom is in town," I tell her.

"Oh my gosh, Katy. What did she do? What did she say? Where has she been?" I roll my eyes at all her questions and lay back down on the bed, looking up at her.

With as little emotion as possible, I say, "I don't know where she has been, and the first time she did look at me and talk to me, was to call me a 'brat' and accuse me of forcing Grandma into leaving me everything. Apparently, I'm a Jedi."

"No," Faye says, as shocked as I was when the accusations were made against me. Shaking my head, I continue.

"That's not even the best part. After her accusation, she slapped me in the face. Told me Grandma had been keeping her informed of my life, and then decided that she was going to protest Grandma's will while living at her house."

"Oh, no she didn't," she says unbelieving. Faye was mad for the both of us. I could see the fury etched all over her face, but I just didn't care. "Did you tell her she was crazy if she thought she was going to march in there after eleven years," she stood up and started pacing back and forth, "and think that she had some sort of rights? Who does this woman think she is? I mean-"

"I told her to stay," I interrupt her. She stops pacing and stares at me with disbelief.

"Katy. Why would you tell her to stay? Maybe you're

the crazy one." She crosses her arms and gives me a serious look. Maybe I was.

"I just didn't want to fight. None of it, the house and Grandma's things, it doesn't mean anything without Grandma in it. I don't even want it. I just want to be done with it. Besides, everything is in limbo right now until paperwork is signed, and stuff like that. That could take weeks—even months."

"Your uncle is a judge, Katy. Fight it. And what do you mean you don't want any of it?" She sits down on the bed next to me. Her voice is calmer than before. "You may not want it, but Grandma gave it to you. Out of all the people in her life, she trusted you with her house and her things. A house that she has been living in and making her own for thirty-nine years." I had never thought of it that way.

"Yeah, but it's a house with bills. And if things get broken, I have to get them fixed. I won't even be home to maintain them. We're supposed to go to college in August." With a heavy sigh I throw my arm over my eyes. "I don't think I am ready for this." I wanted to grow up, but this was fast.

Faye lies back down on the bed next to me, her anger forgotten.

"You have people here to help with that. Collin, Aunt Rita, Uncle John, and Uncle Henry, they love you, Katy. I love you. You're never alone in this, and I bet they will do everything in their power to make sure your grandma's wishes are followed."

I knew that. They really would fight with me on this; take my side instead of my mom's. Those two days I spent thinking I was alone after Grandma die—seemed stupid now. Of course I wasn't alone. The day I had been adopted, I got a chance to be part of a family.

Thinking about the other issue at hand, I mumble, "I can't go back with Mom staying there."

"You can stay here for as long as you need. Or, until

you go to New York." She gives me an uncertain look. "Are you still going?" I made up my mind about that already.

"Yeah, but I'm not running. It's a good opportunity." She looked as if she didn't believe me.

"You're not going to give in to your mom, are you? Grandma didn't want her to have that stuff. You should fight for it."

"Yeah, I guess you're right."

"You *guess*, I'm right?" she says in mock shock. "I'm your inquisitively intellogical best friend, and I'm always right."

"Intellogical is not a word, Faye."

"Sure it is. It's a hybrid of intelligent and logical. Intellogical. I'll add it to the dictionary," she says, sounding sincere.

"Uh, huh. Are you publishing your own dictionary."

"Yes. I shall call it the Faye Funtionary. Only fun words allowed."

I laugh, because she is insane, and I love her. There isn't anyone in this world that can make me laugh the way Faye does. She can take my mind off anything that's bothering me.

When I stop, she places a hand on my arm, and her voice turns serious. "It's good to hear you laugh. It's not your normal lighthearted laugh, but it's a start. Right?" I smile and nod my head yes.

But no one knows that my laughs are still tainted with pain. Sometimes, it's hard to cover up what I am really feeling, but the thought of someone examining my mind, makes me cringe. Because right now, I'm thinking that I want to crawl in a hole, and just stay there forever. It's because of people like Faye and Collin, that I don't.

~~~

The next three weeks are full of legalities and unwanted battles between me, Aunt Rita, Collin, my mom, and the courts. In the end, she got exactly what Grandma had wanted her to have; the twenty thousand dollars from the life insurance policy. It still wasn't enough for her, but I already knew it wouldn't be.

In the middle of all the chaos, was my eighteenth birthday. Collin, Faye, and Micah made me a cake and we celebrated under the gazebo, surrounded by Grandma's garden. With everything going on, that was all we did. It didn't bother me though. It was perfect. Everyone got me something that I could take on my trip.

"Open mine," Faye said giddily, pushing a box into my hands. It was wrapped in pretty silver wrapping paper with a silver bow on top. Pulling the paper away and opening the box; I was baffled.

"What is this?" I say, pulling the bottle out.

"A keepsake. I don't want you to forget me when you are in New York. Two months is a long time."

"It's beautiful, Faye." And nothing like her usual gag presents. Every year for my birthday, I got a graphic tee with something ridiculous written on the front. But this, this was one of those gifts that you keep forever. That you can never grow out of.

It was a clear, long-neck, glass bottle that had been stripped of its label. The words, 'Best friends are sisters at heart' was etched onto the front of the bottle. Inside were all sorts of things that were reminders of what we had done over the years. Dances, sleepovers, soccer games, Halloween costumes that we attempted to make ourselves one year, a giant pencil that we had used to tick off our math teacher because it was 'distracting'. Fabric from shirts that we had both worn over the years, because it was our favorite.

She had kept all this stuff. Some of these patterns were from shirts that we shared when we were ten. She put more thought into this gift then I could have ever imagined. So many memories were stuffed in such a tiny bottle. On the back of the bottle was a picture of Faye and I when we first met at the age of seven. I laughed at that, because Faye had braces. Even though she hated this picture. she knew it was my favorite. It was the first time I had made a true friend. Wrapped around the neck of the bottle was a ribbon that said 'Fermenting since 2002.'

I break out in laughter. Everyone looks at me like I'm deranged, so I pass the bottle around earning snickers from everyone and a huge smile from Faye.

Leave it up to her to use terminology to her own accord. I love her so much. Putting the bottle back into the box, I set it carefully on the table and pull Faye into a tight hug.

"Good present?" Her voice is a little shaky and sad. I'm a little sad that she can't come with me, but she has Micah. She wouldn't give up that time, and I wouldn't ask her to.

"Great present," I say. It was the first present that she put so much thought into.

Micah handed me a small bag with tissue paper sticking out everywhere. Inside is a picture of Faye, Micah, and me from sophomore year. We are sitting at the back of our English class making goofy faces. I have a feeling Faye helped with this gift.

Micah never really was a good gift giver. He actually gave Faye a teddy bear for Valentine's Day one year. She had to tell him that it was cute... if she was five. I don't think he put much thought into the gift.

"Thanks Micah," I say.

"Well, no one can compete with Faye's gift, but I thought that you would like a picture to remember me by," he says with a tight lipped smile. I smile back and say thank you again. I don't know why, but things have always been uncomfortable between us. Secretly, I was happy that he had gone so far away to college, so that I could spend more time with Faye.

Collin hands me a bag and inside is a Nikon camera

with different zooms on it. I'm surprised that he thought of something like this. It was perfect, and a little confusing, since I knew he didn't want me to go to New York. But, I assumed he was making the best of a situation that he knew he couldn't control. I couldn't wait to start taking pictures with it.

We stayed out under the gazebo all night talking and joking around with each other, enjoying the peace and quiet. It was a great night considering the last couple of weeks. Mom had been out, so we were able to avoid her for the whole night.

I hadn't seen much of her, but when the papers finally went through we didn't even have to tell her to leave.

Collin, who stayed in the house to keep an eye on her, said she left late one evening, or early in the morning one day. She slipped out when he was sleeping. She took some of Grandma's things with her; jewelry and about five hundred in cash that she kept in her closet in case of emergencies.

It didn't make sense, because she already had a twenty thousand dollar check in her hands. I was just glad that I had taken the teardrop necklace with me to Faye's. I blamed myself for not being there and telling her she could stay. But Collin understood why I did what I did, and he wasn't mad at me. He knew I didn't want to be like her.

What she took from me, and Grandma was irreplaceable. But I still had Grandma's house, and the garden in the back was full of memories and life. Thankfully, she couldn't pack that in her suitcase and carry it out the door.

~~~

The day before I left for New York, and Collin went back to California, we were sitting in the living room on the couch, going through old mail that Grandma had in every nook and cranny in her study. Aunt Rita had been over just about every day when Mom was here. She would help go through the piles of mail in the study, trying to find all the bills so that we could pay them.

She didn't like that Mom was staying at the house either, but her husband had said no when she asked if my mom could stay with them. She didn't know what else to do with her. That was her sister; she didn't want to throw her out on the streets. Mom wouldn't have left anyways.

Collin and I had carried a huge box out to the living room, sat in front of the TV, and started going through as much as we could before our departure. I was thinking about all the decisions I had made in the last three weeks when Collin spoke to me.

"Look at this, Katy." He holds a photo album up and starts flipping through the pages. I lean over to take a look.

They're pictures of Grandma and her brothers when they were my and Collin's age. She was so beautiful.

He kept flipping through page after page until he came upon pictures of Grandma with her kids. Then just pictures of my aunts and uncles. Class pictures of them from every year; my mom as a baby, as a toddler, a pre-teen, and a teenager.

Collin stops on a picture of my mom when she was nineteen. She was standing outside this house, leaning against a tree with her arms crossed. She was laughing, but I couldn't see what she was laughing about, it was out of camera shot. She looked very happy. Where did that person go?

"Wow," was all Collin could say. I was speechless, though. It was like looking in a mirror. I didn't know how to feel about this, but I look just like my mom did all those years ago.

We had the same bright green eyes, sandy blonde hair, and short frame. I wondered if I would look like her when I turn the age she is now. I didn't know for sure, only time could tell. But I did know one thing; every time I look in the mirror, I would see her, and it made my gut twist. I didn't like the person she was, and I certainly didn't want to look in the mirror and see her staring back at me.

My feelings for my mom were so confusing. I wanted to know about her and longed for a relationship with her, but I didn't want to be anything like her. And the thought of seeing her every day in the mirror was not pleasant.

Collin didn't say anything else. He just closed the album, set it in the 'keep' pile, and started going through the rest of the box. I couldn't shake a thought that flitted through my mind unbidden, *Would I be like her?*

The next morning, Aunt Rita came over early to take Collin to the airport.

Collin and I said our goodbyes, but not before he tried to talk me out of going to New York one last time. It was just too unsafe as far as he was concerned. I wasn't backing down though. I had to make my own decisions. He told me to call him as soon as I landed in New York. I agreed as he gave me a big hug and walked out of the door.

Aunt Rita and I said our goodbyes as well. "Please be safe. Call me when you get back, okay." She pats my cheek then gets a sad look on her face as she gives me a quick hug and pulls back.

"Of course," I reassure her.

She gives me another long look then says, "You're grandma was so proud of you," then turns and walks away.

Faye and Micah came over to take me to the airport an hour after Collin and Aunt Rita had left.

I already had my bags packed and sitting by the door. Arrangements had been made for the house in my two month absence. Faye had agreed to come over and check things out, daily. In return, I had to agree to call her at least once a day. That wasn't a problem; I didn't plan to completely abandon my friend.

I was looking at this trip as a way to clear my mind and keep going, even after the tragedy in my life. After all,

Grandma wanted me to live life to the best of my ability; to see things, do things, and I would.

Micah carried my bags to his car and put them in the trunk while Faye and I took our seats. The car ride was short, and before I knew it, we were pulling up to the airport. Micah took the bags out and carried them while Faye and I walked in front of him.

"Did you pack some of that mace that Grandma gave you every year?" Faye says, looking at me with a sideways glance.

"Yes, of course." I give an exasperated sigh. I made sure to pack plenty of them for the worry wart.

"I'm just asking. New York is a crazy place. Remember, don't walk alone at night," she checks it off on her finger, "don't walk down any dark alleys," she checks that off on another finger, "and don't go out with strange guys. If a guy asks you out, stay in a public place. New York men can be very scummy."

"So can any man. I don't think it matters where you live." Micah places my bags on the turn style and falls in line with us as we walk toward the gate. He has been extremely quiet; trying to let us say our last goodbyes. Faye pulls me into a hug.

"Don't worry about anything here, okay. I'll take care of the house and stuff. You just go and enjoy yourself, get some culture and stay safe." I hug her back.

"Thanks, and I will." When she releases me I see tears starting to form in her eyes. "Don't cry. It's only two months. When I get back we'll be college bound, together." Hastily wiping the tears from her eyes, she smiles at me.

"I know, but my girl is all grown up," she screeches. "Call me as soon as you land. Okay?"

"I will, and stop being so loud you lunatic. You're drawing attention to us," I say, laughing and looking around. Micah walks over, gives me an awkward hug, and hands my small carry-on bag over.I turn and take two step away from her before turning around and walking backwards.

Putting two fingers in the air, I say to Faye, "Two months. Be good."

Turning, I walk down the gate hallway. I find my way onto the plane, shove my carry-on into the overhead compartment, and take my seat next to the window. When we take off, I can see the sky and clouds right next to me.

It was beautiful, and even though I was a little nervous, with this being my first flight, I ended up watching a movie and we were landing in New York before I could finish it.

When the plane touched down everyone was packing up the things they had out, but I just stared out the window. There was water on both sides of us. I thought we were going to end up in it, but we landed on the runway, right in the middle with no problems at all.

Getting off the plane with my carry-on, I stroll over to baggage claim to get my things and head for my apartment. I decide to just flag down a taxi. I heard New York traffic was horrible, so taking a taxi for the next two months seemed like the best way to get around.

The drive was short, but it took a long time to get to my destination. Pulling my bags out of the trunk of his taxi, the driver hands them over, and I thank him with a smile and payment.

The apartment was wonderful, it looked just like the pictures. Walking in, everything was light and airy. The kitchen was to my immediate right. It was so small a full size refrigerator couldn't even fit in there. But everything was clean and like new.

Walking up a small flight of stairs into the living room, I set my bags down. The floors are hardwood; causing my heels to clink as I walked across it. One whole wall to my right was made out of a light colored brick with a fireplace in the center.

Above and behind me was the loft area. A set of stairs

would take me up to a small bedroom with only a desk, closet, bathroom, and a twin size bed in it.

But straight ahead was the balcony. This was the reason I had liked this apartment so much. The view from the balcony was breathtaking in the pictures I had seen. I was eager to look, and see if the view was the same in person.

Walking over, I open the French doors and step out into the crisp, warm air. The sun beating on my face felt nice. The breeze from ten floors up is strong, but it made the sun bearable. I could see the whole city from up here.

At night, everything would be lit up. This is where I would be sitting most nights. The only thing I had trouble with, was the fact that I couldn't call Grandma and tell her how beautiful everything was and thank her for giving me this opportunity. Closing my eyes, I inhale deeply and smile in contentment.

I went inside and started to unpack what I could while calling Collin and Faye to reassure them that I had landed safely. Faye wanted to talk forever about what it looked like and if I had seen any hot guys yet; which I heard Micah snort in the background at.

After I hung up with Faye, I got ready for bed. It wasn't late, but I wanted to get a good night sleep, so I could enjoy every day I was here.

I planned on making my first stop in the morning to a coffee shop I had seen a couple of blocks over on my taxi ride here. Then, I was going to hit up every single museum that I possibly could from there.

It was going to be an exciting couple of months in New York. I would enjoy it the best I could, make some new friends, and try to figure some things out about my future; mainly my career. My major was undecided.

I let things fall away, like my mother's hatred for me, and let Grandma's last words lead me, *There is so much for you to see in life, so much to be lived. Go enjoy it!* I planned to repeat that to myself every day I was here, and enjoy the heck out of the Big Apple.

Chapter Five

New York is amazing.

I spent the first month visiting every museum and tourist place I could. I had to remind myself that I had twenty-four hours in a day, and had to sleep at least six of those hours. I visited Central Park, Times Square, and the Statue of Liberty. It was endless.

But nothing could beat the view from my balcony at night. It was were I spent most nights, wrapped in a fleece blanket, staring out over the city with every building lit up. It was beyond exquisite. At night, the city was just as busy as it was during the day. It was like no one ever slept here.

There was so much to see and do. I quickly realized that two months was never going to be enough. I'd have to plan another trip; maybe Faye could come with me.

Ellis Island had been my favorite place to visit. There was so much history in this one place. I could have spent my whole trip at Ellis Island, and I wanted to know more about everything.

History had always been fun for me when it was boring for others. Maybe that was my calling. It would be amazing to be an anthropologist. I could travel, and learn about so many different things. The thought made me a little giddy.

As promised, I talked to Faye every night. Giving her the run down on what my day was like. She and Micah were having a good summer too. I was happy that she could spend it with him, even though I wanted her to be here with me. I started to miss her almost immediately. She was happy that I could have this experience after losing my grandma. She thought that I would be antisocial and withdrawn.

I didn't have a lot of friends in New York, but I did

meet one girl. Her name was Amber. She was a student at the New York Academy of Art, going into her second year in August. She was also the complete opposite of me, but she was nice, and she reminded me of Faye a little.

I met her a week ago at the coffee shop down the street. She walked over and introduced herself with a lively lilt to her words. We met every morning for coffee at the same coffee shop, since that first time.

Tonight, we are going to see Wicked. I had wanted to see it for some time now, but kept putting it off for some reason. Amber had offered to go with me and bring a few friends. This would be the first time meeting her friends and my nerves were getting the best of me. I didn't know what New York night life was like, because I hadn't been out at night.

Wrapping my fingers around the sapphire that hung below the hollow of my neck, I close my eyes and willed the nerves away.

Picking up my purse, I shove a can of mace into it and head toward the door. A knock comes before I can make it across the living room. Looking through the peephole, I see that it's Amber.

"I thought we were going to meet downstairs?" I ask after opening the door. She has on a very tight black dress and red heels that make her at least five inches taller than me. I felt like Raggedy Ann next to her in my navy blue, knee length pencil skirt, brown silk blouse, and half-inch heels. She gave me the once over and didn't look impressed either.

"Your doorman really creeps me out." She walks in past me heading up the short flight of stairs, plopping down very un-lady like on the couch.

"Did Frank let you in?" I say, referring to the very old doorman. I think anyone would be able to slip past old Frank.

"You do know that Frank won't be able to keep anyone out of this building, right?" She gives me a leveled look.

"Yes, I know that, but he isn't security he's just the doorman. Still, he should have buzzed me before letting you up at the very least."

"I kind of slipped past him when he went to the bathroom."

"No." I say, walking over and sitting next to her. "He left his post without having someone relieve him?" The shock isn't hard to read in the sound of my voice.

"Yeah, he doesn't take his job seriously," she says, picking up an art magazine from my coffee table. "I wasn't the only one either. Someone was standing outside, and as soon as he left, they ran inside. It looked like a girl, all I could see was her blonde hair though."

"That's odd...and frightening." I didn't think much about it. There was a lot of teenagers that lived in this building. They probably were sneaking someone over. I made a mental note to tell Frank about it tomorrow.

When Grandma and I had looked at places, we had looked at only buildings with a doorman, at the very least. Even if the doorman doesn't qualify as security, people were less likely to bother with a building that had constant supervision. She would be furious right now. I wish I could call her and talk this out.

The thought of my grandma brings back that old familiar heart wrenching feeling, but I quickly force that away. I was getting much better with it, and the last thing I want is for Amber to think I am unstable and mentally ill. She notices my hurt anyways. Her brows draw in, and she gives me a questioning look, but she doesn't ask me what caused the hurt.

"Well," she says standing and pulling at the hem of her short dress, "let's get out of here. The guys are going to meet us there." Wait, what? I don't remember her saying anything about guys.

"Amber. You didn't set me up with someone, did you?" I say unsure.

"Of course not." Her tone says she is lying. She did set me up. I roll my eyes, but all she can do is grin. It might be nice. I didn't see why I couldn't date. I remember Faye's comment about staying in public places when on a date.

We head down to the lobby where Frank opens the door for us. He narrows his eyes at Amber, but doesn't say anything. I give him a tight smile, and he gives me an apologetic look. I won't let him escape though; he'll be hearing an earful from me tomorrow.

It's not that I didn't want Amber in my apartment; I just didn't know her well. Three days is not long enough to invite someone up to your place—male or female.

The only reason she knew where I stayed was because she lived close to me. When we left the coffee shop every morning, we walked the same way back, my stop was first. I don't even want to know how she knew which apartment I lived in. Either way, she was harmless, a little ditzy and sneaky, but harmless none the less.

Haling a taxi was pretty easy. I tried not to think that it was because of the way Amber was dressed. A few minutes later, our taxi pulled up to the Gershwin Theatre with ten minutes to spare. Getting out, I followed closely behind Amber as she pushed her way through the throngs of people.

Two guys stood outside of the door entrance. Both were extremely tall, and I had to admit very cute in their suits and ties. The guy on the left was loosening his tie as he looked around the crowd, he had that laid back look. But the guy on the right had his tie pulled tight, shirt perfectly tucked in, and was looking at his watch.

Walking up to them, Amber hugs the guy on the left. Reaching up and pulling his head to hers, she gives him a quick peck on the lips. Turning to me, she points to the guy she is holding onto.

"This is Holden," she says, her smile radiates affection. "And this," she points to the uptight man next to Holden, "is Dallas." Dallas walks up to me and extends his hand.

Smiling tightly, he says, "Hello." I shake it reluctantly. I might as well make the best of this. Whatever it is. I was lucky to get the tickets I had; no one was going to make me miss the show.

"Katy," I say. He nods his head in acknowledgement but says nothing.

We step through the revolving door into the lobby. People are scarce in here due to Showtime being in a few minutes. But it looked the same as the movie theatre back home, just on a larger scale.

There was the same dark colored carpet with funky patterns on it, and same atmosphere in here as a movie theatre. I waited for the smell of freshly popped popcorn to invade my senses, but it didn't.

Lines and lines of names adorned the walls. I wanted to ask Amber what they meant, but when I looked at her she was deep in conversation with Holden. I let it go for now and tried not to be annoyed by her disregard.

Our seats were on the second floor, so I followed Dallas onto the escalator while Amber and Holden trailed behind us. I was treated to a map of the Emerald City on my ride up making the anticipation increase. It would have been nice to share this experience with Faye. She would have loved this.

Taking our seats, Amber and I sat in the middle and the guys sat next to us on each end. We had really good seats in the front row, middle section. The lights had already gone down, so I wasn't able to see anything but the stage; which blew my mind.

The background on the stage was a huge map. I couldn't see every detail, but I could see that it was a map of the Wicked world, with OZ smack dab in the middle glowing green. Hanging above that was a gigantic beast. Its appearance was similar to a dragon, and its wings spread the whole length of the stage, as it hung ominously from the ceiling.

From start to finish, I was captivated. The singing, dancing, and acting drew me in like I had been sucked through a narrow pipe; ignoring everyone and everything around me.

I found myself making comparisons between Elphaba, the Wicked Witch of the West, and myself. It didn't matter how much I wanted to compare myself to Glinda, the Good Witch. Elphaba had a tough life growing up and a horrible father who was mean to her. It sort of reminded me of myself, and my own life; if you swapped the father for the mother.

It was a hard truth to swallow, knowing that my mother didn't want me enough to fight her urge to self medicate. I always held out hope that someday she would come to her senses and be a mother to me.

At intermission, Dallas asked me if I wanted to go down to the bar for a drink. Looking at Amber, I decided that it sounded better than sitting next to someone who didn't know I was even there. She hadn't even said a word to me since she had met up with Holden, except to introduce me.

The bar was busy. Dallas exuded a certain presence that said, back away, so everyone cleared a path for him. However, people bumped into me without so much as an 'excuse me' or glance in my direction. It was like I was invisible. I didn't let it bother me though. I was doing my fair share of bumping because it was so packed. Everyone was trying to get in a quick drink before the show started back up.

"What would you like?" Dallas asks.

"I'll just have water, thank you." He looks like he may say something. Instead, he just turns and orders my water and a scotch for himself.

After handing me the water, we walk over to a small table. With about ten minutes left before the show starts up again, Dallas strikes up a conversation about Amber, surprisingly, or not.

"How long have you known Amber?" Taking a sip of his scotch, he waits patiently for my answer.

"A week," I reply.

"Really? That makes sense. She is a very charismatic and outgoing person." His fondness with her alarms me, leading me to think that he would rather be up in the balcony with her then down here with me. Noticing the questioning look on my face, he elaborates. "She's my cousin." I nod my head passively.

"Are you from New York?"

"Washington," he says. "I moved here three years ago to attend Columbia for school. Amber moved here last year. She wanted to go to school somewhere away from home but still wanted to have family close."

"What's your major?" I expect him to say business, or something along those lines, but he surprises me.

"Art History." He smirks at me. Noticing my astonished look, he places his elbows on the table and leans in close. Intrigued by what he might have to say next, I lean in too.

Looking at him up close, he has a handsome face. High cheekbones, and a light dusting of stubble that is perfect on him. His blue eyes are the color of the sky and his smile is nice—when he isn't smirking. The mix of scotch and cologne coming off him is strong making me want to retreat, but I don't want to make him feel bad, so I stay.

"Not what you were expecting?" he says, smirking...again.

"I took you for a business major. You have that disposition," I respond then take a sip of my water.

"Well, most of my family is in business, but I decided

to go a different route, even though it was the opposite of what was expected of me. My father wasn't happy, but it's my life. Besides, I like to do the unexpected," he says, shrugging his shoulders carelessly. "What about you?"

Trying to bide time, so I can decide what to reveal to this stranger, I take another drink of my water. Setting it down, I take a deep breath.

"Do you want to know why I really ordered water?" I say very seriously, looking him straight in the eye.

"I guess so?" he says confused.

"I am a terrible alcoholic. Have been since I was thirteen, but," I lift my glass of water in the air, "I'm recovering." I take another drink of my water while eyeing his scotch. Noticing the change in direction he downs his scotch and places the glass on the tray of a passing waiter.

"I'm so sorry. I didn't know." He looks visibly stricken as he runs his hand through his hair and adjusts his tie. He may actually bolt out of here. I can't help but laugh. His uneasy look turns into understanding, as he realizes that I was joking. Grinning, he shakes his head in disapproval, then joins in on the laughing.

"Katy, you are not what I expected either."

"I'll take that as a compliment. And you should know, that I am only eighteen, I can't even be served."

"That doesn't stop most people," he says with a gleam in his eye. I love the back and forth banter. It's nice to be out with people.

We return to the theatre for the rest of the show. Seeing how the Witches, the Tin Man, the Lion, and the Scarecrow came to be was mesmerizing. It made me question what I already knew about The Wizard of Oz; having watched it several times growing up.

The lines between good and evil were blurred. Each scene just got better and better. Seeing the love between Elphaba and Fiyero made me yearn for love of my own.

Looking over at Dallas sitting next to me, he was just as into the show as I was. He was even chuckling at all of Glinda's wittiness. I was more aware of his presence this time. I didn't understand, when did this change from an inconvenience to a casual date?

Thoughts of Caleb washed over me unexpectedly. It was the strangest feeling as my belly fluttered uncontrollably. How could just the thought of him do that? When I was with Josh, I got some occasional butterflies when I saw him, but nothing like this.

When I looked at Dallas, there was no flutter and no anticipation. He was really nice, and I liked talking to him, but it just wasn't there. Still, it wouldn't be so bad to get to know him a little over the next month while I was still here. Trying, with very little success, to push thoughts of Caleb out of my mind was almost...painful.

After the show, we took a taxi to Old Town Bar. I went along just for the experience.

It was a very small bar, packed shoulder to shoulder with no sitting room. It looked rich with history. To our left, the bar made of mahogany and marble, stretched almost the full length of the building. To the right, the wall was covered with tons of pictures. Chandeliers hung from the aluminum ceiling, and the lighting was dim.

The only spot semi open was a place in front of the bar almost at the back. We ordered drinks, mine a cranberry juice, and stood there until a booth or some stools became available. Holden and Amber were in their own little world, pressed up so close to each other it was uncomfortable to look at.

"What did you think of Wicked?" Dallas yells at me over the noise.

"It was great! Not at all what I expected," I say, smiling over my double meaning.

"Yes, it was," he grins at me. "Great, I mean. I have actually seen it three times."

"Does it ever change for you each time you go?" I ask, sliding closer to him so I can hear better.

"It does. There is always something different to see, something that I didn't catch the other time. But it never gets old or boring. I have seen plenty of shows in the past three years, Wicked is my favorite." Taking a sip of his scotch, he says, "Was this your first?" I nod my head yes. "I could tell," he says grinning.

"Oh really, and how?"

Smiling widely, he leans in. "You had drool dripping from the corner of your mouth every time I looked at you." He touches the corner of my mouth.

"Uh huh," I say unbelieving, and surprisingly liking the attention he is giving me. I didn't flirt, that was usually Faye's thing. I don't know where this is coming from; this boldness. Maybe it was because I was in a different city with unknown people and circumstances.

"You never told me what it was that you planned to study. Amber said you recently graduated." Leaning against the tight space between him and the bar, I relax my shoulders.

"I planned to go to college in the fall, but I'm not so sure anymore about going out of state. I had to fight just to keep my house. I don't want to just leave it sit for years while I am away at college. As for what I will study, that's undecided." I shrug my shoulders. "I love to learn about the history of places, people, and things. Maybe something that will allow me to do that."

"You don't have anyone who can stay in your home for you?" He leans against the bar next to me, his elbow propping him up.

"No. My brother lives in California, and everyone else has their own house. My best friend and I are planning to go to college together. I thought about asking her to stay and go to college in town with me. It's not her first choice, and now that I have said that out loud, it sounds extremely selfish of me, doesn't it?"

"No," he says shaking his head slightly. "She can make her own decisions. You should at least bring it up, but there is another option. Maybe you can rent the house out?"

"Huh," I say raising my glass up to my lips for a drink. "I hadn't thought of that. It's not a bad idea."

"I know. I'm an unexpected genius." Oh my gosh, I am with the male version of Faye. I smile at his self appraisal, because he says it with a goofy look on his face.

"So, what type of art do you study?" I question.

"Architectural. It's fascinating. I've always loved finding the value in something beyond dollar signs. My brother always thought I was off kilter, but money just doesn't interest me the way the history of something does. Something we have in common, I see."

Setting his glass on the bar, he stands up straight and looks toward the booths. With his hand he widely gestures around the room.

"This is one of the oldest bars in New York. Most of the structure in here is original." He is gazing around the room appreciatively. "That's why I love New York. There is a lot of history here."

"It's not the celebrities?" I joke.

"I don't pay any attention to them." He waves dismissively.

A booth frees up for all four of us to sit down, but Amber and Holden are gone when I look over. Desperately searching the bar for Amber, I start to feel a little nervous. She wouldn't leave without telling me, would she? I don't even really know Dallas.

Dallas leans down and whispers in my ear, "They already found a booth, up at the front." He points to where they are sitting.

We spend the rest of the evening talking about Architectural Art and my college plans. Dallas desperately tries to talk me into schools in New York, but I hadn't applied for any. It's sort of cute the way he wants me to stay so we can get to know each other better. Or maybe its something stalker would do; I haven't come to a conclusion just yet.

After three hours of talking and laughing, Amber and I split leaving the guys at the booth. As I stand to leave, Dallas grabs my hand.

Looking at him, he smiles and asks, "Can I see you again?"

There really isn't a reason to say no, beside the fact that I have been thinking about Caleb all night, which is very strange. Dallas is fun to be around and nice to talk to despite my initial reaction. He has also been in New York longer than me; he may know some places around town that I haven't been to.

"I'd like that," I say with a smile. He gives me his number, and we make plans to watch the sunrise over the East River and go for coffee in the morning.

The taxi drops me off first. I wave to Amber, who didn't stop talking to me about Holden until I got out of the car, and make my way up to my apartment.

When I get inside the lobby, I notice Frank is gone; probably in the bathroom. I shake my head and take the elevator up ten flights to my floor. Walking into my flat I take my phone out of my purse, dial Faye's number, and drop the purse on the coffee table. Heading toward the balcony, I leave my heels in the living room, and open the sliding doors.

Faye picks up on the first ring. "Oh my gosh, I have news!" she shrieks in my ear. Before I can react, she continues. "Wait, tell me about your day first, because you will not want to follow what I have to say. It's pretty eptastic!"

"Eptastic?" I say smiling.

"Yea, yea. I'll add it to the dictionary." This dictionary could possibly be a best seller.

Sitting down on the chaise lounge, I find the fleece blanket and pull it over me. The stars are so visible tonight for the first time since I have been here. They resemble tiny shards of glass reflecting in the dark. Grandma would love this.

I tell Faye about Wicked and Old Town Bar finishing with Dallas.

"You met a boy. Awe, Katy that's great."

"Gosh, you make it sound like I'm pathetic."

"No. You just haven't dated anyone since Josh, and well, I was starting to think you might be depressed again. You've been in New York for a month, and not one guy has asked you out or talked to you. I can't exactly come over there and check for myself."

"I haven't really been anywhere for a guy to ask me out."

"What sort of venue, exactly, constitutes as a date making place? I don't think it matters, Katy. You are a beautiful girl with lots of spunk. I just can't believe no one has asked you out." I didn't have that same spunk as I used to. I was trying to get it back though; my time with Dallas tonight proved that.

"This conversation is pointless Faye," I say exasperated. "Remember...Dallas. I'm going out with him again."

She sighs. "I'm so happy for you, having a summer fling. Just be sure to use protection. You remember what happened to Victoria last year and-"

"Faye," I groan. "He is a complete stranger. Who do you think I am? You know me better than anyone, I'm not going to just lay myself out there for him and say 'Come here big boy.'" I try that last part as seductively as I can. She starts chuckling, but it turns into full blown laughter quickly.

"I-just-I can't. 'Big boy'" she says mocking me. "Who

are you?"

I sigh, "That's all you got from that, wasn't it?"

"It's just-" she's laughing harder now. "I have never heard you talk like that. Maybe you have a bit of me in you after all."

Changing the subject, I knew that's what needed to happen, or I would never hear the end of it, I say, "Stop laughing. Tell me your news?"

"Oh yes! Are you ready for this?" Her laughter has turned to extreme excitement; it makes me excited for her even though I haven't a clue what this is about. "Micah-asked-me-to-marry-him!" She says it like it's one word and squeals so loud that I have to hold the phone away from my ear.

I'm not entirely surprised. They act like they are completely and totally in love with each other. But, I can't help but feel worried. She is so young. I'll be happy for her anyways, as long as she doesn't rush into it, because being in love means that you can take your time. And this deep nagging in my mind has me thinking that love doesn't last. When it does, it just leaves your heart open for heartache.

"You haven't said anything." Her excitement deflates just a little.

"That's great, Faye. So, how did he propose?" I lay back anticipating a long response. She didn't disappoint—neither did Micah.

Micah did a fantastic job with the proposal. He took Faye to the amusement park and suggested they ride the Ferris Wheel. But when they got to the top, the wheel stopped. Micah pointed to a banner that hung huge over the entrance to the park. It said 'I could stay here with you forever. Marry me, Faye.' When she turned to look at him, in shock, he had a ring in his hand. It was beautiful by her declaration. Without words, she told him yes.

"It was magical and just perfect, Katy." She had a

dreamy tone to her voice. I couldn't help the huge grin that spread across my face. When Faye was happy, I was happy. "You'll be my maid of honor, right?" Who was I to turn that down?

"Of course I will." We ended the call, but not before Faye reassured me that the garden had been taken care of, and the house was fine.

After changing into shorts and a t-shirt for bed, I remember that I had wanted to talk to Frank, but made plans in the morning with Dallas. I probably wouldn't catch him tomorrow since he works the overnight shift.

I head down, hoping he is there. He was about to hear an earful from me. I can't believe he just left his post earlier and let someone get past him. There's not usually someone at the desk this late at night, because we have such a stealthy doorman, *yeah right*, so the lobby is completely empty. Frank isn't even down here. I hope he is okay.

Walking over to the front door, I open it and look out, thinking maybe he stepped outside for a second, but he wasn't there either. Huh?

Taking a seat in the lobby, I wait for him to return. Twenty minutes later, Frank's still gone, but a woman walks- or is being dragged- into the lobby by a man. He looks like a bouncer at a club, wearing a pair of black jeans, black boots, and a black t-shirt. His face is cleanly shaven and his black hair is slicked back. His arm muscles are being strangled by his t-shirt and are covered in suggestive tattoos. Gross.

He gets her into the elevator, haphazardly, and asks what floor. She slurs out something and starts giggling ridiculously as he punches the number in. *A reminder why I don't drink*, I think. As the doors slide closed, he looks right at me sending goose bumps down my arms.

Trying to rub the goose bumps away, I start to worry about Frank. I try checking the bathroom, but he isn't in there. That's it, that's the last place to check. I'll just look outside again and take the stairs back up. I don't really want to be in here when the man in black comes back down.

I jog to the door and open it—no Frank. I'm not sure where he could have gone or why he would leave his post. It isn't just for a short period either, because I have been sitting here for twenty minutes, and he wasn't here when I came home. This is serious. I'll have to call management tomorrow, even though I don't want to get Frank in trouble.

Giving up, I turn to take the stairs up. Half-way there the elevator doors open, and the man in black steps out—eyeing me.

The goose bumps return as I pick up my pace across the lobby. His eyes follow my path, and the need to get out of there quickly takes over. There really is nowhere to go but up the stairs or up the elevator, and he's blocking the path to the elevator.

Taking the stairs is a bad idea, it's ten flights before I reach my floor. At least the elevator would close me in and move quickly. The stairwell has so many entry points that anyone can burst through at anytime, but it's my only option.

Reaching the door, I open it forcefully and step inside. But not before I take one last glance behind me, just in time to see the man in black take one step forward—toward me.

This is not good, so not good. Fear creeps down my spine and adrenaline kicks in. I take the steps two at a time, darting as fast as possible without stopping. As I reach the second floor, I hear the door open. Dread pours over me making my body feel numb. My mace is upstairs in my purse where I usually keep it.

My Krav Maga training has helped me build some endurance, which is why I'm not out of breath right now, but this man is twice my size, and I've never used the Krav Maga skills in real life. I'm silently cursing myself for not going to class the past month and not taking Caleb up on that self-defense offer.

Taking deep breaths to compensate for the amount of

running I am doing, I look behind me to see how close he is. I wish I hadn't. I wish I had just kept running. He is directly behind me.

I reach the landing and prepare to go through the door on the seventh floor, but not before the man grabs my ankle, bringing me down. My head hits the concrete hard causing me to be temporarily dazed. Feeling the man release my ankle makes a false sense of hope shoot through me. But his hands return quickly, wrapping around my upper arms and pulling them painfully tight behind my back. This is the worst position to be in; lying down on my stomach.

Feeling his body cover mine, I try to scream but he frees my hands pinning them between his body and mine, while he covers my mouth, so my scream comes out muffled. He's too heavy, I can barely breath.

Trying desperately to get the upper hand, I throw my head back hoping to hit him. But, I don't connect.

Tears stream down my face, and my stomach turns. His big sweaty hand runs down the length of my body ending at my knee. I wiggle under him trying to get him to shift off of me, but it's no use, he's too heavy. All of my Krav Maga training is worthless in this position.

Pushing my knee to the side, he repositions so his hips align with mine. I feel him as he pulls down my shorts. No, no this can't be happening. Why me? I'd rather he bang my head into the cement, shoot me, throw me down the stairs, anything but this. I have never truly wanted death as much as I do now.

The thought of what is about to happen, and the fear that overtakes me, causes me to tense up. I start to see spots in my vision. *No please don't pass out.*

I have to keep fighting even though it's not getting me anywhere. The spots deepen right before complete darkness overtakes me. I hear a thump followed by a loud 'Ugh', and then—I am gone.

Chapter Six

I was in a forest. Trees loomed over me big and tall, blowing freely in the wind. As I walk, the sticks under my bare feet snap, but they never hurt.

I step into an opening. Flowers surround me smelling like lavender and looking brilliant. The sun is shining a bright light of hope in the sky. As it hits my skin warming me, I feel at peace. Laying down in the meadow, a bird chirps a lullaby overhead. It's one that I have heard many times as a child; one that my grandma used to sing to me before bedtime.

Frolicking in the meadow the doe plays as if there had been no yesterday. Full of energy, with no worry in sight, they belong to the one who is strong and will keep them safe in the night.

As I continue to listen to the birds with a smile on my face, the sun starts to disappear, overtaken by dark grey clouds. The heat leaves my body making me feel cold as ice, and I start to shake uncontrollably. The birds with their beautiful lullaby, whistle a different tune—of pain. Dread starts to descend filling every limb in my body making me feel heavy. When I try to get up, I can't

My smile fades away and is replaced with a frown. Looking around, the forest is dark, and the trees are no longer green and lush, but they are barren. The leaves are being carried away by the whipping of the wind. The white flowers, that once surrounded me in the meadow, have turned into a dull colorless shade. When I reach over and touch one, it turns to dust in my hand.

When I look back to the sky there is a black hole where the sun was. It looks closer than it should be, so I reach out attempting to touch it. It is close, my hand disappears in it, and as soon as it swallows my elbow, it sucks me in entirely.

~~~

Hearing a constant beeping, I open my eyes, blinking at first so that they can adjust to the light. I'm in a hospital.

My head feels like it has been crushed flat. When I try to move it, it's too heavy. My mouth is so dry. I need water. I look around to find a cup sitting on a swivel tray, but it's just out of reach. Sitting up a little and reaching for it, the pain is too much to bear. I try just reaching it by extending my hand as far as I can, but when I lift my arm, I notice the dark bruises that lay across my bicep.

Long dark bruises that resemble fingers. It looks like I have been touched by death. Then I remember what happened and why I'm here. Remember the way the man in black looked at me, his hands gripping my upper arms too tightly. I remember the way he felt on top of me and then complete darkness taking over.

My chest tightens painfully, and breathing becomes hard. Panic starts to take up residence, and I start to gasp for air but none seems to find its way in. The beeping noise quickens its pace.

Left over fear from the incident has me looking around the room as my panic increases. What if he followed me here? What if he comes back? The pain in my chest spreads and my head starts to ache too.

Sitting up, I forget the IV, and it's ripped out of my arm in my hurry to flee. The floor is cold under my feet and my legs tremble. As I try to take a step forward it causes me to lurch into the swivel tray, but I don't fall. Instead, I hold onto it tightly and try helplessly to regain my footing.

I look behind me, feeling that I will be attacked at any moment, just as someone pushes through the door. There is a bright light, and then a man in black. Black boots, black shirt, and a smug smile on his face. He's walking toward me. A scream rises up out of me, as I push myself up and try to back away. No, not again. I plead for someone, anyone, to help me.

My legs will not hold me up, so I fall as I am trying to retreat from this man. I push myself back using my hands and feet, refusing to turn my back on him again. He is right in front of me now. Shaking my head, I try to plead again.

"Please, no, no. Please don't. Please, please," I beg as my tears fall. He reaches down, so I close my eyes and scream louder, throwing my hands out in front of me to stop him. I feel a pinch in my upper arm, and my head starts swimming. No longer able to scream, no longer able to hold my hands up, I drop them to my side.

This is it, I'm going to die. He has injected me with something. What will he do? Where will he take me? There is nothing more daunting then the uncertainty of your circumstances.

My eyes grow heavy, and I start to forget what was happening. Finally, my body cannot withstand it anymore, and I sink back into something familiar—the dark.

~~~

"Katy." Hearing my name being called, I open my eyes slightly, but I'm still a little drowsy. I look at the woman standing over me, and worry starts to take root. She must notice, because she takes a small step away. I relax, but not enough for my heart to stop hammering in my chest.

"Katy. Do you know where you are?" the woman asks. She has a Middle Eastern accent, but that's all I notice, because my vision is blurred.

"Yes." I manage to croak out. I know exactly where I am; in the hospital. And last night, I was...I can't even think it. It's too horrible. Instead, I turn my head away in shame and start to sob as quietly as I can. The thought of being violated, and the fear of what happened and what it means, makes my heart turn violently inside of my chest.

Tears pour from my eyes in streams. I close them, hoping it will act as a dam, but my effort is pointless. The woman tries to speak to me again, but I keep my eyes closed and continue to sob, unable to stop.

I feel my life changing in this very moment. Any worth that I had, is gone. Hopelessness and fear override any other feeling that I may have. I cry for hours, sometimes stopping only for a moment just to start back up again. Finally, the sobbing dissipates, but tears still stream down my face. I lay there; lifeless, emotionless, and completely broken.

A woman walks into my room, but I stay in my position, unmoving. She stops a few feet away from me.

"Katy, my name is Doctor Raeanne. I'm a psychologist. Your doctor has approved my visit." I don't say anything; just continue to stare up at the ceiling, but watching her through my peripheral vision. "Katy," she continues, "do you have family we can call? Someone must be worried. You have been out of it for the past two days. I'm sure someone will want to know that you are okay."

My family? I think about Collin, Aunt Rita, and Faye. Faye, I call her every night. The thought of talking to Faye makes me feel nauseous. What would I tell her? I already knew the answer to that—nothing. I would tell her nothing. I didn't want to have this conversation with Faye, but if I didn't even call, then I wouldn't have to worry about that. I knew I couldn't avoid her forever, and that she was probably worrying and blowing up my phone. I'd have to talk to her sooner or later. I choose later.

Turning my head toward the doctor I say, "No," with very little emotion. She pulls out a chair and sits down.

"Katy," she begins. "Do you know why you are here?" I nod my head. "I can see you are not prepared to talk, and that is okay. It's normal to be non-verbal when you have been through a trauma." She crosses her legs and puts her hands in her lap. "Your Doctor needs to come in and examine you, to make sure that you are working properly so that she can release you. Are you okay with this?"

A single tear slips down my cheek. As much as I want to protest, I agree. I just want to get out of here. But, I don't know where I will go when I leave. The thought of going back to my apartment frightens me. It's the only place I have though. Doctor Raeanne rises from her chair.

"I'll need to talk to you, as well. Before you are released," she says as she turns and leaves the room. I can't help but feel relieved. Seconds later, an older woman comes in wearing a white lab coat. She walks up to me and stands a few feet away like the psychologist did.

"Hello Katy. My name is Doctor Feora. I need to examine you. As I do this, I will explain what has happened. Okay?" Her voice is gentle, but it doesn't soothe me.

I nod my head in acceptance. Taking out a small flashlight she reaches for me, and my whole body tightens as I flinch away. A look of pure pity crosses her face, and I hate it. Her pity only puts truth behind what happened, but I wanted to believe that this was all a horrible nightmare that I would wake from soon.

Without touching me, she shines the light in my eyes back and forth as I try not to blink. Satisfied, she moves on reaching for me slowly, grasping my arm with just her fingertips. Touching me as if she was defusing a bomb. My body was tense, and I was on edge. Looking at the dark purple bruises on my arm, that look of pity crosses her face again.

"These will fade in a couple of weeks," she reassures. The bruises are the least of my worries.

She travels down toward my rib cage and pushes lightly. I wince at the pain it causes.

"Katy, you suffered a severe concussion when you fell causing some swelling in your brain. That, coupled with passing out due to the amount of fear and stress you were under, caused you to fall into a deep sleep." She moves to the other side of my ribs. "The swelling was minor and started to dwindle within hours after you were admitted." She walks down to the edge of my bed, pulling my legs from under the blankets, again, touching me with just her fingertips. My ankles are bruised just as badly as my arms. She checks them briefly, then comes up next to me staying a few feet away. My body relaxes a little.

"You need to rest for a couple of weeks. There is a lot of bruising, and the swelling in your brain has completely gone, but no permanent damage. No heavy lifting and please take it easy." She grabs the clipboard from the end of the bed and starts writing. "There is a gentleman here to see you. His name is Frank, he is the one who brought you in." She stops writing and looks at me. "Do you want me to tell him anything?"

I have questions for him. If he had been in the lobby, maybe I wouldn't feel so disgusted with myself. So much anger and embarrassment was building inside me at the mention of his name, because I know what he has seen. I couldn't get the thought out of my head that it's his fault I am here.

"Tell him I'm fine." I shouldn't ask him my questions while I am this angry, nothing good would come out of my mouth. The doctor nods her head.

"The police would also like to speak with you to get your statement. You should know that Frank disabled the perpetrator, and he is in custody." She gives me another sad look before turning to walk out of the door.

"Wait," I yell. Something's not right. She hadn't mentioned anything about doing an exam...or a kit. Isn't that what usually happens in these instances? "Shouldn't you-don't you need to examine- I mean..." Stumbling over my words, I try again. "You need to check, you know to make sure that he didn't..." Understanding what I am trying to ask, she walks over to me. A small, tight smile braces her face as if she can finally tell me something good.

"No, honey. He didn't get that far." I blow out a breath of air that I hadn't realized I'd been holding in. The doctor walks out the door leaving me by myself. I thought I would feel somewhat better, but I don't.

I've had things taken from me before. When I was seven, Bobby Salet took a box of crayons from me. He dumped them all over the floor and stomped on them, breaking every single crayon, as he laughed. But I wouldn't let it bother me. Instead, I just went home, told Grandma, and she bought me another pack. I kept those ones close to me.

My father had been taken by cancer, my grandma by stroke, and my mother took every mother-daughter moment from me that we should have shared.

But nothing compares to losing your sense of wholeness. Feelings I had never felt before started to take over. Thoughts of just how cruel the world can be filled my mind. I had already thought that it was cruel, but now, I felt it was laughing in my face. Maybe I was destined to live a life with one bad thing after another intermingling. I certainly didn't want to know what was going to happen next.

I tried not to think about it. But thoughts of all the bad invaded my mind unbidden, and I had no idea how to make it stop. I reached for the sapphire around my neck, but it wasn't there. I hadn't realized how much I relied on a necklace for comfort.

~~~

It took four hours for them to release me. I wish it had been longer, because every time I thought about going back to my apartment, fear clawed its way out ,and my gut started to clench, but I knew I had to go. After giving my statement to the police, I used the phone in my room to call Amber. She didn't ask a lot of questions; only if I was all right. I reassured her that I was, and she drove me back to the apartment. She didn't talk at all, and I didn't offer any conversation. I had a feeling that she was glad to be rid of me as she said bye and fled.

I ran, literally ran, to the elevator and jumped inside pushing the button over and over again trying to get the doors to close quicker. Frank wasn't here, and I was relieved, but the day doorman was looking at me as if I was crazy. When the doors finally closed, I pressed myself up against the elevator wall.

When I got off on my floor, I run to my door, open it, and close and lock it behind me. My heart was racing as I closed my eyes and leaned against the door to catch my breath. My side and head are throbbing painfully from being pushed too far so soon after an injury.

I go up to the loft and into the bathroom and turn the shower on. Stripping out of the scrubs they had given me at the hospital; I jump in the shower before the water can turn warm. I don't care. I just need to wash the dirty off. I scrub my body till it feels raw. It didn't matter; I still didn't feel clean, so I slid down the wall and stayed under the spray of the water a long time after it got cold.

Afterwards, I grab my sapphire and put it on so that I can feel the comfort that Grandma's gift brings me. Then, I lay down in bed. I start to fall asleep but realize that I have not talked to Faye. My phone is plugged into the charger sitting on the coffee table. But I don't feel like going down to get it. Every move feels like a knife stabbing me in the side. So I drift off.

It isn't long before the phone wakes me. I climb slowly down the steps to the living room and answer it on the third ring.

"Katy, oh my gosh! Are you okay? I tried calling you like a gazillion times. I was starting to worry." Faye's voice is on the other end and it makes me feel a pang of guilt.

I wanted to tell her, and a part of me knew that it was

because I didn't want to hang on to this alone. But I was too disgusted with myself, and afraid that she might think less of me, so I lied instead.

"I'm okay. I just got in late last night and didn't want to bother you. I've been busy sightseeing." I hold my breath, waiting for her reply to see if she'll believe me. I can hear my own tone, and it sounds sad and weak.

She questions it at first saying, "That's never stopped you before. You know you can call me any time."

"Yeah, I know," I say, easing my way onto the couch as I bite my lip so that I don't yelp in pain. She makes me promise that I won't do that again, then launches into a spiel on what colors she wants at the wedding and what the bridesmaid dresses will look like. I listen but give little feedback. If she finds that strange she doesn't notice, because she just keeps going on and on. I just want to go lay down and cry some more. I am thankful that she has something to distract her from my bleak mood.

When we hang up, I go back to bed. I spend the next several days the same way. Only doing what I absolutely have to, and nothing more.

I call Faye every day when I know she won't answer, and leave a message saying that I am having fun, and I probably won't be able to call again until late. She tries calling me, but I don't answer. The fear never leaves me.

Deciding to just go home, and escape this city all together, I book a flight back two weeks early. I book the flight during the busiest time of the day unworried about fighting through crowds. I'd rather be in a crowd of people then alone. *No one would be able to hear my screams if I'm alone.* I shudder at the thought.

When I get to the airport, being around people proved difficult. Every time someone got too close to me, I would jump, and my heart would start a race it could not win.

I hurried as fast as I could to board. When someone sat next to me on the flight, I tried to move as close to the window as I could.

When we landed, I skipped calling Faye for a ride to avoid questions. I hopped on the bus because the thought of being in a taxi alone with a stranger, made me feel sick. I just picked the lesser of the two evils. It didn't matter whether I was alone or in a crowd, I still felt fear saturate me.

I didn't know what I was going to do when I got home or how I was going to feel. The house would be empty because I live alone now, but it was my home. What else was there to do? If I felt safe anywhere, it would be there.

When I arrive at the house, I drop my suitcase on the floor, shut and lock the door, and hurry to my room. Getting under the covers, I pull them up over my head and shut my eyes trying to block out any sounds or movements. The tiniest ping would make my heart race. I felt like I was four again; sneaking into mommy and daddies room, because I was scared of the dark.

No matter how hard I tried, I couldn't go to sleep. This house was different then my tiny little New York apartment. There were an unlimited amount of places to hide. Things could creep out in the middle of the night or come in from several different places.

Instead of falling asleep in my room, I got up and walk back to the front door to check that I *in fact* locked it.

I decide to curl up on the couch instead of going back to my room. But when it got dark, the hallway looming behind me only makes me anxious, so I sit in Grandma's rocking chair in the corner next to the couch.

Grabbing Grandma's blanket, I pull it over me and just stare into the dark. Keeping my eyes open started to become painful. Blinking no longer kept them moist, so I close them and fall right asleep. That really seemed to be the only thing I could do lately—sleep.

~~~

A tapping wakes me up. Faye is standing in front of me, tapping her foot on the hardwood floor, with her arms crossed over her chest. I forgot that she came in every morning to get the mail and check on things. I look at her tapping foot then up at her; she looks angry.

"Number one," she holds up her index finger, "you didn't call me last night. Number two, "she holds up her middle finger, "you didn't tell me you were planning on coming home early. I'm having mixed feelings here. I want to hug you, because I missed you so much, but murder sounds nice too."

Sitting up, I wince at the pain it causes. Her anger fades, and is replaced with worry. Leaning over, she reaches out to put her hand on my shoulder. Not thinking, I cringe away. She looks hurt but still puts her hand on my shoulder.

"Are you okay?" she asks.

"Sure. I just...fell." When did I become such a liar? There has never been anything I wouldn't tell Faye. I feel like the worst friend in the world. I try to tell myself that I'm not ready to say it out loud, that I don't want to put a damper on her wedding news, but it's just my way of avoiding it. I know this, but it doesn't stop me from lying anyways.

"When did this happen?" she says, taking a seat on the couch. I relax when her hand moves from my shoulder.

"I don't know," I say shrugging, "almost a week ago, I guess."

"It's like you have two left feet." Lying back on the couch, she blows out a breath and puts her arm over her head. "Was it serious? Did you get checked out?"

"No it wasn't, and therefore, no, I didn't," I say, looking away from her in an attempt to hide the truth.

"But you're in pain, I can tell."

"Yes, I can never get anything past the Inquisitor," I snap, but she doesn't catch on to my mood.

"So, why did you come home early? Oh wait," she sits

up straight in her chair, "I know. You couldn't stay away from your flamboyant best friend, who just so happens to dress well. And," she draws that word out, "I brought you a gift. I was going to leave it on your night stand. But since you are here..." She pulls out a small purple box and hands it to me.

I open it to reveal a beautifully complex hair comb. A flower adorns the middle with vines coming out of it in all different directions. Small leaves are scattered all down the vines, and tiny flowers with small diamonds in the middle sit at the end of each vine. It looks very expensive.

"Are you getting married tomorrow." I really hope her answer is no.

"Um, no, But," she claps her hands together and bounces in her seat, "we have set a date!" That was quick, but I don't voice my opinion out loud. "January seventeenth!"

"January seventeenth?" I ask to make sure I heard her right.

"Yes, it will be a winter wedding, and it will be so gorgeous."

"That's only six months away? You guys won't even be in the same state."

"Okay, I wanted to wait to tell you..." she says nervously.

"Just tell me, Faye." I'm pretty sure I know what she is going to say.

"I'm going to do a half semester with you, then transfer to where Micah is." That's exactly what I expected. "Are you okay with this? We'll get four months together. By then you'll have settled in, and we will see each other on holidays, and we can do that face chat."

Whatever, that's what I want to say but instead I'm supportive.

"It's fine. You're right, you should go be with Micah."

I wasn't going to college next month anyways, so her decision actually made things easier on me. The fact that she had Micah, made things easier on me. I didn't tell her that either.

"You're not mad?" she asks hesitantly. *At the world*, I think to myself.

"No, of course not."

"All right," she jumps up off the couch with a huge grin on her face, "get up and get dressed." She leans down to pick up her purse. "We are going wedding shopping."

"Can't Micah go with you?" I groan.

"Yeah right. He acts like he's sleeping when I call him, so he doesn't have to go. We need coffee first. I'm having caffeine withdraws."

Getting up from my spot, I try one more time. "Can we do some online shopping?"

"No! Now, go—dress." She points me in the direction of my room. I do as I'm told and come back out wearing a pair of blue jeans, a long sleeve white t-shirt, and tennis shoes.

"Seriously, you have no style girl," she says exasperated while looking me up and down. "It's too hot for long sleeve. Are you crazy?"

"What," I say, looking at what I'm wearing. "It's comfortable."

She rolls her eyes, and we head out the door. I walk slowly to accommodate the soreness I still feel in my side. I know if I told her that I didn't want to go because of the pain she would want to examine me. Then she would see the bruising. So, I decide to stick it out.

It feels nice to be back around Faye considering recent events. I just don't want to be alone.

Going through the drive-thru at the small coffee shop down the street, we grab our coffee and head to one of the biggest bridal shops downtown. It is jam packed with people, all of them with stacks of dresses in their hands. I tense up the moment we enter the front door. All of these people make me nervous.

Faye walks in and heads straight to a rack as she studies each and every dress. I put my back toward her and look around frantically. My heart is beating quickly. I can do this—for Faye. Someone bumps into me, and I scream and back into Faye.

"Katy, what's wrong?" she asks. Her voice is full of concern as she grabs my wrist. But I pull away from her and feel my eyes widen. Knowing I've given something away, I run out the door breathing harshly. When I'm out, I lean up against the outside of the store, and try to concentrate on my breathing; in, out, in, out. Faye comes bursting out of the door with a look of terror on her face making me jump.

"Katy, what was that? You scared me to death." Placing her hand over her heart, she takes a step toward me, but I flinch away from her not thinking, just reacting. She backs away and just stands there next to me, not saying anything.

There is nothing I can do to prevent them, they just come without permission. The tears streak down my face, and soon I am sobbing. I close my eyes like a little kid. If I can't see her then she can't see me.

"Katy, what is it? You're not telling me something, and you are scaring me. Please talk to me," she pleads.

"I-I can't, Faye. I just can't. Please..." I shake my head.

"Listen, let's just get out of here. We can do this another time." She grabs my hand and starts to pull me toward the car, unable to see the terror in my eyes over her touch. When we get in, she doesn't start the car right away.

"Katy," she says, turning toward me, "you have to tell me what's going on. You came home early and didn't tell me. I feel like you were avoiding me every time I called you in New York, you haven't smiled, and every time I reach for you, you act like I'm going to hit you or something. Tell me, right now. What is going on?" Still crying, I put my head in my hands.

"I can't Faye. It's too terrible. Please, I just want to go home."

"Tell me right now...or I'll call Collin," she threatens. But the sound of her voice is what makes me relent. She is just as worried and scared as I am.

Looking up, I stare out at the road not wanting to look at her. After a few moments, I start to shake, because I know that what I am about to tell her will change things.

"I was attacked," I say between sobs. I look over and see her shoulders slump.

"Oh my gosh, Katy." She puts her head in her hands, and I turn away. "Did you get mugged?" she mumbles into her hands.

"No." She looks up, staring at the car that is parked in front of us. Closing her eyes she takes a deep breath.

"Did that guy, Dallas, hit you?"

"No," I croak out.

"Katy, please..." she says gently, turning to look at me.

Staring straight ahead, I start to tell her what happened to me that day in New York. I try to numb all feelings in myself, so I don't break down.

When I start to tell her about being knocked down in the stairwell by the man in black, she starts to sob repeating over and over, "No, no, no." When I'm done, we are both sniffling.

Finally, finding the nerve to look at her, I can see my pain reflected in her eyes that are glistening with tears. I hate that I caused her hurt, but I knew she would figure it out. She is too inquisitive. Not knowing what to say to her, I feel relieved when she starts first.

"I'm so sorry that this happened. I wish I had known sooner." If she had, it wouldn't have made a difference. There really is nothing else to say.

She starts the car, and we drive back to my house. Things feel tense between us. This is what I was afraid of.

She feels weird around me. Faye sits on the couch, and I sit down next to her.

"Do you want to watch a movie?" I ask, trying my best to get things back to normal. *Things will never be normal again,* I thought.

"Sure," she responds flatly. I pull the first movie off the movie shelf, not caring what it is, and put it in.

"Katy?" Faye says. I turn to look at her pale face. "I think you should see someone."

I let out a huff. "I talked to someone at the hospital. I can't tell anyone else. I mean, look how uncomfortable it's made you? I don't want people to act weird around me. It's bad enough I have to live with this. No one else should have too."

"But, you need help, Katy. I can tell you right now you don't want to be touched and people freak you out. It's like someone has sucked the life out of you."

"I won't talk to anyone. Please, just drop it." Shaking her head she relents. This isn't over. If Faye is anything, she is persistent.

We watch the movie in complete silence. It is suppose to be a comedy, but neither of us laugh. When it's over, she stands up and stretches.

"I'm supposed to meet Micah, but I'm going to call him and cancel."

"No, don't do that. Go ahead and go. I'll be fine. But," I hesitate. Asking this next question will most definitely be like saying 'you're right and I'm wrong'. "Will you come back tonight, and stay with me? I couldn't sleep last night. That's why I was in the chair." Without hesitation, she nods her head.

"Of course." Picking up her purse, she heads toward the door calling behind her, "I'll be back at eight. Call me if you need anything," and then she's gone.

Walking up to the door, I lock it and head to my room to take a shower. Pulling open the dresser drawer, I grab a pair of flannel pajama bottoms and a t-shirt. When I pull out a pair of socks, I notice a card on the bottom. Taking it out and turning it over, I read: Caleb Mathews, Self-Defense Instructor.

Thinking back to that day at the diner, it seems like a lifetime ago. He handed me his card in hopes that I would call, or maybe he was just trying to be polite. I didn't know then, and I don't know now, what his motives were or why he approached me that day.

Self-defense may not be a bad idea considering my Krav Maga was useless. What was it Caleb said about his class, *Yes, well this is completely different, I think you would like it.*

Maybe I would, but my gut clenched just at the thought of Caleb. I remembered how he knew about my grandma without me saying it. He was attentive by his own admission. He would definitely know what happened to me. He would see right through my facade, and as soon as I flinched or ran because someone bumped into me, he would know, and he would look at me with disgust.

It doesn't matter. Faye was right, I don't want to be touched, and I do feel lifeless.

Wrapping my fingers around the tiny sapphire around my neck, I squeeze it and close my eyes. Walking toward the bathroom for my shower, I throw the card in the garbage. But, I'm not able to push past the gnawing in my head that throwing the card away was probably a bad decision.

Chapter Seven

Faye came over just as planned last night. We fell asleep in my bed talking about college. I told her my plan to take a year off. I knew Faye; in normal circumstances she would have been all over me about the statistics of students who actually go to college after a year off. She didn't even protest. "I think that's a good idea," she had said.

She was nervous around me and avoided any kind of contact. No matter how hard she tried to act normal, it didn't work. It made me regret telling her. Eventually, she would have noticed the change in me, and I wouldn't have been able to avoid it. Maybe that's why I told her, because of the inevitability of her figuring it out.

When I woke up, I felt well rested. It had been so long since I had a good night sleep. With Faye here, I felt a little safer. It took an unusual amount of time to fall asleep, but when I did sleep, it was without nightmare and soundlessly.

I walked out to the kitchen where Faye was making breakfast. She had two plates sitting out on the breakfast bar piled high with strawberries and blueberries and two pieces of whole wheat toast. The smell of melted cheese carried over from the stove where she had made egg white omelets. She was pouring coffee into two mugs when she spots me.

"Good morning, sunshine," she says happily. Surprised by her cheery disposition, I give her my best confused look, but she ignores it. Instead, she hands me a cup of coffee. "I made breakfast," she says, as she scoops the omelet out and onto my plate.

"I see that. Why?" I study her as I walk to the stool at the breakfast bar.

She shrugs and mumbles, "You look like you haven't

Fractured Heart (The Redemption Series)

eaten in weeks." Then from under her breath, "I should have seen that."

"Faye," I sigh, "don't do that. Don't start blaming yourself." She sits next to me and starts cutting into her omelet.

"You looked stressed yesterday," looking up at me she continues. "and you looked like you hadn't eaten and your eyes were, *are*," she corrects herself, "a little sunken in. Why didn't I notice those things when I first looked at you?" She looks down at her plate, and her shoulders slump. "When I talked to you that last time in New York, I heard the sadness in your voice, but I did nothing. I didn't say anything. Instead, I chose to ignore it. I assumed that you were homesick. What kind of a friend am I?" Looking at me again she says, "Not a best one, that's for sure." She sounds dejected. I hadn't thought she would blame herself.

"I'm sorry, but as much as you would like to think so; you cannot read minds. How were you suppose to just guess what was going on? And, you are my best friend, Faye. There is no one in this world like you." Grabbing her hand, I squeeze it tightly. "There is no one in this world who can replace you." She has an innocent look in her eyes when she glances at me.

"Okay, remember that when you hear what I'm about to tell you." Oh no, this can't be good. Releasing her hand, she looks at it, then at me. I sit back waiting patiently. "I called Collin," she confesses.

"What!" I yell so loud it makes her cringe. "I specifically asked you not to do that!" Standing, I start pacing back and forth. "Why did you do that, Faye? I thought you were my best friend? Best friends don't do the opposite of what is asked of them."

I stop in front of her, and she says, "I had to. I didn't know what else to do or how to deal with this. And best friends do what's best for each other regardless of what the

92 | P a g e

other says or thinks," she pleads.

"You," I say pointing at her, "don't have to deal with this. It was never yours to deal with. It's mine. You had no right to make that decision for me." Putting my hands on my head, I start pacing again. "He's probably on his way here right now, and I'm just not ready to see him or talk to him about this."

"No." she says standing up. I stop pacing and look at her. "I talked him into staying in California. He did want to come out here, but I told him that you probably didn't want to talk about it right now. I promised to look after you." Watching her twist her hands in front of her, I realize that she is very nervous. Letting out a long breath, I cross my arms over my chest and look away from her.

"Who else did you tell? Because I swear Faye—"

"No one!"

"Micah?" I ask between clenched teeth.

"No, of course not." Satisfied with her answer, I pull her into a hug. A tense hug, but it's a start.

"This is hard for me to accept, Faye. You can't go around telling other people. You have to let me deal with it in my own time."

"I was scared," she says softly. With that, I feel my anger fall away.

We finish our breakfast in complete silence. It's so good when you compare it to what I had been eating just to curb my appetite. I try to savor every bite, but I have eaten so little the past week that I can't finish, not even close. I notice Faye eyeing my plate disapprovingly, but she doesn't say anything.

"Your brother wants you to call him," she says before taking a sip of her coffee. Crap, I didn't want to talk to my brother right now or possibly ever. All I can think of is how disappointed he will be or even disgusted. I'm not ready to deal with our relationship changing. "I told him that if it were me," Faye continues, "I wouldn't want to talk to my brother right now." She knows me so well.

"Thank you," I say. She nods her head, gets up, and takes our plates to be washed; dumping my barely touched food into the trash first.

She turns swiftly after loading the plate into the dishwasher. Startled, I glance at her.

"I think I should move in," she says. I hadn't thought about that, but her suggestion doesn't surprise me, and it's not an entirely bad idea.

"I think you're right," I agree. Smiling widely, she turns around and starts to load the dishwasher again.

"Also—" I groan and throw my head back. See, she always does this. She hits me with something good to soften the blow when she has something bad to say. "When I talked to Collin earlier he had mentioned a self-defense instructor, I think his name was Caleb, he thinks that it would be a good idea for you to see him, and maybe learn his type of self-defense." Turning to look at me she is wringing the kitchen towel in her hands. "He said the kind of self-defense he teaches will help when your attacker is bigger then you." I start to shake my head no, start to remember that I can't be touched, but she interrupts me. "I'll go with you. We can learn together. It might be fun."

"I don't know," I say unsure. "How does Collin know what type of self-defense Caleb teaches?"

"Research, and he said he knew his brother." That had me curious enough to want to call him. "How about we go, I'll take the class, and you can just watch? If you feel comfortable, you can take my spot, and maybe next weekend we can both do it?"

This conversation is just freaky. I literally just told myself yesterday that I could not see Caleb as I threw his card in the garbage. It wouldn't have had any less effect on me if the card had mysteriously appeared in my hand right now. Maybe this should mean something, but I didn't know what.

Unwillingly, I agree. Faye called Caleb and made the arrangements for this Saturday, only registering herself like we had agreed. We walked out to the gazebo and sat out there for most of the early afternoon. Micah called so she talked to him forever, laughing and grinning the whole time. I only wished I could laugh and grin like that again.

Since Grandma passed, I hadn't been able to get that back fully. Grabbing the sapphire around my neck, I squeeze it tightly. I try not to think about Grandma because that leads to thinking about what she would have done if she knew what happened to me in New York. Probably find the guy and chop off his arms and other body parts that shall remain nameless. That makes me smile a little. I miss her so much it hurts. When I look up at Faye she looks baffled.

"Micah, I have to go," she says, hanging up with him.

"Why don't you just go see him? I'll be okay."

"No, it's all right. Maybe I'll ask him over; if you're okay with it?" But I can tell she wants to go.

"Really. Go. You're starting to annoy me with your cheesy grin and inappropriate suggestions over there. I'd rather not be present for them."

"What are you talking about? We didn't say anything remotely suggestive. We were talking about pleated table cloths." She laughs, then sighs. "Fine, but I'll only be gone for an hour."

"Ugh, you don't have to babysit me."

"I know that." She gets up to head inside. I follow her, closing and locking the back door."An hour, I'll be back in an hour."

"Make it two, and I'll think about letting you in when you get back."

"I have a key. And I'll be back in one." She gives me a pointed look. I forgot about her key. Rolling my eyes, I lock the door as she leaves.

Wanting to call Collin, I walk over to the phone and pick it up. That's as far as I get before I set it back down. I'm not ready. Instead, I grab my laptop and go to Grandma's study.

Pulling the curtains closed and locking the door, I sit at her desk in the corner for the first time. Memories start to run through my head like a movie reel. Me sitting on Grandma's lap, her reading to me, her showing me how to do fractions. She was really good with numbers. She could calculate big numbers in her head; it was scary.

Opening the laptop, I pull up the internet to research Caleb's self-defense class just as Collin had. This is the next best thing to actually talking to Collin.

Typing Caleb's name in Google, I get thirty-thousand hits. The first link reads, 'Mathews Private Security'. I click on it, and it brings me to a page that lists customer testimonials, all very good of course. On the left side of the page there is a brief biography.

"Caleb Mathews is the founder of Mathews Private Security, a business that he strives to perfect in every way. Always putting his clients in front, he believes that every life is worth living and wants to help protect every single one, as he feels he has been called to do.

"He started his business in the midst of a tragedy when his brother was shot and killed at gun point." Oh. My. Gosh. He had lost family just like me, but his attitude was so much better than mine. I admired him for that.

I remember him telling me about his mother but nothing about his brother. Wondering if his brother was the Dillon Mathews that Collin had gone to school with, I go back to Google and type in Dillon's name.

"Dillon Mathews was twenty-one when he was gunned down in his apartment. He is survived by his father Paul Mathews and his brother Caleb Mathews," the obituary reads.

As I scroll down there is a picture of Dillon. I am

beyond shocked. The man in the picture looks like Caleb but underneath, it says Dillon Mathews. Dillon and Caleb were twin brothers. I wanted to know more, but I also didn't want to learn about Caleb's life from the internet either. So I closed the laptop.

What would something like this do to someone? Certainly not make them friendly, but he was really nice. When my mom had abandoned me and my brother, it made me wary of all adults, including Grandma at first.

I still felt a deep pain when I thought about Mom's cruelty the day she came back into my life. Every time I thought about her, my heart ached with sadness because of the way she had left me.

And the thought of what happened in New York, just makes me sick to my stomach. I feel angry, disgusted with myself, furious with life. But here is this man, who has had horrible things happen to him, yet he says life is worth living.

I can't even think about something happening to Collin or Faye. They are the two people in my life who make it worth living. If something did happen to them, I'd probably step off that ledge of sanity and plunge head first into the deep dark waters of death.

When Faye returned, I was still locked in the study just sitting there with my ear buds in. I didn't hear her until she started banging on the door. Running over, I hesitate for a moment, but when I hear her call my name again. I unlock the door and pull it open. She is breathing hard and has her hand on her chest.

"Katy, I thought you were dead or something. I knocked like fifty times."

"I had my ear buds in; I couldn't hear until you started pounding." Her brows draw together as she looks past me at the closed curtains.

"Why are you in the dark with the door locked?"

"I guess it's just a habit. How was your visit with

Micah?" I ask as we walk into the living room.

"Fantastic. We just stayed in my room..."

"Okay," I say, waving my hands in front of me hoping to avoid hearing anything gross. "I don't need to know the details. Just fantastic will do."

"Don't worry, nothing happened." Oh, thank you. I didn't want to hear about her love life when mine was non-existent, and probably would never be normal with my new issues. "Besides there wasn't enough time for that. He likes to takes his time and explore."

"Ah! Stop please," I beg, covering my ears with my hands. She smiles wickedly at me. She always joked about that stuff.

In the living room she has about five suitcases and a box with her.

"Did you just pack all this?"

"Yup, with Micah's help. I thought I'd take Collin's room." She turns to look at me. "You okay with that?"

"I'm okay with it, but you may want to call Collin and ask him."

"Already did. He says it's fine." Picking up a couple of suitcases, she starts to lug them back to Collin's room. I pick up the box since it's the lightest.

"This seems like a lot of stuff for two weeks? You'll be moving into the dorm then." Sitting the box on Collin's bed I look over as she is shoving the suitcases into the closet.

"I'm taking the first semester off," she informs me.

I stare at her back, unbelieving. She knows this will make me angry. I don't want her to stop living her life. But, I don't say anything, it's no use.

I am, however, determined to convince her that I'm fine if she goes about her life. She is not obligated to stay with me. But the thought of being alone makes my insides tremble.

~~~

Saturday, we wake up early for self-defense class. My nerves are ridiculously off the charts, even though I am just going to watch.

Faye put on a pair of shorts and tank top because of the heat. It was one of the hottest summers we've had. I, on the other hand, put on a pair of black yoga pants and a long sleeve shirt. My bruises are still visible, even though they were faint, and I wanted to do my best to hide the shame.

We go to a little place down the street from the class to grab a coffee and muffin. Faye encourages me to eat more, since I wasn't actually going to be the one tossed around, but my nerves won't allow me. No matter where we go, I am always frantically looking around and pressed up close to Faye, waiting for something bad to happen.

The class is held in a dance studio for kids. There are little girls everywhere dressed in little pink tutus. I'm not hyperventilating, that was good. Kids apparently don't bother me so much. It's large crowds of grown adults that really bother me. Faye was safe too. I would tense when she touched me, but I wasn't frightened.

We head to the back of the studio to a closed door marked studio D. The studio looks like a gym. It has the same hardwood floor as a gym, and mats are laying out in even intervals across the floor. Bleachers sit against the wall across the room.

The whole place was empty though. Caleb wasn't even in here. Walking in a little further, I see him lying on his back, with his legs up on the bleachers, and a well worn brown book hovering over his face. He must be really into it, because he doesn't hear us walk in.

Faye closes the door a little too hard, which prompts him to look back at us. Closing his book, he sets it on the bleachers, gets up, and starts walking over to us.

Smiling, he says, "It's good to see you again, Katy." He sticks his hand out, and, like a ditz, I just stare at it. The thought of touching him makes me queasy. His smile falls.

Faye walks up to him and puts her hand in his to shake it.

"I'm Faye, Katy's friend. We talked on the phone the other day." His eyes shift from me to her.

"Yes, I remember. It's nice to meet you."

"Same here. Katy never told me what a babe you are," she says smiling. I blush; she did not just say that. He looks at me then back at Faye.

"I'm humbled, but I don't compare to the two beautiful ladies standing in front of me." Gesturing to the mats he says, "Do you want to start?" He turns and walks toward them.

Faye looks at me and rolls her eyes. She obviously thinks Caleb is putting on a show. We follow him over, and Faye stays on the mat where Caleb is. I decide to sit against the wall with my legs crossed. I listen and watch.

"Do you have any experience?" he asks Faye. She turns around and looks at me with, a sly look on her face. Oh no.

"Yeah, I have experience," she says smugly. He nods.

"What kind?" He had to ask.

"I've been known to wield a mean chopstick." He chuckles and shakes his head.

"That's not a martial art, or even a weapon used in martial arts, but I think you already knew that. I'm going to assume that you know nothing."

"Hey, I know plenty," she says, annoyed.

"About martial arts or self-defense?" He raises his eyebrows.

"Oh, no. I don't know anything about either of those," she says, yielding.

"Okay, we'll start from the beginning." I watch as Caleb demonstrates several moves that Faye could use if someone was to try and grab her. He then tells her to try to attack him. When she reaches out to grab his shirt, he grabs her hand and slowly twists her arm toward her body and pushes it up with force. She falls back on the mat with a thump.

"Man, you could have warned me." She doesn't sound annoyed, just a little shocked. Getting up, she moves her wrist in circles. "I didn't think you were going to take me down."

Moving on, he shows her how to use an attacker's weight to her advantage. Using very little force, he flips Faye over, and again she lands on the mats with a thump. I wait for the complaint, but instead she starts to laugh.

"Oh. My. Gosh. That was exhilarating! I want to do that one again." She stands up and bounces on the ball of her toes.

"Let me demonstrate how to do it slowly, because I want you to try it on me."

"You want me," she points to herself, "to flip you?" She points to Caleb.

"You can do it, trust me."

At first, Caleb shows Faye how to do a couple of slow motion wrist twisting and body spinning. Then, he goes in for the attack.

At first, she isn't doing it right. Twisting his wrist completely around, instead of half way, then cutting up toward the ceiling. When she does get it, to my surprise, she flips him. Not perfectly like he had done, but he was on the floor, so who cares.

I can feel my eyes widening as big as saucers as Caleb lies on the floor. Faye is doing a happy dance.

"Good job," Caleb praises Faye, as he rises off the floor dusting off his pants.

"Yeah, that was really amazing," I say, clearly astonished.

Caleb glances in my direction and walks toward me. I tense up. A chill runs through me, and my heart starts to beat violently inside of my chest. He can tell there is a shift in my mood from moments ago, but says nothing. *He's just getting his water,* I think to myself.

Faye is jumping around on the mats like a crazy

woman. I look over at Caleb and notice that he's looking at my legs. *Ankles*, I think to myself. My bruises are showing. They're not as prominent as they were last week, but the yellowish green tint is very visible against my pale skin.

Quickly, I fold my legs under each other making sure my ankles don't show. When I look at him, he's looking straight ahead like he is concentrating on something across the room.

Feeling foolish, and ugly in my own skin, I stand, walk across the room and out of the studio. Finding a bench right outside of the building, I sit and attempt to calm my racing heart, but it's useless. I just need some time alone. All of these people walking around aren't helping.

The bruises mock me and serve as a reminder of what happened that night. If Caleb had seen me naked, I would have been less embarrassed. Those bruises, they'll go away, fade into nothing, but I can never forget how they got there and the man who left them.

When the door opens, I expect to see Faye but it's Caleb that walks out. People are passing by on the sidewalk, but he walks out there and sits down in front of me; right in the middle of the sidewalk. There is a whole bench and plenty of room right next to me, but he chooses to sit five feet in front of me on the ground—thankfully. Blowing out a breath, I look away from him.

"What did Faye tell you?"

"Nothing. What did you think she told me?" he asks, concerned.

"Nothing." I just want to leave, go home, and not come back. This was a really bad idea, but I let Faye talk me into it, because I knew it would make her feel better. I was doing this to get better, so that Faye didn't feel like she had to babysit me.

"Faye doesn't need to tell me anything. I work private security, remember? I'm very attentive to my surroundings."

Feeling self conscious I look down at my ankles to

make sure the bruises aren't showing again. I don't look back up, but Caleb is sitting down in front of me, and I'm sitting up high; putting him clearly in my line of vision. I have a feeling he did that on purpose.

"Katy, you don't have to tell me anything. But I would really like to show you a few things that may help you." His voice is soft and filled with concern—for me.

Isn't this what I wanted? Help. Faye had been acting like a mother hen since she found out, moving in with me, only leaving me for an hour a day to see Micah, taking the first semester off college. I had to show her that I was at least attempting to get better. Taking a deep breath I relax.

"Okay," I relent. Looking at him finally, he wears a huge grin. It's a nice one, and for some reason, I don't feel that same queasiness that I felt when I came in. His blonde hair is messy just like the day I met him, and his blue eyes twinkle. He truly is beautiful.

As we fight our way back to the studio, through all the little girls in pink tutus, curiosity starts to pique my interest.

"What's up with the dance studio?" He glances back at me.

"It was my mom's studio. My aunt ran it for awhile, but she passed away three years ago. I didn't want to make any changes, so I kept it the way it was and hired Miss Jill over there," he points to an elderly lady at the check in desk, "to run the place. I just cleared out the back which used to be storage and made that my training studio." Opening the door, he steps aside to let me pass. "I train all of my employees here on weeknights and teach women's self-defense on the weekends." When I don't walk in, he walks into the studio, and I follow him in.

"Do you usually have this small of a class?"

"Usually, there is anywhere from twenty to fifty women here. But that class is held in the evening at six."

"So you had a special class just for us?" A ray of hope washes through me. Feeling foolish, I quickly clear it from my mind. We stop in front of Faye, who is eyeing me in shock, and he turns toward me.

"Yes, I did," he replies with a smile. I feel it deep in my chest. Why do I have to feel this way about Caleb? All of these feelings are out of place in my life right now. I know that I am not ready for any sort of relationship with a man. Thoughts of complete and utter brokenness and shame that course through me are far more prevalent than hope and heart.

"You ready to try?" he asks. I nod my head and trail behind Caleb to the mats. Faye's just sitting on the bleachers with a shocked look on her face. "Okay, we'll start with the hand motions," he continues. I am already tensing up, and the courage that I thought I had is crumbling. "Then, I'll show you how to take someone down regardless of their size and strength."

"I remember you telling me that you know Krav Maga. This is nothing like that. Krav Maga is about beating your opponent quickly, with force. It's about releasing your anger on your attacker. What I am about to teach you will let you use your attacker's size and strength against them. Because nine times out of ten, the person attacking you is going to be bigger and stronger. You can't let that person get the upper hand. Most importantly, you can't let them get you on the ground. If you end up on your stomach it's nearly impossible to get back up." I flinch due to his highly accurate depiction—he stops.

"You just flinched. My intuition tells me that you have been in that position. Your body language gives you away." He knows.

I look down at my feet and cross my hands over my stomach. I don't want him to know. I don't want anyone to know; it makes me feel sick with shame.

"Hey," he says gently. Placing his thumb under my chin, he lifts my eyes to meet his. I don't flinch, because I didn't see it coming. I don't cringe away from his touch either. It's gentle, and he's only touching me with the tip of his thumb. "Don't ever take your eyes off your attacker. Don't ever run from your attacker. If you're running, your back is to him. I'll teach you how to disarm or disable him. You don't need to be stronger, and you don't need to be bigger than him. All you need to know is where the pressure points are and which way to move so you are deflecting his movements. Let him do all the work, you just anticipate. Are you ready?"

"Yes," I say, sounding feeble and uncertain.

"Okay, you're the attacker. So attack me." He is so patient as I work up the courage to do what he is asking of me.

Reaching out in the same way that Faye did, he grabs my hand, twists it up and toward my body. My heart starts to race, so I turn and look for Faye. She is still sitting on the bleachers with her elbows on her knees and her chin in her hands. She smiles at me as encouragement, so I do my best impression of a smile. Caleb releases my hand quickly.

"Do you see how I did that?" I nod my head. "Okay you do me a few times, then I'll do you again." A sudden burst of laughter from the bleachers has us turning toward Faye. She looks up from her bout of laughter.

"Oh, sorry. That sounded really naughty. Maybe you should consider rephrasing it." Still smiling she shakes her head. Caleb and I look at each other.

"Your friend has a really dirty mind," he says.

"I know. I tried to wash it once, but it just made it worse," I say, shrugging my shoulders. Faye is the queen of inappropriate innuendos. I've learned to look past them, but for as long as I can remember she has been like that.

We go back to the lesson, me as the attacker a few times. When Caleb takes over as the attacker, my heart feels like it's going to jump out of my chest. He reaches forward, so I grab his hand like he has been doing to me, and twist it perfectly the way he had. After a few more of those, he looks at me and smiles.

"That's fantastic."

"Hey, I only got great job, but she gets fantastic?" Faye says perturbed.

"I call them like I see them," Caleb says to her jokingly. I like him.

"Ready to move on to the flip?" Not really, but I'm doing a pretty good job now, and I don't want to stop. My side still aches a little, but I think I can handle it. Nothing was broken, just bruised. I'll push through the pain.

"It's just the same as the hand movements we have been doing. Only, I'll bring your arm around my head and up between us, flipping you completely over. When you're ready, attack me."

I stick my hand out and he grabs it, starting to twist it up. At first, I think it's going to be fine, but then he lifts my arm over his head, and my body brushes against him and panic settles in.

I scream, as I try pulling my hand out of his, and back away. He let's go after I tug a few times, causing me to fall to the ground. I back away still, screaming and shaking.

When I look at Faye and Caleb, they are both standing in front of me, worry etched into their beautiful faces. And I put it there.

Caleb looks as if he wants to pick me up and wrap me in his arms. He reaches down for me, but I pull my legs up and huddle further into myself.

This will never work. I'll never be able to get that close to a man. I put my face in my knees and cry like the awful and tainted person I am.

Chapter Eight

"This is worse than I thought," I hear Caleb say.

"What do you mean? What do you know?" Faye asks him.

"She has obviously been through some sort of massive trauma. This won't help her."

Sobbing quietly into my knees, I listen to Caleb and Faye talk about me as if I'm not there. I might as well not be. I'm useless to them. That makes me cry harder. I'm so sick of all the tears. I wish that I could just drown in them.

"Katy." Faye kneels down in front of me, so I peek at her. "Let's go." I shake my head no.

"I need to get over this. If Caleb can help, then I need to stay here. I need to do this. I don't want people to look at me like I'm a kicked puppy. I don't want people to stop their lives for me. This is my life, and the people around me shouldn't suffer because of it."

"Is that what you think?" Faye says, taking a seat next to me. "You have no idea what I would do for you, Katy. None. And you know what? This is my life, and I don't let other people make decisions for me." When she touches my knee, I jump. "I do what I do, because I love you, Katy. When you love someone, you make sacrifices for them. Not because you feel obligated, but because you just genuinely want to."

She says it, but I don't feel it. All I can think is, *Why.* Why does she do these things for me? Why does she stick around? I look at Caleb, and he looks just as worried as Faye does.

"Go on Caleb, tell her you love her too," Faye says in complete seriousness. Caleb and I both look at Faye with rounded eyes. She smiles and starts to laugh. "I was kidding. I wish I had a camera. That look was a photo op. Oh man, you two."

"Katy," Caleb starts, "you should go home today. But, if you're serious, I do have some ideas."

"Yes, I'm serious." Wiping my eyes with the sleeve of my shirt, I try to control the shaking that has started.

"Alright, meet me here tomorrow morning at eight thirty." He looks like he wants to say or do more; as a look that I have no words for crosses his face. Instead, he turns and walks away reluctantly.

"I'm sorry," I say quietly to his retreating back. He turns around and waits until our eyes meet.

"You have absolutely nothing to be sorry for. Don't ever think that you need to be. I'll see you tomorrow. Wear something nice but comfortable. Bring your workout clothes in a bag." With that, he walks out of the studio.

"I tell you what, that man is a mystery to me. But, he seems like a good guy." Turning to Faye, I watch as she packs up her things.

We spend the rest of the day looking at bridal magazines in the living room. I picked out some bridesmaids dress', but she made this face where she stuck out her tongue and scrunched up her nose and made a gagging sound. So in the end, she picked them out

I still couldn't believe that she was getting married in six months. It seems too soon. Micah was nice to her, but I really didn't want my best friend to be with someone who was *just* nice to her. I wanted her to have the perfect guy. Someone who could love her completely and support her. Someone who could understand her. I don't think that I even understood her, though.

She kept a lot hidden, and underneath her snarky and inappropriate comments, was something else. She kept her emotions carefully guarded; only letting show what she was comfortable with.

Her relationship with Micah seemed forced to me,

though. I always wondered if they stayed together because it is comfortable for them, or if they truly want to be together. But he did ask her to marry him, so it must be true love, right? They have been together for a long time, but still that didn't mean they had to get married all ready. There was plenty of time for all of that.

"Hey, you didn't go see Micah today," I say.

"Oh, he went to a game with Sean." Absentmindedly, she flips through the next bridal magazine.

"What game did they go see?" She looks up in thought.

"I'm not sure, I didn't ask. Are there any games going on around here?"

"They usually have a baseball game at Bently field right around this time of year. It's for couples. You didn't miss it so that you could stay with me did you? Because you know that—"

"He didn't ask me to go," she says, clearly puzzled.

"I'm sorry, Faye. Maybe he went to another game, somewhere else. I'm not sure when the couples game is. It could be at the end of the month." I try to fill her with hope, but it's no use. Her mood is changing swiftly, so I change the subject. "Want to get some dinner? I'm starving."

"You mean like, go out to eat, where there are people?" The surprise in her voice is almost comical.

"Well, maybe we can just order it and bring it back here. What if we run into someone we know? I don't want to talk to anyone."

"When are you going to start talking to someone other than me?" It didn't sound mean, but the tiny bit of annoyance in her voice was transparent.

"Well, I'm sorry that my crappy life gets in the way of your perfect wedding planning and social life. I didn't ask you to come and move in. This is exactly why."

"No, you didn't ask me, but Collin did." She flips the magazine page a little too roughly.

"Since when do you listen to Collin? The last time you guys talked for longer than ten minutes, was six years ago." Perplexed by her guilty expression when mentioning my brother, I wait for her answer. Throwing her head back on the couch dramatically, she groans and looks at me.

"That isn't the point. You need me here."

"I don't need you here, Faye. I can take care of myself." My tone is harsher then I intended.

"So, if I just leave, right now, and don't come back for a few days, you're going to be okay?" I hoped she didn't do that, because I probably wouldn't get much sleep, and I'd miss her. But I was stubborn.

"Of course." We stare each other down, but I finally relent. "Fine, I need you. I can't sleep when you're not here. Is that what you wanted to hear?"

"No, I don't need to hear anything." Her voice is softer.

Letting out a long, heavy breath, I say, "We need to get out of this house. It's making us crazy, and you're starting to annoy the crap out of me." Turning to look at her she has her eyes closed and a big smile on her face.

"That means that my work here is done. I shall die a happy person." Jumping off the couch quickly, she startles me, and I flinch. "I have an idea." she says a little giddy, not even acknowledging my flinch.

"What?"

"No, I'm not telling. Do you trust me?"

"Is this a trick question?"

"Whatever. Just throw your shoes on and let's go." She glances at her watch. "We have three hours before they close. We'll grab dinner on the way."

I do as I am told reassuring myself that Faye knows what I can and can't handle at this point. She wouldn't take me somewhere that was unbearable. Did I trust her? Yes, with my life. That's why I had to do better. For her, for Collin. I could do this.

Hopping in her car, we drive out as the sun starts to

fade behind the horizon. It would only be light out for another hour. The hope I had that we would be back before it got dark, was not looking good when she merged onto the e-way.

"Where exactly are we going?" My voice sounded a little panicky. I didn't like where this was going, but that's where trusting her came in.

"It's a surprise. Just sit back, relax, listen to Kelly Clarkson, and trust me." It was ironic that Kelly Clarkson was singing about loving someone's dark side.

In the past, I would have never thought I had a dark side. But now, with the route my life had taken, I thought that maybe everyone had a dark side. It was just buried deep, and certain life events pulled it out of hibernation.

I wondered if there was anything that could bury the dark side again, or if one had to just learn to live with it. That led me to thoughts of my mom. She embraced her dark side. Would I?

Driving for about thirty minutes, Faye gets off on exit thirty-seven. There is only one thing out here, so the jig is up. I groan internally but let her have her moment, not saying anything. We pull up to the little toll shack and pay the parking fee to get into Fantasy Amusement Park

"What's your game?" I ask. Looking out the window at all the cars packing the tiny parking lot, my nerves already start to tingle.

"Just trust me." Turning into a parking spot, she grins.

Walking the short distance to the ticket booth, she pays the fee, refusing to accept my money when I try to hand it to her. People rush by us trying to make a quick exit so they can avoid the long lines at closing time.

Stopping at the front entrance, I plaster myself against the wall, the stone feeling like ice on my back. My breathing starts to escalate, and my heart hammers in my chest. Faye, seeing my distress, grabs my wrist and turns toward the crowd.

"Watch out, she's going to puke!" she shouts. I probably have a look of horror on my face, which convinces people that I will be sick, so they clear a path for us immediately.

We stop at the Top Runner, the highest coaster in the park. I have never been one for roller coasters the few times we have been here. I was the person that held everyone's stuff as they got on and rode. I just didn't delve into the unknown. Faye stood behind me acting as my bodyguard, as I stopped a good distance away from the person in front of me. The line wasn't that long, we probably would get to the front in ten minutes. I took that time to plead with Faye.

"Faye, this isn't a good idea. I haven't been on a big coaster. I may get sick for real." Panicking, I try to pull her out of line, but she doesn't budge. "Please, Faye." I think she may have a change of heart, but then she shakes her head in protest.

"When did you stop trusting me? It'll be fine," she says, drawing out that last word. "I have a theory." That does nothing for me.

"Is this like the time you theorized that if we used enough gum we could hang pictures on the wall in my room? Because Grandma didn't like that."

"I thought that was a great idea—for a seven-year-old. It was inventive and it worked." Proud of her theory, she beams at me.

"Yes, well I was the one that was stuck scrubbing it off the walls. Gum doesn't come off easily after a prolonged period of time." Looking at the coaster reaching toward the sky, my heart drops to my feet. I swallow the lump in my throat and look at Faye again.

Guessing what I am about to say she puts her hands on my shoulders causing me to tense up.

"Trust me?" she says.

I'm not sure what the best thing is in this sort of

situation. Do I completely ignore the giant death trap in front of me, or check it out for off centered tracks and stuff? Why couldn't we just go on the Apple Dipper in the kid's area? There were at least eight hills on this one, five of those high enough to make me plan my escape.

By the time we make it to the front and are being ushered on, it's too late. Faye pulls me to the front car. She hops into the very first row, but all I can think about are the eight other strangers that will be behind me. Then I realize that not only will we all be locked in, but we'd be going close to eighty miles per hour, so I jump in next to her.

As the shoulder harness comes down, I reach up to assist its drop until I hear a click. Then, for good measure, I push up as hard as I can to make sure it is secure. The ride attendant standing to my left gives a thumbs up to the man in the box at the other end of the platform. This was it, I took a deep breath and look at Faye. She smiles and mouths 'Trust me.'

With a jolt, the ride was in motion. And all I can think is, *trust is more difficult than I thought when it is your life on the line.*

As we are being pulled up the lift hill, that familiar quickening starts in my chest, so I grab the metal bar in front of me for dear life, but my hands are so sweaty they just slip off. Fear starts to claw its way to the surface, and I do my best to push it down. I try not to think, instead I listen to the clinking of the car being pulled up. The closer we get to the top of the hill, the more I feel my body tensing, my heart pounding, my stomach twisting and turning.

This is it, we are at the top. And then, we are sailing down so fast it knocks the wind out of me. I let out a blood curdling scream, as it seems like we are dropping into oblivion, but quickly, we straighten out and twist to the right.

As we take the next hill, I think I have a minute to gain

my composure, but it came and went so quickly that was not the case.

My head was tossed in so many different directions, it was a wonder it was still attached to my body. First left, then right, then left again. As we climb another hill, I anticipate it this time and try to enjoy it.

My breathing is erratic, my heart is thumping so loudly I could hear it in my ears, and my body feels high like it had been lifted into another world.

This was not the same erratic breathing and heart racing that I had become accustomed to. This was different, because it was not born out of fear—it was born out of excitement.

The thought had me smiling and throwing my hands in the air. This was Faye's game, she wanted me to endure those same feelings I've been having the past couple of weeks, but for a different reason.

She was trying to direct those emotions to something positive, in hopes that I could call on them the next time I was in a situation similar to that in the studio. She really was a genius, and I was glad that I had trusted her.

The next five hills are similar, my excitement grew with each one. When the ride was over, we jump off while patting our hair down. We both wear the same never ending smile. There wasn't time to go again like I wanted to, so we jump on the e-way and head home.

The sun had dropped below the horizon all ready, and the night was dark with the new moon lingering. Turning to Faye, she still wore that smile.

"Thank you." It's the first time I've said that to her since coming back. She deserves more, but I don't know how to give her more right now. She seems more satisfied with the 'thanks' then I would have been. She looks at me, and her smile grows bigger.

"I wanted to ask you," she hesitates, "do you want me to go with you tomorrow morning? I thought maybe you could try going by yourself though. I'll keep my phone close, so you can call me if you need to." She adds quickly.

I had forgotten about my morning plans with Caleb with the excitement from the roller coaster still lingering. I look out the window as I think about her question. Earlier in the studio proved how unready I am at being touched by men. He just merely brushed up against me, and I had a panic attack. I wasn't sure what he had planned as I think back to his 'dress nice' comment. He seemed like a decent enough guy to keep his hands to himself knowing that it sets me off.

Should I consider tonight's roller coaster ride a breakthrough? I guess time would tell me the answer to that. Making up my mind, I look at Faye.

"That sounds like a good idea." I think she lets out a short breath, but it was too dark in the car to tell, and it was too quiet to hear. I can do this; for her.

~~~

The next morning, I wake early, nervous about my meeting with Caleb. Faye is still sleeping, so I tiptoe quietly to the kitchen making sure to check every dark corner the sun is not yet shining in.

I slept really well last night, but as soon as my eyes opened the same feeling that washed over me every morning took hold—dread. Maybe it was because I couldn't shake it after the same feeling reprised every morning for the last two weeks. *Or maybe I wasn't getting any better.* The thought depressed me.

Either way, I was determined to get through the whole day without needing Faye. She should be starting college in a week, and if I had my way, she'd be going.

I start the coffee pot and pour a bowl of cereal, taking it to the living room foregoing my normal seat in the sun room or under the gazebo. Those places felt too open for me.

My mind drifts back to Caleb and where he might be taking me this morning. I run through every possible scenario; breakfast maybe. Oops, I'm already eating. Maybe he is taking me to meet someone. I have no clue, and trying to guess is getting me nowhere, so I click on the television to stop my wandering mind.

Flipping through the stations, I stop on a news channel, but with mostly bad news it becomes too depressing, so I just turn the television off. The coffee is done brewing, so I walk over to make a cup just as Faye emerges from the hall.

"That smells good. Pour me a cup," she says, walking out to the sunroom. After pouring us both a cup and fixing it up, hers with a little vanilla and cinnamon, I join her in the sunroom.

Looking at the table in the center of the room, I ask her gently, "Can we maybe move the table to the corner?" She looks at the corner and back at me with a confused look. Moving the table to the corner would defeat the purpose of the sunroom since we will no longer be in the sun. But she nods her head and helps me move it. We sit there, my back against the wall, in the shadows.

"Are you sure about today?" she asks.

Blowing out a breath I say with confidence, "Yes, I can do this." As long as no one touches me.

"Okay," she says, nodding her head.

"What are you going to do today?"

"I'll probably invite Micah over, if that's okay with you."

"Of course it is. This is your house too. Even if you weren't living here, I would consider this house partly yours."

After we drink our coffee and have a brief conversation about poached eggs, I don't even know how that one got started, we set out to get ready for the day. In my room, I rummage through my closet, trying to pick out something nice. Since Faye's plans consisted of staying in and watching movies with Micah, she was done getting ready before me, which is how she ended up in my room helping me decide what to wear.

"You should wear this one," she says, pulling out a top. It was a chevron sleeveless top, black in the back with a small opening between the shoulder blades. The front was a royal blue except for the shoulder straps which were also black, and had a series of V like stripes alternating between soft thick pink V's and thin black V's. It was light and airy, a nice choice for the summer, and really cute.

Taking it from her, I slip it on. I was already wearing a pair of black slacks, so I walked over and pulled a pair of black heels out that were blue on the bottom.

The final touch was the sapphire necklace that Grandma had given me. I hook it around my neck and look in the mirror. I check my arms for bruising, but they had pretty much disappeared. With the blue on my shirt and in the necklace, it was the first time I had looked composed since that night in New York.

"You look fantastic, all dressed up," Faye says from behind me. I look at her reflection in the mirror.

"Thanks. So what's your theory on where he is taking me?" Walking over to my closet, I pull out a gym bag and go through the task of grabbing workout clothes. Faye, sitting on the bed, looks off into the distance as if she is trying to decide.

"Maybe he's taking you to the park where he'll lay out a blanket, and a basket full of ripe fruit. You guys will sit in the sun watching the kids play and dogs catch Frisbees." She has a dreamy faraway look in her eyes. Finally, snapping out of it, she looks at me. I just stare at her.

"You have been thinking about this, haven't you? That's a little farfetched, and way too detailed to have just come out of nowhere." Shrugging her shoulders she sighs.

"Maybe, I just really want to see you happy. And, maybe...in love," she says, hopefully. Startled by her statement, I try to brush it off with a joke.

"Are you naming our kids too?" She smiles at me and falls back on the bed. Walking over and sitting next to her I say, "It's not like that, Faye. Even if you want it to be, even if I want it to be," I place my hand over my heart, "I'm just not there yet." And I don't know if I ever will be. Looking at me, she nods her head.

"I get that." There is a sadness in her voice. I know she is thinking about my attack.

~~~

Driving to the studio, I park in front of the building. Taking a deep breath, *or five*; I open my car door and head inside. This time there aren't any little girls running around in pink tutus, but Miss Jill is sitting at the reception desk. I walk over to her.

"Hello, dear," she says when she notices me.

"Hi. I'm—"

"Katy. Yes, I know." She smiles a little as she looks over the rim of her glasses. I notice her glance at my neckline, and I remember I'm wearing the sapphire necklace. Her smile fades. "Where did you get that necklace? It's stunning." She moves in closer to examine it.

I touch it self-consciously, and because she is looking at it like she may rip it off my neck.

"My grandma."

She looks confused as she continues to stare at the necklace. It's making me uncomfortable. I'm just about to say so, when I see Caleb come walking out of the backroom behind Miss Jill.

"Hello, Katy." He smiles causing my stomach to flutter, so I ignore it. "I'm glad you're here." He looks around and then back at me. "No Faye?" he questions. When I look at Jill again she's staring at her computer screen instead of my necklace. That was really weird.

"Nope. I thought I would go it alone. So, where are we

going?"

Walking from behind the counter, he stops about ten feet away. Good, he knows what he is dealing with. *A lunatic*, I think to myself.

I notice that he is wearing black slacks and a royal blue, button up, collared shirt. We match; isn't that crazy. He looks nice with his usually messy dark golden locks tamed and combed to the side in a wave. His face was smoother in contrast from the scruff that he had yesterday.

Putting his hands in his pockets he says, "If you don't mind, I'd like to just show you."

"Sure," I say, pointing toward the door, "lead the way."

Deciding that it was best to take separate cars, I follow him closely down the road. He was hard to lose because his truck was huge. I could see it over the top of anything, with the exception of a semi truck.

After about twenty minutes, we pull into a parking lot behind a building. I park next to him and jump out to meet him around the back of our vehicles. There are people everywhere getting out of their cars, all dressed nice. No certain type of person: young, old, couples, women with kids, teenagers. Wherever we were, they didn't discriminate.

I watch as the people walk across the lot, and then across the street, to a large three story building with white doors. Some people stood outside and lingered, talking to each other, while others walked inside.

There are a lot of people. I wasn't sure if I could do it or not. That familiar tightening sensation started to build in my chest.

"We can wait outside until everyone has gone in, if you prefer?" Caleb offers. He can probably see how tense I am. I make a physical effort to relax.

"I don't know, Caleb? There are a ton of people." I can hear the nervousness laced with fear in my voice.

"Don't worry. It's not like that here." His voice is soothing, and it helps, so I take a step forward—then stop.

Seeming to know exactly what I need, he walks in front of me.

It doesn't matter; I still frantically look around, especially behind me. I can only imagine what it looks like to others; like a have a nervous tick or something. Well, I guess that's kind of right.

As we get closer to the door, people start piling in. Walking up the few steps and looking in, I can see that we're at a church. Of all the places, I hadn't thought of this one. I looked at Caleb, and tried to determine if he was the church going type, but really, how can you tell that kind of thing by looks alone.

Glancing back at me as if he knows that I am watching him, he smiles. "Ever been to church?"

"Yes. When I was like seven." I remember Grandma pushing me to go, telling me that I would meet some nice people and make friends. That sounded good to me, so I went. Only, the people weren't nice. The adults scared me, the kids were cruel, and I felt ignored.

I usually took the bus to church on Sunday mornings, leaving Grandma at home. I dreaded every minute of it. It all started with a little girl who used to taunt me. If I even glanced at her, she'd stick her tongue out at me. Most of the time, though, she was throwing stuff at me. Things like beads, marbles, and chocolate.

I came home after church one day, stripping my nice clothes off to put my play ones on. Faye was coming over and we were going to ride our bikes. When I pulled my shirt over my head, chocolate fell out. It smeared all over me and melted into my shirt.

People where just cruel. Grandma told me that things like this would happen all the time; you just had to pray for that person who is lost and that you will have the right reaction to those lost souls. I never prayed, but I did stop going to church after that.

One of the worst experiences of my childhood was

when the leader on our bus was telling us that we all had a part of our dad and mom in us. I started crying, so she walked over and sat down next to me on the bus.

"What's wrong, Katy?" Her voice was pleasant. She was the only one who was ever nice to me at church. I looked up at her through my blurry eyes.

"I don't want to be like my mommy." Even at seven, I knew I didn't want to be like her. She was a sorry excuse for a mother, and a human being. The thought of being like her made me sad then—but scared me now.

As Caleb and I walk into the church, I can see rows and rows of people already seated. Collin directs me over to a row of chairs that are lined against the back of the church's wall. It was perfect, and weird at the same time. It's like they knew I was coming.

Sitting down, he leans in a little and says, "I've been coming to this church for a while now. I started coming here during the darkest time in my life."

Surprised by this piece of information he has divulged, I just stare at him. He gives me that small smile, the one I remember from the first time we met, and my nerves calm a bit."Surprised?" he asks.

"Yes, very." This whole morning was surprising. First, my easy morning with Faye, then the weird conversation with Jill—the receptionist. And now, I was sitting here in a church for the first time in eleven years. And guess what? It doesn't make me feel uncomfortable at all.

Chapter Nine

As I sat there, listening to this man who I had never met, something occurred to me. What he was saying, spoke true to my life. He had no idea what I was going through, or what challenges I faced in the past, but I felt like he was talking directly to me.

The first thing he said was my life in a nutshell.

"Life can take you, build you up, and then break you down." That was true. In fact, I had experienced that over the span of my life. When he started talking about not being able avoid life, because every day you wake up, you're in it; I wanted to say 'duh', but his next statement made me shiver.

"But life is not in you." His voice was quiet, and I could have sworn that he was starring straight at me. It was unsettling that he seemed to know so much about me. Did I not have any life in me too?

"How do you let life in?" he said. I wanted to know, so I sat forward. "There are so many people out there that have been beaten, thrown away, broken, and battered. Life has put you through the ringer, and you become lost. But sometimes, we have to face all of those struggles that life brings us, to experience His grace. What you experience here, on Earth, let it be just that, an experience. Benefit from it. And know that He is always with you."

Something in my chest ached at that. Could it be true, that the struggles we face in life help balance everything? It didn't seem right. Why did I have to lose my dad and my grandma? Why did I have to have a crappy mother, and why did I have to be attacked? Did God let those things happen to me, so I could experience His grace?

The Pastor ended the sermon with a prayer; something I had done very little of in my eighteen years. Everyone closed their eyes and bowed their heads. There was no way I could keep my eyes closed as he prayed. Instead, I took a peek at Caleb sitting on my left.

I could see his thick lashes as they lay on his cheeks, his head leaning slightly forward, as his hands sat on his thighs. He was an oddity, with his private security business and dance studio. Those seemed like they didn't go together in the least.

Then, there was this church thing. I had never pegged him for what—a Christian? He was a good guy, and I-well, I couldn't even keep my eyes closed during prayer.

As if he heard me, his eyes flick open, and he looks at me out of the corner of them. I turn forward and close my eyes as if I am doing what I am supposed to be doing, but not before I catch his grin.

After prayer, the band comes on stage. The lights go dim as the first notes from the keyboard fill the silence. People in the pews start to close their eyes and sway to the music; some lifting their hands into the air like they are reaching for something.

I couldn't stop staring at it all. I had never seen this before. Not that I had anything to compare it with, besides a movie, and it all seemed so stiff, monotone, and forced in those. It was a different picture than I was seeing here.

Looking over at Caleb, I watch as he sings with the music. Straining to hear just his voice, I realize that it is a lost cause. There were too many people singing at once, but I didn't stop wondering what his voice would sound like.

Not knowing the words, I just stood there and watched the band. The sounds were beautiful and the words were encouraging. They sang about losing yourself and thinking that you can never be found. *But you can change who you are at the foot of the cross*, they sang. It gave me hope. But as the people in the pews reached for the sky, I didn't know what they could possibly be reaching for. The ache in my chest returned at that thought, but I ignored it like I had been ignoring everything else in life. I didn't want to feel like this.

When the song was over, we stayed in our seats and waited for everyone to clear out. Several people came over to say hello to Caleb and shake his hand. He introduces me, but when they offer their hands for a shake, I just stand there. They didn't look at me differently. There was no judgment in their eyes. They simply dropped their hand and smiled. Could they see how broken I was?

Afterwards, Caleb and I walked side by side back to our cars. I didn't feel the need to look behind me. For some reason, I felt safe with him. Maybe it was seeing how friendly he was to everyone in the church.

Giving me an address, we took our separate cars and head onto the expressway. He said it was about a forty-five minute drive until we arrived, and he was spot on.

Pulling up to a large park, I thought that maybe Faye was right about the picnic. However, we haul our gym bags out and walk across the park and down a set of steps that lead to a beach. The ocean was spread out in front of me and waves crashed onto the shore. A flock of seagulls wailed above us. Caleb leads me to a small cabana.

"You can dress and store your duffel in here." Walking in, he flips a light switch on and backs out leaving room for me to step inside. "There are towels in the basket on the floor, you'll want to grab one. And there is a small fridge in the corner with plenty of water." I nod my head and walk inside, closing and locking the door.

The cabana is surprisingly spacious. There are two armchairs against the back wall with a small round table in-between. A vase of yellow calla lilies sat on top of it. Suddenly, I was thinking about my grandma. She was everywhere even though she was gone. I still missed her so much.

After changing into a pair of drawstring grey pants and a white t-shirt; I grab a towel, a bottle of water, and make my way out. Caleb is sitting on a beach chair a few steps in front of the cabana. Jumping up, he walks into the cabana and changes into his black jogging pants and black A-shirt.

We walk down the beach together. My toes sink into the warm sand as people lull around, sun bathing and splashing in the water. I notice everyone and everything.

"I haven't seen you in a while? What have you been up to?" Caleb asks.

Shrugging my shoulders, I say, "I went to New York for a little while at the beginning of the summer. I haven't really felt like doing anything since I got home." My voice trails off, and I look away.

"You know what?" he says, drawing me back to him. "I've been to New York a few times. It's a culturally rich state."

"I enjoyed it for a while," I say hesitantly. "I saw Wicked. It was great, have you ever been to a musical or play?"

"Just local ones. When I was in New York it was on business. I was there for maybe two or three days."

I wanted to ask him about his brother but didn't know if this was the time or how to do it. What if he didn't want to talk to me about what had happened? He hadn't told me about him before, why would he now? But, I pressed my luck anyway.

"Do you have any brothers or sisters?" No, that's not obvious. But my curiosity was too great. He looks at me, questioningly for a minute, but then looks straight ahead.

"I had a twin brother."

"Had?" I ask, urging him on. Hoping he'll give me another piece of his history.

"He was murdered." He says it so quietly, that I almost don't hear him. "Three years ago. He was a great person. Better then I was. He even graduated from high school a year early. He taught me a lot. I just didn't listen to him until it was too late. Sometimes, you don't learn anything from a person's life until they are gone."

Surprisingly, he doesn't sound sad. Instead, he just makes it sound final. It happened, he moved on, and everything will be okay. How does he do that?

Finally, after ten minutes of walking, we stop about ten feet in front of a large group of rocks. He sets his water and towel down next to a huge cement pillar with a sign attached about ten feet in the air that says 'Danger Rocks'. He walks to the space between the huge rocks and the shore. I follow.

"This is the best place to come and practice my meditating and breathing techniques. I do this every Sunday after church. It helps reduce stress." Walking over to him, I listen intently.

He places one finger on my forehead. "It's all about connecting your mind," he says, then he places that same finger just below my neck, "with your body." On cue, I tense from the touch, but my stomach also flutters with excitement. I'm so conflicted. He pulls away quickly. "It's fairly simple and slow, so you should be able to catch on just by watching a few times." He places his hands on his hips. "Ready?" I nod my head, yes.

He gets into position and stands with his left foot out, so his leg is bent at the knee, and extends his right foot straight back. Reaching forward with his left hand straight out, he brings his right all the way around from front to back ending back in front, so his arms are side by side straight out in front of him. Bringing his feet together, and standing up straight, he makes a fist out of both hands and brings them in next to his side, elbows down.

He moves slow, soft, and gently, as he pushes his palms all the way down in front of him and brings them back up over his head while taking deep breaths and blowing them out.

Looking over at me, he says, "Tai Chi. It's all about

focus and breathing. When I'm practicing Tai Chi, my mind and body become one. I concentrate on the movements of my arms and legs, emptying my thoughts. It gives me the time I need to be alone with God."

I stand there, watching him, mesmerized by the gracefulness that he can pull off. He extends his left leg to the side and slowly turns his body in the same direction, his arms held out in front of him like he is defending himself.

His muscles flex with every fist clench ,and he catches me staring. My cheeks burn from the embarrassment of being caught, but he just smiles.

"Don't tell me this intimidates you? You know Krav Maga, remember?" he says mockingly, as a smile plays on his lips.

"Well, I'm just afraid I can't live up to your gracefulness." Standing next to him, I wait till he is back at the beginning and mirror his stance. He repeats the movements. This time I follow, only slightly behind. After a good twenty minutes of this, I can do it on my own.

"Not too bad. And your right; you can't live up to my gracefulness," he says with a smirk.

"I'm sorry that I'm not as feminine as you. I have a wonderful collection of purses if you're interested." He chuckles deeply, reminding me of just how masculine he is.

"I confess that I have a man purse. I use it as an overnight bag. It's very spacious and easy to handle." He sounds like he is selling me something.

"Wow, I'm learning so much about you today."

"And I don't know much about you," he says. I know he wants me to talk about what happened. I breathe in through my nose and out through my mouth, circling my left leg around before planting it firmly in the sand.

"My life is complicated. And not very interesting." I try to put it off for even longer. Pull, push, swoop, and breathe.

He doesn't say anything for a while. All I can hear are the seagulls overhead and our intermingled breathing with the crash of the waves.

"It doesn't matter if you have an interesting life, Katy. What matters is how effectively you live your life. There is something in you, just waiting to come out. If you don't let it go, you'll shut down."

I choose not to examine the depth of the meaning behind his words. I may not like what type of person it will make me if whatever is in me, comes out.

For another thirty minutes, we continue the Tai Chi. It is relaxing, considering my eyeballs were roaming everywhere when we first got here. Now, as we finish, I just concentrate on my breathing and the movements.

"I think that's enough for today." Caleb walks over to his water bottle and takes a few big gulps of it. I do the same, and sit in the sand. Coming over, he sits next to me and looks out over the ocean.

"This is a beautiful spot. I've lived here my whole life and never realized it was this close," I say. I had been out here plenty of times, but never seen the beach.

"It is, but beauty is everywhere," looking at me, he says, "in everything. It's not hard to find if that's what you're looking for."

"So, one day you were walking around thinking, 'I'm looking for something beautiful' and presto!" I spread my arms out toward the beach surrounding us.

"It's all about how you think," he smiles a little. "If you choose to see the pain and ugly in something, then that is all you are ever going to get from it. I actually saw this part of the beach several times before I actually *saw* its beauty," he says. Leaning back on my hands, I look up at the blue cloudless sky.

"What about the things that are truly painful and ugly: death, murder, abuse, kidnapping? How can you ever see something beautiful and good in those things?"

"There is nothing beautiful in those things, especially when the wounds are fresh, but you can recover fully from them and turn them into something positive in your life. That's what I have been telling myself every day since my brother's death. There is no greater trial in life then the death of a loved one." Our eyes meet for a moment. There is a contentment in them that I have never known.

"What about being physically attacked? What good comes from that?" I ask. He looks at me long and hard before he answers.

"Nothing—but what you choose." Feeling embarrassed, I turn my gaze back to the sky. I focus only on breathing in and out, not about he might be thinking.

Maybe I should clarify, and tell him what happened. But I feel so disgusted with myself, and when I think about that night, it brings feelings of shame and dread.

My eyes burn as I struggle to keep the tears at bay. I can feel a single traitorous tear slide down my cheek. My face remains neutral, not changing, no emotion. Then, I feel his hand slide over mine in the sand; his fingers intertwining with mine.

It was unexpected, and I didn't flinch. His touch feels familiar, and I feel dazed. Maybe my hand is a safe zone, or...maybe Caleb is a safe zone.

"Katy," he breathes softly. I don't want to look at him, too embarrassed by my tears and my past.

"Katy, I would never judge you. It doesn't matter what happened to you in the past. Because it's exactly that, the past. All that matters is the present- right here, right now- and the future. The decisions you make in this exact moment and beyond—those matter."

I look down, pull my hand out from under his, and cross my legs. Grabbing a handful of sand, I let it slip between my fingers; anything to avoid his gaze. I can feel his eyes burning into me.

"If you ever want to talk about it, I'll listen," he continues. "It won't change the way I look at you." *How does he look at me*, I think.

"Maybe some other time," I say, shaking my head. "It's not easy to talk about. Can I ask you a question?"

"Anything."

"How much do you know?" I ask self consciously.

"Nothing, Katy. I know nothing; except what I can see visibly. Your bruised ankles, the sadness in the tone of your voice, the dark circles under your eyes, tears you shed, the way you don't like to be alone with people or have to have your back against something." He clears his throat and shifts in the sand. "You don't like to be touched," he says softly.

"Very perceptive," I say, smiling a little. "You have a different affect on me, though. My body and instincts respond differently with you each second we spend together."

"Then we'll have to spend more time together," he says victoriously.

I think of Faye, and how I want her to go on and live her life; not being trapped by me and my issues. Would I do that to Caleb? Hanging around him, would he do the same and sacrifice for me? He doesn't really know who I am, but in the short time I have known him, he definitely seems like the type to make sacrifices for others.

"Maybe," is my response. I don't want to do to him what I have done to Faye.

"Have coffee with me tomorrow?" he ask, surprising me. I stay quiet, contemplating if it's a good idea. Again, he asks, "Have coffee with me, and then I want to take you somewhere."

Thinking of Faye, I say, "Okay."

After packing up our stuff, Caleb walks me to my car, staying close behind, guarding me like Faye does when I start looking around frantically. It doesn't bother me that he is behind me; it's oddly comforting. Caleb is in private security so that only makes sense, right?

We say a friendly goodbye as he shakes my hand and

taps my nose, saying he'll see me tomorrow. I smile and get in my car while Caleb stands there and waits for me to start up and pull away.

Taking the expressway home was a mistake. There are cars backed up two exits behind me, and I'm only half an exit away from the off ramp. I briefly consider driving on the side of the road over the white line, but with my luck, I'd be caught and given a ticket. So, I turn the music up and wait—not so patiently.

Ten minutes later, my phone rings showing Faye's name. I hit talk and put it up to my ear.

"I'm almost home," I say right away. "There is a ton of traffic, but I should be there in about ten minutes," I ramble quickly.

"Katy," Faye says hesitantly. By the tone in Faye's voice, I can tell that something is up. Immediately, worry starts to seep in. "Oh my gosh, Katy," she says sadly. "I was gone for like, thirty minutes. Micah and I went to get lunch. Oh, I don't know how to tell you this."

"Just spit it out, Faye. You're freaking me out." Looking around now, I am trying to see if I can maneuver my way in between cars so that I can speed this slow race along. But it's useless.

"We got back, and I was in the kitchen putting leftovers away." She hesitates again, and I get even more frustrated with her for acting like she did something wrong. "When I looked out the window there was something wrong. All the color that you can usually see from the kitchen window— was missing. When I walked up to the window to get a better look," she pauses, "the garden is gone, Katy. The whole thing. Flowers, trees..."

I can't hear the rest of her words. The phone slips from my hand, and I feel numb. I try to convince myself that she is exaggerating, but deep down, I know she is not. The garden that my grandma and I worked on together, labored in together, shared together—gone. Why? Who would do that? And then my mind wanders to my mom and what she said. She didn't want me to have anything. But why would she do it now? She had a month while I was in New York. I know nothing about her, or why she does these things, though.

Traffic finally moves, and I am finally able to take my exit. I drive way too fast. If I were to get pulled over, what would I say? 'Oh sorry officer. My garden is dying and I need to get home to it.' That would sound ridiculous. So I make a conscious effort to slow down.

I get home, jump out, and run up the steps and into the house; barely catching Micah and Faye sitting on the couch.

Running out the back door, I stop dead in my tracks. She wasn't joking. No early April fool's joke. It's gone. Every single last bit of it—ruined. Dead and colorless. The stones from the waterfall are everywhere. The tubing has been pulled out, it doesn't look repairable.

I just stare at it, unable to move or speak. This is it, this is my breaking point. *I'm about to lose it*, I think as my temper flares.

Why would she do this? Why? I want to lash out at my mom in some way. Any love that I felt for that woman has evaporated into thin air. The need to scream is powerful. As I prepare for that scream, I feel a hand on my shoulder. Looking up, I see Faye standing there. Always there to keep me grounded.

"You know who did this, right?" I say angrily. I try not to direct it toward her, but it's useless. She only nods.

"I can't believe she had the nerve to do this," I lash out. "What is her problem? I don't even know why she hates me so much. All I ever did was be born. She didn't even raise me, so I wasn't her problem." Fury devours every single cell in my body, and I let it.

Getting up, I stomp in the house, unable to look at anymore death. My inhibitions have been stripped, I act without thinking.

Grabbing the small vase of flowers that sits in the middle of the breakfast bar; I lift it, and with a roar, throw it with a force I didn't know I had, across the room. I push the dishes that lay in the strainer off the counter and rip every single picture, postcard, and magnet off the fridge.

I can hear Faye saying my name from a distance as I continue to the living room to ruin anything that is in my way.

I tip the movie shelf over, and the movies come tumbling down and spill all over the floor. Grabbing another vase that sits on the small table by the front door, I go to throw them and see that they are yellow calla lilies, and it stops me dead in my tracks. Grandma's flower.

For a moment, I feel a pang of hope, was this all a dream? The last calla lilies that Grandma and I had bought were dead. I threw them in the trash several weeks ago. So, how did these get here?

Setting the vase back on the table, I just stare at it. I would give anything to be able to hear Grandma's voice right now. But it's not Grandma's voice I hear—it's Collin's.

Turning around, he is standing there in the hallway. I don't know what to do. He knows what I have been through. Does he feel differently about me? Will I have the same issues with him as I do with others? He just stands there with his green eyes glistening. He just witnessed my melt down. I don't care about any of that. I missed him.

Running over, I hug him the way I use to. Throwing my arms around him and squeezing him tight; hoping that his hug doesn't feel different. Just when I think he isn't going to hug me back I feel his arms close around me. He lets out a long sigh.

"Katy, are you going mad?" Pulling back, he looks me in the eyes. "Do I need to call the mental institute? Because that was on the verge of psychotic."

I just," I look down at my shoes, embarrassed. "I'm tired. Of everything. Did you see the garden?" Looking up at him, I continue. "Mom, she did this," I say, the fury returning. Micah speaks up from the couch, forcing me to turn my gaze from Collin. I forgot he was here.

"We found a few bottles of empty weed killer under the gazebo. There wasn't anyone here when we got back," he interjects. I turn back to Collin.

"I know it was her. It's the only thing that makes sense after what she said to me. Why would someone go through all that trouble? I mean, every single flower, plant, and tree is gone."

"You don't have to convince me," he says, shaking his head. "I believe you."

"That woman is a crazy-" Micah starts to say, but Collin looks at him with annoyance.

"What are you doing here?" he asks firmly. "This is family business." The look he is giving Micah could burn a hole through a wall if he stares long enough.

Micah gets the clue and stands. "I'm just going to go. You guys have enough problems," he says, shaking his head.

"What's that suppose to mean?" Collin takes a step forward, his fists clenched. What is going on? I put my hands on his chest to hold him off, but I don't know why. The anger I had for my mother a moment ago leaves, because this isn't like Collin. Something is wrong.

"Nothing man." Micah raises his hands in surrender.

Faye, walking over from the kitchen, says, "Collin, he didn't mean anything by it. Why are you acting like this?" She picks up her purse and keys from the table, and her and Micah head toward the door. But Collin's face remains on Micah. With a hard look in his eyes, he doesn't take them off Micah until he is gone.

"Collin, what was that? Since when don't you like Micah?" I have never seen Collin react this way—ever.

"I just don't like the guy," he mumbles, but doesn't elaborate.

"Well that was rude, and Micah was a guest. I wish you hadn't done that."He just shrugs his shoulders and goes to sit on a chair in the living room. I follow and sit on the couch. "Why are you here? I mean, not that I'm not happy to see you, but you flew almost a thousand miles, and I know you have your job and Chelsea."

"I wanted to come home and make sure my baby sister was okay. I don't see anything wrong with that."

"What about your job and Chelsea? Wasn't she upset that you left, and how did you get off of work?" I hate giving him the third degree, but I can feel the tension in the air. He's not telling me something. Blowing out a long breath, he tells me the real reason he came back.

"I wasn't planning on coming home, yet. I know you're not ready to have me around."

"No, it's fine. I just felt sort of weird around everyone. Still do, but I'm working on it. Just tell me what's going on. We'll work it out."

"I quit my job, Katy. I had to get out of California; it was suffocating me." He sits up and tugs on the collar of his shirt metaphorically.

"Did Chelsea come with you? I know she really doesn't like coming here." I knew he would not just leave her. Sitting forward in the chair, he places his elbows on his knees and folds his hands together in front of him.

"I caught Chelsea with another man. I was out with the guys, at a baseball game, but we got rained out. Well, Chelsea didn't hear that, because she was too wrapped up in some guy I had never even seen before." His voice is laced with pain and betrayal.

Sitting back restlessly, he continues, "I caught them in the act. It was the most gruesome thing I have ever seen. She didn't even see me at first, and I was too stunned to move, so I saw more then I would ever have wanted to. I just wanted to scratch my eyes out of their sockets. When she finally realized I was there, she jumped up and started pleading with me to stay. Can you believe that?" he says desperately. "I grabbed my stuff and fled, disgusted by what I had to see. She had been sleeping with him for months. A neighbor said he stayed at my apartment the whole time I was here," he points at the ground, "trying to figure this stuff out with Grandma's Will, grieving. She kept calling me over and over once I was gone, but I hopped the first plane home, and didn't look back."

I tried to shake the feeling of hate for Chelsea from my mind. So I put my hand on his, trying desperately to be there for him, like he was always there for me.

But mostly, I could only wonder, is Collin home for good? I really hope so. Then, I started to feel his pain. Thinking about how horrible it would be to have seen that. He was devastated. Collin was a good guy, but I wondered what this betrayal would do to him.

In this family, we just have all the bad luck.

Chapter Ten

"What! That's awful!" Faye yells through the phone. Not really the reaction I had expected when I told her about Collin's situation, but what she said next left me even more puzzled. "Is he okay? I mean, is there something I can do?" When did she start caring about Collin? I'm not sure whether to start asking questions or be thankful for her compassion.

"Uh, I don't know. He should be fine, it'll just take time." I was sitting on my bed while Collin took a shower and changed. After talking for a little while, Collin was ready to wind down.

He looked so down and out, that I didn't know what to do. So, I recommended that we watch a movie, eat all kinds of junk food, and invite a few people over. He was game for all of that, except the people thing. It was just going to be Collin, Faye, and me.

"Okay, well I picked up your list of junk food, and yes, I know that I am not allowed to make any grotesque noises when you guys eat this junk," she says exasperated. "One night, Katy, I'll give in for one night, for Collin, but this stuff is going to make us feel like crap tomorrow."

Faye was a health nut. She didn't eat anything that was bad for her due mostly to her familial background of obese women. Her mom was the same way. It was something that they shared and helped them bond. I felt a longing deep inside me for that mother-daughter relationship. It had been worse since Grandma died, but it had always been there. If only I had a different mother.

"Okay, one night, for Collin. How far away are you?" I ask.

"I'm pulling up to the house right now. Hey, I wanted

to ask you something?" she says sounding uncertain. "Do you think Collin will be okay with me staying here still, or do you think he'll want me gone?"

"I hadn't thought about it. I guess you could go home now that Collin is here."

"Oh, okay," she says despondently.

"But, I like having you here. Maybe we can talk him into letting you stay," I say, trying to raise hope in her.

"All right! I'm coming in now can you come and...Oh," she says sounding slightly off, "never mind." She hangs up, so I walk out to the living room to meet her. She walks in with Collin trailing behind her with two bags of groceries and...shirtless.

"Put a shirt on, Collin." I walk over to the breakfast bar and sit down. "I don't think Faye wants to see your bare chest. Gag." I make a gagging noise and watch as Faye's cheeks redden. What!

Collin looks inside the bags and mumbles, "I don't think she minds." Then, to change the subject quickly, "Man, I better go and put on some pants with elastic."

Faye smiles and starts to take the groceries out of the bag with Collin's assistance. He pulls out a bag of cheese and hands it to her to put away. I watch as they work together in unison, putting things away and stocking the cupboards with chips and sweet treats. This is the perfect time to ask my question.

"So, Collin? Since Faye already moved her stuff in, you don't mind if she continues to stay with us, do you?" Walking over, I grab the jar of pickles out of his hand, sit at the breakfast bar, and wait anxiously for his answer.

Faye and Collin look at each other. Something passes between them. I can't quite put my finger on it, because it's there and gone so quickly. I start to think maybe they are hiding something from me.

"No, I don't see a problem with that," Collin replies.

"Great." I pop the lid off the pickle container and start eating one, as I continue to watch them suspiciously. If they're not telling me something, I will find out sooner or later.

After making a giant plate of nachos, and grabbing a bag of sweets, we all plop down on the couch to watch a movie. Faye and I choose a chick flick. After a whole lot of groaning, Collin finally agrees to our movie.

Collin and Faye laugh at the witty banter from the movie, but I couldn't seem to find my laugh. I couldn't remember when the last time I laughed was. I've smiled— sort of— but no loud laughter.

Was I even happy with my life? How could I get happiness? I was happy that Collin was home, even if it wasn't intentional. But there was something strange idling inside me, making me feel uncomfortable. I pushed past the uneasiness and tried to find my own peace, but it didn't last for long.

When the movie was over, and the nachos were demolished, we decided to play a game of cards. We all took seats around the coffee table and waited as Collin dealt out the cards for Texas hold 'em.

Collin and Faye squared off more times than I could count. I wasn't any good at this game. Faye was holding her cards in front of her face, fanned out, as Collin sat across from her waiting for her decision.

"Faye, either you got it or you don't. Please..." he groans, laying his forehead on the table, "just decide. I can barely keep my eyes open, I'm so tired." Faye looks at him mischievously.

"Oh, I've got it all right."

Collin groans again. I sit there and watch this all play out, smiling because Collin and Faye are acting like two little kids with their bickering.

"You know what I meant. Play your hand or I'm going to retract my earlier statement about you staying here,"

Collin threatens.

"What? You can't do that," she says angrily.

"Sure I can. It was my house before it was yours."

"You're just trying to distract me from playing this right. So be quiet and let me think."

"He's right, Faye; play already. You've been staring at those same cards for ten minutes. I promise you, they won't change." She eyes me with discontent.

"Fine." Laying her cards down on the table, she smiles gleefully. "Full house, baby! Read 'em and weep!"

"Dang." Collin lays down his two of a kind.

Faye's victory elicits a dance. She stands up and starts whooping and hollering, pumping her fist in the air while she jumps in a circle. She looks like a little kid who was just given the biggest lollipop in the store.

Looking over at Collin, he is staring at her with a look of admiration on his face. When he catches me looking, he clears his throat, and the look quickly fades.

"All right, ladies." Rising from the floor, he grabs the empty nacho plate. "I'm beat, but I'll see you guys in the morning." He starts to carry the plate to the kitchen, but I remember something.

"Oh, wait." He stops and turns. "I won't be here in the morning. I'm meeting Caleb for coffee."

I watch Faye's eyes widen as she leans in and looks at me like I am about to give her some really juicy gossip.

"You are?" she asks.

"Yes."

"I didn't get to ask you about your day. Oh, you have to tell me," she says excitedly.

"That's my queue to exit. I don't do girl talk." Collin walks over and kisses me on the head. "I'll see you after your coffee date with Caleb, then. I'm glad you're going out and doing stuff."

"It's not a date. It's just coffee amongst friends."

"Well, either way, I'll see you tomorrow. Goodnight,

Faye." He waves to her and she dismissively waves back. I watch him walk away, worried about what his situation will do to him. I don't think it's hit him yet, but when it does, how will he react?

"All right sister, spill the beans. I can tell it went good since you didn't call me, and you're going out with him again tomorrow."

Sighing, I tell her about my day at the beach and the odd visit to his church. When I'm done, she grins widely.

"Oh my gosh, Katy. That's fantastic! So, you didn't feel weird around him?"

"Well at first, yes, but after we left the church, I don't know," I say, shrugging and looking down, "I guess I just feel safe with him. I mean, I still flinched a few times when he touched me, but I didn't have a panic attack. Of course, I couldn't stand the touch any longer than a few seconds."

"Still! That's a start, right?"

"I guess so." And then more confidently, I say, "Yeah."

Earlier, I had told Faye we could bunk together until I prepped Grandmas room for her. It was weird, and she knew it. She started to protest, but I told her it was fine. No one was using it. She relented. So, we went to bed, both of us crammed into my full size bed. She fell asleep instantly, but I had this thought in my head on replay, and I couldn't find the stop button.

If I couldn't be touched for too long on my hand or chin; what did that mean for me and romance? Was romance dead for me? Would I ever let a man hold me or kiss me again? I was broken, my heart was fractured. No man would ever want me.

But then, I remember Caleb's words at the beach today. He said that my past didn't matter and it wouldn't make him feel differently. I didn't know how he felt about me now, But I hung on to those words until I fell asleep.

~~~

I woke the next morning at seven. Caleb had said that we needed to be early. So I agreed to seven, regretfully so.

Rolling out of bed, I brush my teeth, hair, and put on some faded blue jeans and a random shirt.

After pulling the shirt over my head, I decided to try another one. The one I had now said 'Living the dream' on it. It was one of Faye's birthday gifts to me.

Finding another shirt, I pull it over my head trying to make as little noise as possible, so I don't wake Faye. Reading it, I am satisfied. It kind of explains my mood right now.

By the time I get out of the door, and I am heading to the coffee shop, I'm running a few minutes behind. But when I get there, Caleb isn't there either. Sitting out front in my car, I wait for him to show up. After ten minutes he's still not there, and I start to get fidgety.

Finally, when I am just about to call him, he strolls up to my car. I roll down the passenger side window. He slides his sunglasses off his face and leans down to look into the window.

"Hey, sorry I'm late. I had some security issues. We'll probably have to get the coffee to go."

"Okay." I climb out of my car. He waits till I walk around then tags along behind me. "So, any chance you'll tell me where we're going?" I ask, after we walk into the coffee shop.

They're not too busy, there are maybe two people in line. I start to feel uncomfortable and my heart speeds up, my breathing becomes erratic. Caleb is still standing behind me, but I am looking around trying to notice everyone and everything.

I take a deep breath and call on the feelings that were present on the coaster, and remember that I can get those same feelings from excitement. I thought about my day with Caleb today. Wondering where he was going to take me. Would it be another training session? Or maybe he just liked spending time with me. Surprisingly, I really liked that idea. I started to get excited at the prospect, and my terror started to fade away. I stop a good distance away from the people in front of me, still, as the short line moves forward.

"It's a surprise." Glancing down at my shirt, he looks up at me, smirking. "Nice shirt. Not a morning person, are you?" he asks in regard to my shirt that says, 'I'll rise and shine just not at the same time.'

"Not so much." I shake my head and offer him a smile of my own. "Faye gets me these shirts every year for my birthday." I tug at the bottom of the shirt and release it. "Well except this year."

"We'll have to fix that." He points at my shirt. "Do you think you'd be up to riding with me today? It seems like it would be easier."

"Um, yeah sure. I should be able to do that." There is definitely some uncertainty in my voice. But, he doesn't say anything about it.

After we get our coffee, we head to his truck. His very large truck. The tires are as tall as I am. This is a different truck, it's even bigger than his other one.

"Oh my gosh, Caleb. You're one of those."

"One of what?" he says, opening the passenger side door. I put my foot on the running board and grab the door panel, preparing to lift myself up, but Caleb puts his hand on my elbow to assist me in. I tense at first but relax almost immediately. He is touching me with his fingertips and just barely.

Looking at him, I smile. This touch, his touch, hasn't really bothered me so much. I don't want to think too much about it, if I do it may disappear, so I push it to the back of my mind for future examination.

"One of those men that needs a giant truck to feel manly," I continue. His smile is a full 100-watts, and my smile mirrors his. Something in my chest turns. Caleb helps me up knowing that I am in good shape, and I don't need his help, but I don't protest.

Jogging around to his side, he hops in quickly and starts the truck. It rumbles to life, shaking me. I don't feel nervous or anxious about this. I'd say I was making some progress.

On the way to, wherever it is we were going, I tell him about my grandma's garden and my theory on who did it. It's the first time I have mentioned my mother to him, so he is full of curiosity. His questions start simple, asking me where she has been, what she was like, but then he stopped asking because he could see that I didn't know. He asked me where she was now. Again, I stayed silent because I didn't know where, and I hadn't thought about it, maybe I should have. He seemed to sense what I was thinking.

"Is someone at the house now?" he asks.

"I don't know." I say nervously. "Collin came home yesterday. He didn't say he was going anywhere. I don't think he would leave the house without someone being there after seeing what happened. Would he?"

"Call him and see. If he isn't there, I'll send one of my guys over to take a look."

"No, I couldn't ask you to do that."

"You didn't ask, I want to. Besides, if she is using drugs and alcohol, she isn't necessarily in the right frame of mind, so there is no telling what she'll do. I know that from personal experience, trust me." Picking up my phone, I call Collin.

"Katy, what's up? Is everything okay?" He sounds worried.

"Yes, everything is fine. But, are you at home?"

"No, actually. I just left about ten minutes ago. Why, what's up?"

"Was Faye there when you left?"

"Uh, well, no she isn't there either," he says cautiously.

"Katy what's going on?"

"I was telling Caleb about what happened yesterday, and he's just a little concerned. He was going to send someone over to check the area and make sure Mom isn't lingering around. Are you okay with that?"

"Sure, that sounds like a good idea. He won't have to go inside the house, right?"

"No just outside the house."

"Okay, then yes, I'm fine with that."

Hanging up with Collin, I give Caleb the go ahead. He dials a number by pushing one button on his phone and talking to a guy named Mike on the other end. I give him my address and listen as he repeats it to Mike. By the time he hangs up, we are crossing a bridge and pulling to a stop.

"Why are we stopping here?" My internal alarms start to go wild as he parks on the bridge; an abandoned bridge at that.

It's one of the highest in the city, but it's been closed down for years. They were unable to maintain the upkeep so they deemed it unsuitable for use in fear that too many cars would make it collapse. The metal railings where all but gone and the rebar showed through the concrete sporadically.

"This is where I'm taking you," he says, unbuckling his seatbelt.

"Oh, uh, how sweet." I say confused. Chuckling, he opens his door and leaps out.

"You'll see." Coming around to my side, he opens the door and helps me down, only touching my elbow. "A friend of mine meets me out here a couple of times a month."

We walk the length of the bridge, stopping in front of a large, burley man. He's at least six foot tall with a head of curly, red hair. I start to feel uncomfortable, as I tense up. It takes everything in me to keep my feet planted. Knowing that Caleb is here helps too.

"Roger." Caleb shakes the man's hand. "This is Katy. She's going to be going along with me today." Roger offers his hand to me.

"Katy, it's nice to meet you." He has an Irish accent.

Pretending that I don't see his hand, I say, "It's nice to meet you too. What exactly are we doing here?" I turn to Caleb and ask.

"Roger here owns a bungee jumping business."

I feel my eyes widen in fear, as I take a step back and swallow the lump in my throat. There is no way I will be jumping off a bridge.

"Oh, no, no, no." I say, waving my hands in protest. "I have had enough crazy in my life for the past two months," I hold up two fingers, "to last a lifetime. I am not going to jump off a bridge."

"Katy, I wouldn't ask you to do this if I didn't think it was beneficial." He really looks sincere, and I am trying really hard to find how this is going to benefit me in any way.

"How, exactly, is jumping off of a bridge going to help me, except for scaring the daylights out of me?" Crossing my arms over my chest, I raise my eyebrows and wait for his answer. Oh, this will be good.

"Every time I am out here," stepping forward he gazes into my eyes, "and I step off the ledge, I make a decision. When I'm falling; I leave every worry up on the ledge. It doesn't come with me. That's what I want you to feel. When you jump, I want you to leave every horrible thing that has happened to you, every worry on the ledge. The only thing that goes over is you and me."

"That doesn't make any sense."

"Yes it does, because you see, the fall will be so intense that you won't be able to think about all of that stuff."

"What about after? It will just come back afterwards."

"You're right. Your past will always be a part of you,

but you can make the decision to stay in the past, or you can take that leap away from your past, leaving it on the ledge. It's metaphorical, but it has helped me."

Blowing out a breath, I say quietly, "I'm scared."

"This isn't the first time you've been scared, right?"

"No, but why would I willingly step into the fear?"

"This fear is different. It's one that you will be choosing to overcome, on your own terms." He puts both of his hands on both of my shoulders and lowers his head to mine. "Trust me." He's asking for a lot.

I'm not sure I can do it. They can get me all strapped in, and I can be standing on the ledge, but when it comes time to jump, how do I make that decision? How do I choose to plunge to what could very possibly be my death? I know it's highly unlikely, but when I look over the edge, all I can picture is my body lying lifeless on the pavement. While I am standing there, having an internal debate with myself, Caleb is getting his harness on.

Maybe I'll just watch him. What he said though, I want that. I want to jump and leave my worries at the top. Making a decision, I turn to Caleb.

"Okay, I'll do it. But, you won't be mad if I chicken out, will you?"

"Of course not." Smiling from ear to ear, he finishes fastening his harness. Roger goes over it, checking to make sure it's fastened correctly, and puts the ankle harness on.

Walking over to my harness, I pick it up and step into it. After throwing the straps over my shoulders, I tighten the straps around my thighs and hook the rope that connects to the ankle harness to my carabineer. Having a little trouble with the buckle that wraps around my waist, I try to push it in, but it's not catching. I start to walk over to Caleb, hoping he'll help me as I am trying to shove the buckle in, but finally, it snaps into place.

I hear Roger say something about helping me, so I look up and see him walking over. I start to tell him no, that I'll be fine, but it's too late. He's already too close. My natural instinct is to back away from this giant, burly man. As I tense, and take a step back, my foot catches on the small cement lip of the bridge.

And then—it happens.

I fall over the edge, harness not yet completely attached. I'll slip out. A scream so guttural escapes my mouth it sounds like the screeching of a semi truck trying to stop before hitting a car.

I have no idea why bad things happen to people, or who decides when it's someone's time to go, but I do know that I don't want to die. I'm eighteen and haven't really lived my life yet.

I think back to what Grandma wrote on the card she left me for my birthday, *There is so much for you to see in life, so much to be lived. Go enjoy it!* But this is it. I didn't listen to Grandma, and now, I will die. Having not lived my life.

The little time I had, what did I do with it? Sulked, brooded, I lived in the past. Let momentary situations determine my life. No matter what has happened in my past, the journey to death is worst. I think back to when death sounded like freedom that night on the stairs in New York.

Closing my eyes so tightly it hurt, my heart beats rapidly inside of my chest. I don't have time to think about the things I regret, there are too many, so I let them go.

I'm unable to stop screaming. Tears flow freely from my eyes, as I plead for another chance at life if someone somewhere will give me a miracle. I don't deserve it, but I want more than anything to live.

I wait for the moment I will hit the concrete wondering if it will hurt. Will I die fast or suffer slowly?

But the force doesn't come. Instead, I feel surrounded in warmth. I feel like I have been wrapped, and now I am floating up and down. My throat hurts so bad I can't continue to scream. Listening to my own sobbing and harsh breathing, hearing nothing but the thump in my chest so loudly, I continue to plead for mercy.

I can hear my name being called over and over, it sounds soothing. When I open my eyes, maybe everything that has happened to me will have been a dream. I'll open my eyes, and Grandma will be standing over me. Like in the Wizard of Oz.

Slowly, reality seeps into my muddled mind. Through my blurry vision, I can see a chest. Then I realize that I am hanging upside down, and I am wrapped up—by Caleb. Somehow, someway, he caught me.

His breathing is harsh, and his grip is so tight that I can feel his fingers digging into my back, his legs are wrapped tightly with mine.

"Katy, it's okay. I've got you, it's going to be okay. Do you hear me?" He doesn't sound worried, just a little out of breath.

I do hear him, but I can't talk because every breath I take is a stuttered inhalation, so I just nod my head. How is this even possible? When I stumbled he was at least ten feet in front of me? That's dumb to question how a man saved my life, because the reality of it is—he did.

"Roger is going to lower us to the ground. We're too heavy to both be lifted at the same time. It's going to take a minute, so I want you to look at me." His voice reminds me of hypnosis, soothingly trying to get you to break from the trance you're in or put you in one.

Looking up into his blue eyes, the terror I couldn't hear in his voice covers his face. It makes him look more vulnerable. But looking into his eyes, calms me.

Slowly, I start to reign in my hysteria. He seems to have a good grip on me, and considering the situation we are in, I don't think him touching me is a problem. I don't even think twice about it. The thought of letting go makes me queasy, though.

Slowly, we start to descend. The first small jolt toward the ground scares me and I squeal, but Caleb just grips me tighter.

"I'll never let you go, Katy. You're safe with me." There was a double meaning all over that, but I didn't pick it apart in this moment.

Inch by inch we were lowered to the ground. I looked down so I could see how far the ground was away from us still. It looked like twenty feet before we would meet the pavement.

Turning my head back toward Caleb, I rest my cheek on his chest and focus on his heartbeat. The rapid beat was a mirror of mine from the near death experience I just had.

As the ground brings our decent to a halt, I feel the cold seeping into my bones. I shake uncontrollably from the adrenaline rush, so I grip Caleb tighter in an attempt to make it stop. He doesn't let go either. We just lay there for what seems like forever, holding each other, trying to get our erratic breathing under control. He rubs slow soothing circles on my cheek, and my labored breathing comes to a slow halt.

We try to stand, but it's difficult because we both have shaky legs, so we hang onto each other for support and rise from the ground.

"How did you get to me? I was too far away?"

"I saw it before it happened. Roger walking up to you, I knew what your reaction would be, and you were so close to the edge. I started over as soon as Roger started offering his help. I don't know, I just knew I had to move. I was too far away, concentrating on my harness and cables, but by the time you started falling backwards, I was right behind Roger. That's how I was able to go over with you." Blowing out a long breath he says, "Just as you started to go over, I jumped and caught you in mid air about half way down."

I don't think I have ever been so thankful for meeting someone.

"I'm not ready to die," I whisper.

"No one is ready to die, but it's something that we have

no control over."

"Yeah," I laugh weakly, "you're right. But it doesn't stop me from not wanting to die."

"Hey, look at the good that came from this. I'm holding you, completely, and you're not hyperventilating." He holds me tighter.

Looking at his chest, I know he is right. I feel comfort from this, not fear. It's a breakthrough, a major one. All of his simple small touches on the chin, my hand, and my elbow were nice, but to be wrapped in him so completely, is so much better. I hug him tighter.

"Hey." He pulls back a little so that I can look at him. He has been so supportive, not even knowing what I have been through, yet here he is helping me, saving my life, putting up with me.

It's in that moment that I know that Caleb was supposed to be right here, right now. I was supposed to meet him that day at Mel's diner two months ago. Maybe, everything that happened to me from that point has been to bring me here in his arms, and if that's true, I can't regret the absolutely horrible things that have happened to me. I need to embrace them, use them as a tool in the healing process. What else are those memories good for? Nothing. But they are there regardless.

I think I can see Caleb understanding my revelation; his eyes soften, the fear from them gone. Putting his hand on my cheek, there is no flinching or tensing, just longing for his touch. His thumb moves back and forth over my skin.

"Katy," he says in a raspy voice," I'm going to kiss you." *Yes*, is all I can think. I want him to kiss me. And he does, answering my unvoiced plea.

His lips press gently against mine, soft and full. With both hands he holds my head in place as his soft lips press harder. My whole body ignites with awareness, it's a blessing. I have felt so numb for the past month, trying to push things away. Things that I didn't want to hear or do. Things that I didn't want to feel.

But the feelings that Caleb brought out of me, squashed all that. A spark settled in, lighting me up, as hope rises from the nothingness that I had become.

Pulling back from the kiss, he finds my eyes, searching for my reaction, all I can do is smile. The smile stretches from one side to the other. So wide it hurts my face. But I don't care, because my smile elicits a smile from him, and it's beautiful. He's beautiful; inside and out.

Leaning in, he kisses me again, this time a small peck on the lips. Pulling back, he looks at me and almost immediately, he does it again. Just a small, soft peck on my lips. It's all I need. It's everything in this moment.

What just happened on the bridge seems like a distant memory. What matters now is that we are here, we are safe, and I just let Caleb not only hold me, but kiss me; which seemed impossible just yesterday.

"Are you guys okay?" Roger comes running up to us, out of breath.

"Yes, we're fine." Caleb answers him but doesn't turn his gaze from me.

"I'm so sorry, I-I don't know what happened. Maybe I bumped into you," he says nervously, running his hands through his thick, red hair.

Finally, turning my gaze from Caleb, I try to reassure Roger.

"No, Roger. It wasn't your fault, it was me. I tripped on the edge and...well, no, it wasn't you. Please, don't blame yourself." He fights with that, rolling it around in his head, but his voice is audibly shaken when he speaks.

"It's my job to keep you guys safe. It's my job to ensure that you don't die, and here I go and push you over before it's time."

Walking over to him, I put my hand on his arm.

Amazed by that single gesture, I look at Caleb's proud stare. Turning my gaze back to Roger, he looks at me.

"Roger, it really wasn't your fault. I am really clumsy. I should have known better then to walk that close to the edge without my harness completely ready."

I think I have gotten through to him. He just blows out a breath and shakes his head. Then he pulls me into a hug. An awkward hug, but still, a hug. All I feel is shock, that this big, burly man would hug someone. It doesn't seem like something he would do.

I wrap my arms around him and try to sooth him, as he says, "I'm so sorry. I'm glad you're okay, lass."

Standing here, after falling to what I thought was my death, I am hugging a man whom I don't know. Without fear, no hesitation, and no tensing. And I feel free. Free from those memories that haunt me and make me the feeble person I have been. But after an experience like this, I know that life is short, and I want to live it.

Without fear.

Chapter Eleven

My dim life suddenly seemed a little brighter. Letting go of those memories that were binding me to my past; I felt free to move on as something in me loosened, reconnecting me with the person I used to be.

The fear I felt grip my stomach when someone got too close, or when I was alone, was replaced with a squeezing in my chest. My fractured heart was mending. I knew that it was a timely process, but I didn't care, because it was progress.

I was looking forward to talking to Faye and Collin. I wondered if they would be able to see a change in me, since I hadn't been able to wipe the stupid grin off my face. I didn't want to. Maybe if I kept it in place long enough, it would never fade.

It felt so good to genuinely smile from happiness. Life always had a way of bringing you down by pushing you over the edge- no pun intended- but I planned to make the best of every situation. That one near fatal incident had me examining my life instead of avoiding it.

After reassuring Roger that everyone was okay, just a little shaken, Caleb drove me back to my car. Grabbing my hand from where it sat on my knee, he looks over, and the grin is still there. That kiss left me feeling dazed; it had never been like that with Josh.

"We probably look like two Jokers smiling like this. But you know what," I say to him, "I haven't felt anything better in months." His eyebrows lift in question. "Oh...well...I mean. You know, except for that kiss. That was," looking off, I search for the word.

"Amazing, life altering, fantastic, beyond compare, you want me to keep going?" he says jokingly. His sideways glance makes me giggle.

"No, please don't. I don't think there is room in here for your ego." Rolling my eyes, I look at him and admire the simplicity of this moment. His fingers entangled with mine, my body excepting it.

"I have to go into work," he sighs. "I'd rather spend the rest of the day with you, but we've been having some problems with a client. That doesn't happen often, but when it does, we have to all be alert for any possibility."

"So, you can't play hooky?" I tease.

"No, but it's very tempting." He pulls out his phone and pushes a button. "I'm calling Mike to see if he found anything." After a few moments of ringing Mike finally picks up. "Mike, did you find anything around Ms. Laudin's residence?"

"No, sir. Just the usual. The young couple that live there just arrived home about ten minutes ago. They appeared to be having a rather heated argument."

"Oh, they aren't a couple." I felt the need to correct him.

"Are you sure, ma'am? A tall, slender man with light brown hair and a young woman with red hair."

"Yes," I say confused, "but they're not a couple. That's my brother and best friend. They both live there."

"Ok, ma'am," he says unsure. Well, I'm with him on that. "They are at the house now, but everything seems to be quiet around here."

"All right, Mike. Thank you."

"Would you like for me to stay, sir?"

"No. Hart is having some trouble with his client. I'd like for you to assist him with that."

"Yes, sir. Not a problem."

After he hangs up with Mike, Caleb grabs my hand and squeezes it as we pull up to the coffee shop.

"Call me later," he says. Letting go of his hand, I open the door and climb out.

"Why don't you call *me* later," I call behind me. "You're busier then I am, so that only makes sense."

"Okay." He shakes his head and smiles. "I'm glad Faye called me the other day. Thank her for me, will you?"

"I'll do that." I smile and close the door. As I head toward my car, and for the entire ride home, that smile is still in place. I've never smiled so much in my entire life.

When I get home, I find Faye in the sunroom, standing at the back door, staring at her phone.

"What's up?" I ask. Startled, she jumps and starts fumbling with her phone.

"Oh, I-I was just," she stutters. She looks frazzled as she walks over to me, "um, texting Micah. How was your date?" She asks lifting her eyebrows suggestively.

"It wasn't a date, and it was..." not able to contain the smile, I beam at her. "Faye, you will not believe what happened." We move to the table out there and sit.

Taking in the look on my face, she asks me, very cautiously, "Do I want to know?"

Nodding my head, I say, "He took me bungee jumping."

"What! Oh my gosh! Did you do it? Well not *it*, but you know— jump?"

"Well, sort of. I did go over. But, I wasn't strapped in all the way." I tell her the rest of what happened and watch as her eyes grow from little quarters to the size of golf balls.

"I can't believe you almost died. Are you okay?" She sounds like she's in shock.

"I'm fine, really." Once she checks me over for bumps and bruises, she asks me a question I knew was coming.

"You let him kiss you?" She starts rapidly firing off questions. I can't keep up. "What was it like? Was he a good kisser? Did you feel it? Oh better yet, did you like it, and were you all tense? Because being tense could potentially ruin a kiss," she says matter-of-factly.

"There you go again with your twenty questions. I

didn't tense...at all. Which surprised me because it was the reason I lost my balance and went over the edge."

"Ok, great. Now...did you like it?" Her eyes bore into me as she sits there waiting for my answer.

"Yes." It was a simple word, but it elicits the happiest response from her.

She gets up and starts jumping up and down like we did when we were kids.

"Katy," she squeals, "that is a huge breakthrough." Her demeanor withering slightly, she asks, "I wonder if that will work on all men?" She puts her thinking face on, and I get nervous.

"Whatever you're thinking, stop." Getting up, I head to my room. "Besides," I call behind me, where Faye is tagging along giddily, "I shook hands with Roger, the bungee instructor, and he hugged me. It was weird, but I only tensed for a brief moment and there was no panic attack. And I am not kissing a bunch of guys to test your theory," I say sternly.

Walking to my closet, I gather what I need for a shower. Faye sits on my bed.

"What about crowds? Do you think you can handle them?"

"I don't know." That was a good question. I think the biggest hurdle had been jumped, but what about the small ones and my other problems? Does jumping the big hurdle automatically mean that the small ones won't matter, or they will at least be easier to deal with? I didn't know, but I had a feeling I was about to find out.

"I have an idea." Faye's eyes get big and round.

From inside my closet I mumble, "I thought you might." Those words lacked any excitement, but I was willing to try if it meant Faye getting on with her life, and going to college.

"Okay. Get dressed, and," walking into my closet, she says secretively, "wear something flashy." I have no idea where this is going, but when I think about all the times we had each other's backs; the roller coaster and Faye taking time off school and moving in for me, are a few, I don't think much more about it.

Pulling the flashiest thing I have out of the closet, I head for the bathroom and begin getting ready for whatever Faye has in store for me.

As I am putting my eyeliner on, Faye walks in and my mouth drops open.

"What are you wearing?" I ask in disbelief. She has on what can only be described as a short black shirt with sequins all over and a silver sequenced belt. The dress falls off one shoulder, and her black high heels make her legs look longer then they are.

"It's called a dress." She gestures her hand up and down toward me. "What are you wearing?" She sounds displeased.

I look down at my dark blue jeans, black heels, and blue silk halter top. "What's wrong with this? I don't want to look like a hooker."

"What? Are you saying that I do?" She pretends shock.

"Yes, you do," I say sweetly, smiling.

"Good! That's what I was going for." Walking into my closet, she comes out with an old skirt that I had yet to toss out. It is way too short, because I've grown since I bought it. "Wear this one. You'll look hot." Refusing to take it, I cross my arms over my chest and look at her like she is crazy. "Fine," she huffs, tossing the skirt on the chair in the corner. "We're leaving in ten. I'm going to get my clutch. I'll meet the *Nun* at the convent."

As she walks away, I holler, "There's nothing wrong with being conservative."

Faye has always been a little reckless. She said what was on her mind and wore what she wanted. Never really caring what others thought about her. It sort of made people look past my dullness with her bubbly personality around.

Sometimes, her reckless attitude scared me though.

Walking over to my dresser, I put my sapphire necklace on and some clear gloss on my lips, then head out the door. I hear voices floating down the hall from the living room, but I don't want to be sneaky, so I just continue.

As my heels click down the hall the chatter stops. Collin and Faye are sitting on the couch talking to each other. Why they were whispering, and why they stopped talking when they heard me coming, has all my senses on high alert.

"What were you guys talking about?" I ask quizzically. They both smile at me guiltily, and I know something's up, I just don't know what it is yet. All of these heated fights, secret discussions, and questionable looks between them have me wondering if it's about me. I stand there not giving in, not giving up, waiting for an answer, as I tap my foot on the hardwood floor.

Their smiles fade when they realize that no one is leaving until someone tells me what's going on. Collin starts first, clearing his throat.

"Well, Faye and I have been looking into the garden incident; trying to find out if it truly was Julie. Do you remember the woman that lives four houses down, Ms. May?"

Nodding my head yes, I do recall Ms. May, the friendly elderly lady who always gave me cookies when I was younger.

"She saw Julie here yesterday. Didn't think anything of it because she also saw her here after Grandma's funeral. She said she's seen her on and off for the last week. Nothing suspicious; she would just come and grab the mail and water the plants. Ms. May said it seemed like she was taking care of the house."

Sitting down on the chair, I take a minute to take this all in. For the past week my mom has been sneaking around the house. Had she been watching me? Why was she doing this? I didn't know how I felt about this news. The whole situation sent chills down my spine.

"Should I be worried?" I ask.

"We found out that she was staying in a motel out by the expressway. We went this morning and took a look. The guy at the front desk said there wasn't anyone there by her name. We waited around for a few hours and," stopping he runs his hands through his hair, "she *is* staying there, Katy. With some guy. He looks sort of seedy, big guy with lots of tattoos and facial hair."

"What does this mean?" Sitting back in my chair, I think about the garden she ruined and her previous actions, watering the plants and checking the mail. I don't understand, but I think she may be crazy.

"We don't know. But Faye and I had a disagreement on what to do about it. She wants to call the cops, but I feel the only thing that will do is provoke her. She is unpredictable, her actions tell us that."

I agree with Collin. There is no evidence of foul play, but I don't voice my opinion. Instead, I decide to just be cautious from here on out. It still freaks me out that she has been walking around acting like she belongs here. If something is provoking her, it's probably just me—breathing.

"Well, there isn't really much we can do about it, but wait it out and see what happens. But, I think someone should always be at the house," Collin says, looking at Faye, then at me.

"Okay, that sounds like a good plan," Faye says, rising. "We're going out tonight. Which means, you," she says, pointing at Collin, "get to stay home." Grabbing my wrist, she pulls me up.

"She's right, we're going out. You get to house sit. Sorry," I apologize with a sly grin on my face. Collin lights up at my playfulness; something he hasn't seen or heard in a long time. Faye must have told him about my day with Caleb.

"Fine. You ladies have fun. I'll house sit, but be careful," he says sternly.

"Of course we'll be careful. Did you forget that Katy is a master in Krav Maga, and I did take some self-defense classes myself," Faye says.

"It was one self-defense class, and I think we know that my Krav Maga is useless."

"Does it matter? I took Caleb down."

"Yes, it matters. You'll be no help if we are attacked. Now, let's get going before Collin decides to leave while we're talking, then *we'll* have to stay and house sit."

"Ooh, good point," Faye says, and quickly walks out the door. I give Collin a wave and head out too.

When Faye pulls up to Sheba's Bar, I am further confused.

"Faye, there are two problems with this. One, we don't drink, and two, we are eighteen. You have to be twenty-one to get in there."

"Yes, technically, you're right, but we don't have to drink. This is just an experiment .We'll just go in, order something virgin, and sit at the bar; maybe mingle a little." When she takes the keys out of the ignition, I start to have a small panic attack.

"What about the fact that we're eighteen?" I ask, hoping that she would start the car back up and drive away.

"My cousin works the door. I called him when you were getting dressed, he's expecting us." A concerned look crosses her face. "It's going to be okay. You can do this. Besides, I think getting over the whole not able to be touched thing will make all this easier."

I don't tell her how I am already starting to feel a panic attack coming on. Instead, I try to push it down. Taking a step out of the car, I try to call on the same feelings I had on the coaster, thrill and excitement.

The night air is humid and my silk halter starts to stick to me already. I can only hope that there are not as many people inside as I expect. Being hot will make things worse.

Luckily, there are not as many people as I had expected, but there was still a crowd.

People were scattered all over, but mostly they stood near the bar. This bar was merely for social run-ins. I had never been, but I've known Collin to come. I didn't think Faye had been here before; if she had, I didn't know about it.

Walking to the bar, we sit on a couple of stools and look out over the crowd. Small tables with two or three chairs littered the floors. Booths sat against walls and in corners for a more private area. I expected the place to be filled with smoke and people dancing to loud music. None of those things were true to this experience.

People talked and laughed softly, and the air was clean. Everyone was dressed in their business suits. I realized, quickly, this was a bar for people on a higher social ladder.

The bartender comes over, and Faye orders two waters with lime. He looks at us kind of funny; two women ordering water in a bar, but in the end, he brings us our water and doesn't question our age.

For an hour we just sit there people watching and drinking our water. But it started to get busy, and I was beginning to get bored. Out of all the places for Faye to bring me, a bar seemed like the worst. There were usually some shady people at bars. She assured me that this bar was exclusive and the people here were usually pretty sane.

"You've been here before?" I ask. She has never mentioned coming here. We spent most of our time together since we were seven, but she had a life that I didn't know too much about, a life with Micah.

We weren't that fantastic trio, or the three musketeers. Micah liked to be alone with Faye. When we did hang out, we usually watched a movie.

"My cousin works the door, remember?" Taking a sip of her water, she looks out over the crowd. "I use to come here with Micah. My cousin, Jimmy, would let us in." She looks at me with guilt ridden features. "We didn't drink or anything. We just sat in the corner booth and talked."

I wonder why she never told me this. I didn't even know this 'Jimmy', and I knew pretty much everyone in her family. We talked about everything, but Micah didn't seem to come up much in conversation.

After another twenty minutes of picking through the peanut bowl and sipping at my water, a man takes the seat next to me. He smiles at me, and I thought the only thing to do was smile back, so I did.

"Hi, I'm Trevor." He sticks his hand out. He has a nice smile and is dressed in a business suit and tie, but looks could be deceiving, and I didn't trust people the way I used to. I put my hand in his sweaty one.

"Katy," I say over the hum of the music.

"Can I buy you a drink?" he says, pointing toward my water.

"Oh, no. That's okay." Couldn't he see that my glass was full? Looking away, I try to shake that familiar sense of foreboding when someone was close. There was no panic even though my nerves had been on edge all night, and I guess that was a start, but my heart was still racing a little, and out of habit I was looking everywhere but at him.

Trevor must notice how nervous I am because when I look back at him the curiosity is evident on his face.

"Are you waiting for someone?" he asks. I shake my head no and his curiosity vanishes a bit. I look over at Faye to make sure she is still with me, but I find her staring at me instead. Silently, she urges me to talk to him. Turning back to Trevor I say the first thing that comes to my mind.

"I'm not waiting for anyone tonight, but I do have a boyfriend." I give him an apologetic look.

Reaching out, he puts his hand on my bare shoulder, and I tense.

Maybe I've angered him by turning him down, but he smiles and says, "That's too bad, Katy. I would have liked to know a little more about you."

He squeezes my shoulder, gets up, and walks away. I let out a slow breath and relish in the triumphant feeling of getting through that without panicking.

"Katy. What is wrong with you?" Faye throws her hand in the air and asks exasperated. "He was a nice looking guy and willing to buy you a drink."

"We don't drink, remember? And I just wasn't into him." And there's Caleb. I can't get him off my mind.

Putting my hands in my lap and crossing my legs, I wait for her reprimand. It never comes, but her eyes look past me, and the exasperation on her face turns to shock. She gets up and heads in the direction she was looking.

She looks like a woman on a mission, taking long strides toward the back of the room. When I sit straighter to see where she is walking to, I see Micah sitting at a booth. He's not alone, and by the look on Faye's face and the determination in her stride, she had no idea he'd be here.

I get up and follow her, not to be nosy, but for support. Something tells me this isn't going to be good. Faye stops in front of him, he looks at her and the shock transfers to his face. He stutters and rises.

"Oh-uh- Hey, honey. I didn't know you were going to be here tonight." He steps in to hug her, and just when I think she may push him away. she embraces him. Maybe she did know he was going to be here. But the stiffness in her shoulders tells me otherwise.

He wasn't alone at the table. Three men and two women were also sitting there. No one I had ever seen before, so I didn't think that Faye had either. But I was starting to wonder if Faye had lived a separate life with Micah.

"Can we talk?" she asks him. Her voice is softer then I had thought it would be. Micah agrees and grabs her arm, pulling her to another booth. Not wanting to intrude, I turn and make my way to an empty table in the center of the room. Lifting myself up onto the seat, I try not to watch Faye and Micah.

They have been together for four years. I can't believe that they would not know each other completely. But I've never been in love before, I don't know how it works.

The group of people Micah is with didn't seem like the normal crowd they hung out with. In fact, they normally didn't have a crowd, but here he is hanging with these people.

Looking back at Faye and Micah, I see they are holding hands, and Faye is smiling. I am so confused by what is going on here but usually when Micah was around, Faye was deliriously happy, and I kind of was forgotten. But Faye gets up and walks over to me, hoisting herself up onto the chair next to me.

Hesitantly, I speak up. "What was that all about?"

"Nothing," she says, waving her hand. "Just a misunderstanding." I watch as Micah returns to his table but doesn't sit down. "Micah is getting a table for us, if you are okay with that?" Well, who else was I going to sit with? I nod my head in acceptance.

We get up and walk to a table in the opposite corner from where Micah was with his freinds. There is no greeting, just a head nod from Micah, so I decide to return the gesture in the same manner. This feels awkward, and I really want to leave, but Faye is my ride.

I start to think of a ways to get out of here when Caleb walks in through the door. He doesn't look anywhere else, just at me as if he knew I was here.

He smiles and gives a small wave, then shoves his hands into his suit pants pocket; he fits in here. I smile back and give a wave, entirely too happy about seeing him here and in that suit. I secretly hope that he comes over, and he does. He starts to walk toward us, so I lean over to Faye.

"Caleb is here," I whisper in her ear. She is busy talking to Micah but turns my way when she hears me.

"Where?" She starts looking around.

"He's walking this way." Grabbing her arm, I nod my head toward him.

I stand up, and I don't know what I am doing until he is standing in front of me, but I reach out and throw my arms around him, hugging him tightly. His arms wrap around my waist, hugging me back. He presses his cheek against the top of my head and squeezes me just as tightly.

"Well, this is a nice surprise," he says, his deep voice rumbling through him into me. We pull away from each other, but he doesn't let go of my hands. "And an even better hello." His blue eyes burn into mine. Suddenly, I feel silly.

"Sorry, I just, I couldn't..." Flustered and unable to tell him exactly why I just threw my arms around him, like I had some claim on him, he stops me.

Leaning down, he whispers in my ear, "You're cute when you're flustered. I liked the way you greeted me, don't worry so much." My cheeks redden at his words and closeness, but I don't ever want to move from where I am.

"Oh, sorry, you've met Faye?" I say realizing we have an audience.

"Yes, I have. Hi, Faye. How are you?" he says, turning toward her and Micah

"I'm good. This is Micah," she says, gesturing toward him, "my fiancé."

"It's nice to meet you." Caleb says, while shaking Micah's hand.

"Same to you man," says Micah.

"Would you like to sit with us?" I ask Caleb.

"I wish I could, but I'm meeting Mike here. We were going to discuss something that I think you would be interested in. Can you join us?"

"Sure. If Faye doesn't mind." She shakes her head no.

"Go ahead. Enjoy." She smiles at me and wiggles her eyebrows. When Caleb turns to walk away, I give her a fleeting look. Walking over to a corner booth, I sit next to Caleb.

"So, what is it that you are discussing? I should warn you; if it's not about getting out of here, then I may not be interested."

"I can take you away from here, but I do need to talk to Mike. I had him check into your mom. Do you have any idea what she has been up to the past few years?"

This isn't exactly what I want to talk about, and I wasn't sure what he wanted to say or what Mike was going to say. My nerves were on edge just at the mention of my mother.

And the fact that he had looked into this for me, even though I hadn't asked, may have been a little much. Or maybe it was just in his nature.

"No, I haven't really bothered to ask, and I didn't want to know."

"Your mom has been in a psychiatric hospital for the past three years. Apparently, she tried to commit suicide. She was released from the hospital about four months ago. Her records state that she had been functioning normally for a year before they deemed her sane enough to be released. They thought that she could function normally in society as well."

"A psych hospital?" This does two things to me; it puts stock behind Caleb's accusations that she is mentally unstable, and I also wonder if it's something that is hereditary. I remember Caleb telling me that his mom committed suicide, and any thought I had about myself diminishes.

"Thank you for looking into this for me. I had no idea that she was in a hospital. I wonder if my grandma knew."

Putting my hand on his arm, I ask, "Are you okay? I know with what happened to your mom, this must be hard on you."

"I'm fine. I'm just worried about you. I have dealt with this before, and trust me Katy, it's not easy to deal with. I just thank God that we met." He glances down at my necklace, and I feel a tingle all over my body. He always glances at my necklace. I don't know what it is, maybe he just likes it.

I tell him what Faye and Collin found out, and he acknowledges that he found out the same information.

"There's something else, Katy. I don't know how you are going to respond to this, but I want you to know that I am here, and I am not going anywhere. I will be here with you through all of this. No matter what, okay?"

"Okay." I say nervously. What is this all about?

"Your mom has another family. Three other children, one boy and two girls. They live about an hour away."

He continues to talk, but all I can hear is a buzzing in my ear. The only thing I can think is that I must be deficient. Questions start to run through my head. Was I bad when I was younger? Why didn't she come for me? Instead, she chose to have another family, another child. What made her want to start another family but ignore Collin and me? I couldn't get the thought out of my head that I was just not good enough for her.

I wanted her to love me, do better for me, stay with me—choose me. Maybe I wasn't what she wanted in a child, so she had a new family. Was I really that hard to love?

If you already have a family wouldn't you try to make amends with that one? There was so much I didn't understand about this woman. So much that I disliked about her. But I realized that no matter what, I was a part of her. And then I realized that I have a brother and two sisters out there somewhere. And I wondered if they are going through the same thing that I am going through, or went through. Maybe, just maybe, I would get to meet them.

Chapter Twelve

After my conversation with Mike and Caleb, I found myself angry. Angry at my mom for being the person she was. This mean, sadistic, crazy woman was my mother.

No matter how much I tried, I couldn't purge the feeling of abandonment from my heart, and I couldn't forget what she did to the garden, to Grandma, Collin, and me.

And now, she had more kids and a husband. According to Mike, her kids were eleven, eight, and seven. She had left them too. Just walked out, and didn't tell them she was leaving.

Mike also told me something that made chills creep up my spine. Apparently, my mom had been just as terrible a mother to them. She had left them home alone when they were little; too little to watch themselves. History was repeating itself. She still drank too much and was very heavily into drugs.

"Where is their dad at?" I ask.

"Well," Mike says, looking at me from across the booth. "Their father had no idea what was going on. He worked most of the time. He knew she drank but didn't know she drank as much as she did."

"How is it possible that he didn't know his kids were being left alone? Did they not speak up. Couldn't he see? He's not blind, is he?" My anger apparently extended for my half siblings.

"Most nights when he got home, he said the kids were already in bed. Plus, when you are an addict you tend to hide it well," Caleb says.

"So, she just left one night three years ago? Did the father ever try to find her?"

"No. When she left he learned what she had been

doing. He actually took a restraining order out on her. They found her in a hotel room; she had overdosed. They took her to the mental hospital after they pumped the drugs out of her system and did an evaluation." This is all so sad. I don't know how to feel about it.

When we left the bar, Faye and Micah were still sitting in the back talking. I waved goodbye when I walked past, and she smiled and waved bye too.

It was still pretty early, but I was ready to go home and go to bed. Caleb drove me, stopping outside my house. The bed was calling me, but I wanted to stay with Caleb for as long as I could.

He turns the truck off, and we sit there for several minutes. I stare out the window thinking about this new information. I'm preparing to turn around and ask Caleb if he wants to come in to watch a movie or something, when I see movement on the side of the house. Sitting up straighter, I press my forehead to the glass.

"What's wrong?" Caleb is leaning forward, trying to see out the window over my shoulder. "Is something out there?"

"I don't know," I say quietly, shaking my head. But then I see it again on the right side of the house. "There!" I point the best I can with the window up. Caleb must see it too, because he takes off his seat belt and grabs something out of the glove box.

"Stay here." Opening his door, he starts to climb out.

"Wait." I reach out and grab his arm. He stops and looks back. "It's probably my mom. Don't hurt her." His brows draw close as he holds the gun up. I can see clearly now, that it's a stun gun. I blow out a small breath.

"I already thought of that, but she's unstable so I'm not going unarmed." I nod my head and watch as he climbs out and slowly crosses the street with stun gun in hand. My heart is beating erratically, as I wait for something to happen. I can still see the movement on the side of the house. Whoever it is doesn't see Caleb coming, but when they take a step back, I can make out another person, bigger, way bigger, standing next to them.

Thinking of Caleb, I get out and head toward him, pushing the fear that's bubbling up inside, deep down. He is outnumbered and that scares me even though I know he is well trained. I think I may have a heart attack when my heart speeds up even more.

"Excuse me," I hear Caleb's deep voice. Authority rings in his tone as he stops about fifteen feet away. My mom steps out from the shadows looking at Caleb with disgust on her face.

"This is my house. I locked myself out." Pointing to the large bearded man who has also stepped out from the shadows, and looks at least twice the size of Caleb, she says, "My boyfriend is helping me in." She spots me, and a sly grin crosses her aged face. "See. Here is my daughter. She'll tell you. Right, darling?" she says through gritted teeth.

"I happen to know Miss Laudin, and I also happen to know who you are, so I am going to ask you to leave," Caleb retorts. His stance is guarded like he is getting ready to defend himself against an attack at any moment.

My mom, knowing the game is up, puts her hands on her hips that jut out under her extremely tight orange leather skirt. Her lips form a line as she walks toward me. I freeze, remembering her slap. Then I remember the garden and I see red.

"Hello, daughter." The words are not at all nice, they are threatening and my body reacts.

I step forward to meet her the rest of the way. Grabbing her wrist, I spin her so her back is to me and my forearm is pressed against her throat cutting off her air.

She grabs my arm, trying to pull it away, but my grip is too tight, so she just scratches skin off my arm.

"You have absolutely no right to be here, ever." I yell

so loudly she squints her eyes and flinches. "If you think you can come around here freely, thinking I will submit to your crap, you are sadly mistaken. You have no idea what I am capable of."

"Katy, let your mom go, you're choking her." Caleb reasons, but it sounds far away, and in my muddled angry brain, I don't care what he says. The large man that my mom came with steps forward, and Caleb steps in front of him. They exchange words, but it's jumbled. Caleb turns to look at me, and walks forward a few steps toward me.

"Katy, she isn't worth your integrity. Let her go." His voice is stern, and hearing my mom's choking breaths, I realize that I let my anger cloud my judgment and release her. She stumbles forward while holding her neck. She looks at me and smiles cunningly. If the devil had a smile, it would look like that. She laughs hysterically, sounding like a hyena.

"You're more like me then I thought, girl." Walking over to the large man she came with, she takes his hand and walks away, laughing as she goes.

I hadn't noticed Caleb next to me until he touches my face. Unfortunately, I flinch. I hope I am not back tracking. Looking at him, his face is filled with concern.

"Katy, are you okay?" I think so. Maybe I wasn't a few minutes ago because all I could think about was making my mom pay for what she has done. Not just to me, but she seems to taint everyone's life she enters.

In all eleven years that I lived with Grandma, I thought about Mom every day. Where she was and what she was doing. I wondered if she missed me and if she would come get me someday.

I was a little girl tied down to a fantasy. Sitting by the window at times, practicing what my reaction would be if I ever saw her walk up to Grandma's house. Living in those unrealistic moments that life would allow at the time.

As I got older, I came to understand that she wasn't

coming and would probably never come for me. I quit waiting at the window. I replaced those little girl fantasies with realistic ones. I never gave up hope that she would come though. Every girl needs her mother.

Right now, all I felt was anger and hate, and I wished that she had never come back. Rage built up, and I could feel my face getting red and hear the erratic beating of my heart. Feel the pounding in my head. My breathing was harsh and heavy. She was gone, but the effect of her presence was still here.

"No." It is all I can say to Caleb, because I wasn't okay, and I wasn't sure if I ever would be.

Walking over to the side of the house where she was, I investigate. Nothing looks out of place, but when I look at the window sill that would lead to the dining room, I see the scratch marks in the paint right below where the window locks. She tried to break in.

The only reason she hadn't succeeded was because we interrupted her. What was she planning to do? Steal from the house? Wreck it?

"Is Collin here?" Caleb asks. He starts toward the front door, and I follow. Pulling out my key and opening the door, we step in. The smell of liquor is so strong it hits me in the face like a slap. Collin never drank, maybe he spilled something?

Walking into the living room, Collin is sitting there, television on, his feet propped on the coffee table, and a bottle of liquor in his hand. It's pretty much empty and he is obviously passed out. Putting my head in my hands I rake them both through my hair and let out a disgruntled 'Ugh'. What I really want to do is scream. Do I really need this right now? No, but he is going through a lot, so I let him have this one. That doesn't mean I'm not insanely mad or that he is off the hook.

Caleb helps me take Collin back to his room. He never wakes, just mumbles incoherently then starts snoring. After covering him with the blankets, I turn out his light, and close the door. Caleb is waiting for me in the living room, starring at the photos that cover the wall above the couch. One in particular catches his eye.

Reaching forward, he runs his fingers down the photo of my grandma, Collin, and me. I was about seven and Collin thirteen. We all lay flat on our backs looking up. Grandma's head was tilted toward mine and she held my hand between us. Collin's smile didn't really radiate happiness. I hadn't realized it before, because I didn't usually look at the pictures this closely, but I could see it now.

We had been with Grandma for almost two months at this point. Collin was more excited about coming to live with Grandma then I was, so the picture confused me. I guess the memory never goes away of what happened. He had understood better than I did back then what was happening. At twelve, he had so much responsibility, trying to take over those household things that Mom didn't want to do.

But what shocked me the most was the way we looked sick. Our eyes were sunken in. We looked frail and weak from the lack of care during those four months when we were with Mom, after Dad died. Looking at the picture now, I wonder why Grandma put it up. It reminds me of sad days.

Walking over to it, I pull it off the wall and Caleb gives me an unsettling look. I set it on the kitchen counter and turn to face him still standing in the same spot.

"I never noticed before, but we don't look the best in that picture." As I start to walk out back, I change my mind realizing that I don't have all the beautiful flowers to look at. That comfort no longer exists. So, I unceremoniously plop down on the couch lifting my feet to the coffee table, they land with a loud thud. Throwing my head back, I blow out a breath.

Caleb walks to the kitchen, grabs some paper towels,

and cleans the spilled liquor from the table.

"I can do that," I tell him.

"I've got it, don't worry." He finishes and tosses the paper into the kitchen garbage then sits down next to me. "I think you guys look happy. Your grandma obviously thought so too or she wouldn't have put it up. I can tell she really loved you guys just from the pictures."

Looking down at my hands, I say, "She did." I meet his eyes not understanding why he is here dealing with the craziness that is my life. I'm glad he is though. I grab his hand and hold it in mine while it rests on the couch in between us. "I was lucky to have her in my life. That's why when she died, I was so devastated. I felt like anything bad that could happen to me—would." Taking a deep breath I work up the nerve to continue. I want to tell him everything, but I'm afraid that if I do, he'll act differently around me. Maybe he won't want to touch me anymore or kiss me. I'm slowly talking myself out of telling him about that day in New York, when he turns his body toward me, instinctively, I do the same.

"It doesn't matter what happens to you, you can come back from it." He leans his forehead against mine. "It's about you, and what you take from your circumstances."

"It's not that simple, Caleb."

"I know that. You don't think that life has pushed me. That my circumstances have been great? No, they haven't. You haven't had an easy time in life, but there are people who love you like Faye and Collin. You could be alone, have no one to love you. No matter what your circumstances are, they can always be worse. I rely heavily on God for understanding and control. I could never do it alone."

"You don't know what I have been through, Caleb. If you knew, you would think differently." I take a deep breath and prepare to say what I have only said to one other person. "What if someone is almost raped? How does that person bounce back from that sort of violation?" I wait for him to get uncomfortable or release my hand, but surprisingly he scoots closer and pulls my head to his shoulder.

I lay there with my head on his shoulder, his arm slung around me while he rubs circles into the top of my hand. We don't say anything, but the way he has me right now is so soothing, I close my eyes and start to dose off.

"I was waiting for you to tell me what happened?" he says in a low voice. My eyes fly open, and I tense up. This is it, he's going to bolt. "I waited for you to trust me enough to tell me." After a few more minutes, he whispers, "Thank you." I can hear the relief in his voice and it does something to me. His relief—is my relief too.

I feel like I should be the one saying thank you. This man has been more to me then he could ever possibly know. I was lucky he drove me home tonight. I don't want him to leave because, honestly that man with my mom scared the crap out of me.

"Can you stay for tonight?" I ask.

"For as long as you need," is all he says. I have another question, but it's lost on my lips as I slip into sleep.

~~~

The sounds of clinking and voices wake me in the morning. Blinking my eyes open, I'm not sure where I am until I notice that I am laying on my couch with Grandma's blanket pulled over me. I slept soundlessly considering what I learned last night and what happened.

The clanking continues so my eyes find the sounds. Collin and Caleb are in the kitchen, passing pans and plates back and forth.

"What are you guys doing?" I ask groggily

Collin's head flips up at the sound of my voice. He puts his plate down and walks over to me. Sitting up, I pull my legs under me so he can sit on the couch.

"Katy, I'm so sorry about last night." He looks down and closes his eyes, shaking his head back and forth. "I talked to Chelsea yesterday, and she said some things." He takes a deep breath and releases it. "I'm really sorry. I went for one drink, and every time I thought about the conversation with her, it made me so mad. I kept taking drink after drink."

He knows how it hurts me to see him like that. Our mom has a drinking problem and we both spent time with her while she used alcohol and pills to medicate herself so she didn't have to deal with life. To see Collin do the same thing was heartbreaking.

"What happened that made you want to drink that much?" I start to pick imaginary fuzz off the blanket waiting for his news.

"Chelsea, she wants me to come back. She spent an hour yesterday crying into the phone, begging me to come home, telling me that she loved me, that she made a mistake."

"What did you say?" I didn't want him to leave, but I would respect his decision either way. Besides, I was better. I had Caleb now. Glancing at him he isn't even looking in our general direction. He is putting food on plates, letting us have our moment.

"I told her I didn't want to come back. That I couldn't trust her. She called me several nasty names, and said some things that make me want to throw up even as I think about them now, and then she hung up on me." I give him a sad smile then lean over to hug him.

"Next time, call me. We can talk it out, okay?"

"Okay, I'll do that."

I tell him about Mom and her friend being outside the window last night. Of course, he heard nothing because he was passed out.

"I'm sorry, Katy. Being drunk is like not being here at all." We move to the kitchen were Caleb has three plates piled with food on the breakfast bar.

"No Faye this morning?" I ask, looking at Collin.

He doesn't look at me. He stares at his plate, and says very quietly, "No, she didn't come home last night."

"She must have stayed with Micah." Sitting down in between Collin and Caleb, I take a sip of my orange juice. Then I remember what I was going to ask Caleb last night before I fell asleep.

"Don't you think we should call the cops and let them know what happened last night?"

Caleb, who just shoved a fork full of eggs in his mouth shakes his head no. He continues to chew and swallow.

"There really is no evidence and they did nothing wrong. If we call the police they would probably just visit her and issue a warning. For some reason, I don't think that will stop her from doing whatever it is she wants. It would probably just make her more irritable then she already is. But I'll go down to the station and talk to the officer there." He takes a sip of his water and looks back at me.

"I'll call Mike and have him follow her for awhile. In the meantime, it would be nice if someone was always here, and you," he nods his head toward me, "are never alone."

"Okay. Oh Collin," I say, turning toward him. "I have something to tell you it's about Mom, and I'm not sure how you will feel about this. It's pretty big." He nods his head but seems disinterested as he continues to shovel food in his mouth. "Mom has another family." He halts with his fork in mid-air, closes his eyes briefly, and sighs with exasperation. "A husband and three kids. They are eleven, eight, and seven. They live about an hour away."

Trying to gauge his reaction, I sit there and watch as he starts to shake his head then opens his mouth to say something, but he closes it. He opens it again, and a strangled sound comes out.

"Who would have kids with that woman?" He is angry. I hadn't expected that. I assumed he wouldn't even care. But he asks questions, wanting to know everything I know. I tell him everything, which isn't much.

"Maybe she was sober for a while when they first met. I mean, they had three kids together. If they kept going don't you think that she must have been a decent person?"

"That's incredibly naive, Katy." Collin looks at me as if I am a child. He has never looked down on me, but that's what he is doing now, and it hurts. I immediately feel the need to defend myself, but Caleb speaks up from next to me.

"Well, I need to get going." He stands, takes his plate to the sink, and rinses it off. Ignoring Collin's jest, I stand and walk Caleb to the front door.

"Thank you for staying last night, and I'm really sorry about Collin."

He nods once then grabs my hand and brings it to his lips, softy kissing it. Then he grabs my head and pulls me to him. Planting his lips on mine, pulling me in even closer. He leans his forehead on mine.

"I don't want to leave you here. Collin isn't in a good mood and there is just something about that guy your mom was with that gave me a bad feeling. I think I'm going to check into it more."

"I'll be fine. Besides, I will see you in a couple of hours."

"Can I pick you up?" he asks hopefully.

"I'd love that," I say, smiling.

Giving me one last peck on the lips, and a long hug, he leaves. When I turn back to the kitchen, Collin has fled.

I decide to call Faye. She usually calls me if she is even going to be late, but checking my phone, I realize she hasn't called me. I start to dial her number when the front door opens, and she walks in wearing the same clothes that she wore last night.

She sets her keys in the bowl and drops her purse on the floor next to the table. Looking up, she notices me for the first time.

"Oh, hey. I didn't see you there."

She looks different, a little confused even. But I don't have time to ask her about it, because she heads to her room taking her heals off as she goes.

"I'm just going to take a shower," she says yawning. "Then we can talk. I want to know how your night was." Her smile says that she has her own ideas. Collin comes out of his room just as Faye makes it to her door. I listen as they have a conversation.

"Out all night, Dunbar?" Collin says using her last name. He smirks and leans against his door frame.

"What's it to you," she says maliciously. Then she enters her room. What was that? A look of shock passes Collin's face and...hurt. But it's gone just as quickly as it came. He walks into the living room, grabs his keys, and heads toward the door.

"I'm going out," is all he says.

"I kind of figured that out," I say under my breath, as Collin closes the door behind him.

I need something to do to pass the time, so I go into the study and turn on my laptop. I'm looking at garden landscapes, imagining what I can do to the garden to rebuild, when Faye comes in fresh from her shower. She sits in a big chair in the corner, sighing dramatically.

"What are you doing?" she says, looking at me. I peek up from my laptop.

"Planning on replanting the garden." Closing it, I let out a long breath. "I'm thinking it's going to be too big of a job for one person, though."

"Well I can help."

"I've been meaning to talk to you about that."

"About what? Helping you?" she asks, clearly confused.

"Well," I think about it for a minute looking into space, "yes, actually." Getting up, I squeeze next to her on the chair. She throws her legs over both of mine and leans her head on my shoulder. I take a deep breath and tell her what

I need her to do.

"I think you should start college next week."

"What? I already told you that I wasn't doing that. I'm staying here, with you. You need me."

"I'm better, Faye. I don't want you to stay because you feel obligated to take care of me. Besides, Collin is back, and Caleb is helping me out."

"Collin isn't any help. He got wasted last night. What if he does that again?" she asks despondently.

"How did you know that he was drunk?" I say with surprise.

"He drunk dialed me."

"He did?" Sitting up, I look at her. She has her eyes closed and her forehead wrinkled in concentration. "What did he say?"

"It's not important. I was with Micah, and it upset him, so I just hung up after I knew Collin was at home and safe." She yawns then snuggles into me some more.

I don't press the issue—for now. It seems like something is going on with Collin and Faye. They have been making snide remarks back and forth to each other for the last two days, and it's really starting to annoy me, because I have no idea why. But I need to concentrate on one thing at a time, so I keep on about college.

"Back to you going to college. I should tell you, that I don't like you anymore, and you are the worst friend ever." I sit back in my chair but lean away from her.

"That was so, *not* convincing. You are a horrible liar."

"You need to go, enjoy being in college. Don't let me stop you from doing that. I would feel terrible if you stayed on my behalf. No. I would despise you, make your life miserable."

"You could never, intentionally, make anyone's life miserable."

"That's not true. Remember that hamster I had when I was ten?"

"Oh my gosh! You would put him in that green ball and chase him around the house with a broom, pushing the ball as you went. I think that hamster died of a heart attack."

"Maybe, but I made his life miserable. See, it's possible, and I'll use the same tactic on you if you don't go to college." She starts laughing, but I don't know why.

"Sorry, I just got a visual of me in a big green ball and you hitting it with the broom, taunting me."

I laugh along with her. Taking the pillow that I am sitting on I hit her with it.

"Stop laughing."

"You first, and that hurt. I think you hit me with the zipper." Laughter pushed aside, she says, "You wouldn't be mad?"

I knew she wanted to go. It made me happy that she felt I was okay with Caleb and Collin close by.

"No, of course not. I told you I want you to go. Just visualize the green ball and broom when you don't believe that."

"I'll do that. So, last night, you and Caleb, huh?" She nudges me in the side with her elbow. Smiling, I shake my head. "Did you guys have sweet, hot, passionate-"

"Faye, for real. We fell asleep on the couch and Collin was here."

"I figured that when I seen the blankets on the couch. You're no fun," she pouts.

"What happened to you last night?"

"Micah and I slept together?" she says bluntly.

"What!" I say, jolting upright. Faye and I had decided a long time ago to wait until we were married. If one of us would feel the urge, we'd call the other and talk them out of doing something stupid. I couldn't believe that she did this.

I didn't know how to respond, so I just ask, "Why? I thought our thing was that we were going to wait? Did he pressure you?" I ask defensively, and a little angrily.

"No, no, of course not," she says.

"Faye, I wish you would have called me. Remember. That's what we were supposed to do."

"What's the difference." She shrugs her shoulders as if this isn't a big deal. It's huge. "We'll be married in four months anyway."

"The *difference* is that you're not married yet." This decision was not made lightly, yet she is acting as if it's fine. It's not fine, and I am very worried.

"Ugh. Katy, it's no big deal. Really." I didn't want to argue with her anymore, so I let it go. Just the fact that she says it's no big deal, makes me realize that it wasn't as special as she had thought. It breaks my heart that she gave that part of herself away without being married first, but there really is nothing I can do. She made her choice. At this point, I can only be there for her.

"Well, how do you feel today?" She thinks about it for a moment before speaking.

"I feel...okay, I guess. It wasn't at all what I thought it would be like." I nod my head, acknowledging her remark. "We just kept thinking that we only had a few more days before he goes back to school, and I'll be starting classes in a few days. We'll be in two different places."

That's something at least. With a big smile on my face, I let her know how happy her college decision makes me by giving her a big hug.

"So you *are* going. I'm so glad you didn't cancel your classes," I practically shout.

"Geez, I can feel the love right now. I didn't know you wanted to get rid of me that badly."

I can't even talk. I 'm so excited for her to start this new journey. By Monday, Faye will be moving into her new dorm two hours away, and I'll be trying to deal with my mom and the revelations that have come to light.

I decide not to tell Faye about what happened last night or about anything else. She definitely wouldn't leave then.

Chapter Thirteen

Faye and I spent the next two days packing. She had so much stuff and was devastated when I told her she couldn't take everything. I hadn't seen much of Collin. He had come in and out, but when he was home, he spent most of the time in his room.

Faye and Collin seemed to be avoiding each other for the most part, and I thought I had better ask about it before she left. I didn't have much time. She was spending today with Micah since he was leaving in the morning for school.

Faye decided to leave Saturday morning so it would give her an extra day to finish getting things together and hang out with me. We were in her room, at my house, packing up the little knick knacks she had set out.

"Faye, your room is the size of my closet, and your closet is the size of my glove box. You can't take all of your stuff. Just pick a few things, you know, like pictures." Picking up the picture from her nightstand in her room, she holds it out to me.

"You mean, like, this one?" she says cheerily.

It's a picture from her birthday party. She had just turned sixteen and had decided to utilize the makeup case that her mother bought her. Only we were just joking and ended up making ourselves look like clowns instead. I laugh and take it from her.

"No, not this one. In fact, I'll bury this one in the backyard while I'm replanting. It will be safely hidden from eyes there."

"I love that picture." She tries to grab it from me, but I pull it back. She crosses her arms over her chest and sticks her bottom lip out. "Fine, but we need to take a new picture to replace that one," she adds.

"Are you still spending the day with Caleb?" She folds a t-shirt from the clothes basket and places it in her suitcase.

"He's making me dinner tonight, over here." I pull the next shirt off the pile, fold it, and put it in her suitcase.

"Ooh, a man that cooks. What's he making you?"

"I'm not sure. I didn't ask, and he didn't offer. I guess he is just going to surprise me."

Every day Caleb and I were together, with every word that we spoke to each other, we grew closer. He was quickly becoming more to me then I had intended. It was scary because it was unknown, and I also wasn't ready for a serious relationship. There were too many people in my life that had let me down, that made me weary of any relationship that wasn't pre-existing.

Even those relationships were difficult. With my brother's bad attitude and change in demeanor, I had to put our relationship at the top of my priority list.

Caleb and I had created a routine over the past two days. He would pick me up in the mornings, and we would ride over to his studio before dance classes started for the day. He would teach me Aikido. It was mostly about self control and doing moves similar to the ones on the beach, just in a quicker motion. Afterwards, he would bring me home, and check the inside of the house.

I had to pretty much stay at home, because Collin seemed to be unpredictable at the moment. I hadn't seen him drink, but last night he came home smelling like alcohol. He didn't talk to me. He just went straight to his room. I was always worried about turning out like my mom, following in her footsteps, but now, I watched Collin repeat her actions.

Caleb was there and hesitated leaving me alone with him. I assured him that it was fine. He accepted that, unwillingly, and headed home.

He would call me or come pick me up for lunch, and call me in the evenings mostly. He was busy though;

running two businesses and researching this mystery man who was with my mom. Caleb couldn't shake the feeling that he was bad news. He devoted a lot of his extra time to searching for this man's identity. We just didn't know anything about him, so it was difficult.

I also had not decided whether to contact my half siblings. Did I leave them alone? Not knowing if they even knew that I existed was making the decision difficult. If it were me, and I had known I was out there somewhere, then yes, I would want to know. I had this internal fear that they knew of me, but thought I didn't want to be around them. At that age, I knew what it was like to feel abandoned. And because of our mother, they did too.

"What are you thinking about?" Faye interrupts my train of thought, as she closes her suitcase. I follow her out to the living room where she is stacking her stuff by the door. I still haven't told her about my mom and the things I've learned, so I just go with simple.

"My mom," I sigh.

"Why do you torture yourself like that?" Putting the suitcase down, she turns toward me and puts her hands on her hips. She gives me a stern look while tapping her foot. "Well?" she insists.

"To tell you the truth, I've always thought about her. I just never told anyone," I say, looking at my bare feet on the hardwood floor. "She never stopped being my mom, she never will. But, there were times as a little girl, when I would wait for her. I knew she would never come, but I could dream. Right?"

Walking to the sunroom we sit at the small table that has been pushed back in the middle of the room.

"What about Grandma? She was a great replacement," Faye says.

I thought about that, I really did. Grandma was great, and I thank the Lord for her big heart; the one that had enough room in it for Collin and me. But no one can really replace your mother. All those little girl dreams never went away, they just got more realistic as I grew up. Instead of tea parties and girls night with my mom, I thought about spending time with her in the garden that Grandma and I had built, the garden that she had destroyed. Having coffee and lunch, talking to her about my problems and her helping me move into my dorm room for college, giving me away at my wedding.

She'd never be there for my wedding. It was completely impossible. I thought about all the things that Faye would get to do with her mother for her wedding. I'd never get that.

My emotions were so conflicted, like they were in a fight for good and evil. I felt longing for that mother-daughter relationship, but also hatred for someone who could be so vicious. Not only to Collin and me, but also to these other kids that she brought into this world.

It seemed irresponsible to have more kids when the ones you already had were living a life without you. But she was psychotic, and those were the doctor's words.

"Yeah, she was great. The best Grandma a girl could ask for. There will never be anyone else who can compare to her." And every word of that was the truth.

~~~

Faye headed out an hour later at about two-thirty. She and Micah were going to a shop looking at tuxedos for the wedding. I hadn't thought about it till now, but she hadn't really talked to me about the wedding much, lately. I wondered why that was.

When Faye left, Collin came out of his room. Moping around, smelling like..."Is that cigarette smoke?" I ask appalled. He stops mid stride and sniffs his shirt.

Shrugging, he continues toward the kitchen and grabs a bottle of soda out of the fridge. He starts back toward his room. I know I should leave him alone. I've never seen him act this way; he is like a ticking time bomb waiting to explode. He's been distant, and I'm so worried about him, so my words tumble out without a filter.

"Hey!" I yell. Okay, maybe that's not the best way to get a mad man's attention. He turns, clearly annoyed that I am speaking to him at all. His eyes are rimmed red; he looks tired like he hasn't slept in a few days. Maybe he hasn't. I wouldn't know, because he hasn't been around much.

Rubbing the back of his neck, he mumbles, "I'm not really in the mood." He turns, but I don't let him off that easy.

"You better talk to me Collin. You can't keep avoiding me. I thought we were okay." That last part gets cut short by his door slamming. What is going on with him? He is so closed up, and I know from experience that not talking about it is the worst possible solution.

His door swings open, and he rushes out. This time, I don't say anything, but watch as he grabs his keys and slams yet another door, this time the front door. With everything going on I didn't think he would have left me by myself, but here I am standing alone in the living room.

My thoughts drift to my mom and her recent attempt at breaking into the house. Then I remember her friend, and anxiety takes hold. Every single thought of something going wrong flies through my mind.

I decide to call Caleb and let him know what's going on. The phone rings and rings with no answer. Leaving a voice mail, I let him know I am fine, but tell him about Collin's erratic behavior and his swift, silent exit.

Going into the study, I close and lock the door. Walking over to the heavy curtains, I close them quickly and turn toward the desk. This whole scene seems familiar. I remember, not too long ago, doing this same thing but the fear was born out of a different reason. I had gotten past that mostly, but now my own mom was eliciting the same feelings in me.

Sitting down, I put my forehead on the mahogany desk. I just couldn't win. Fear was a constant side kick in my life. My karate lessons had helped none. It didn't even help subside the fear. That Krav Maga instructor I had should not be teaching classes. Besides, Caleb had some formal Krav Maga training and his techniques were foreign to me.

The day that I could live without feeling fear seemed nonexistent. Collin didn't seem to be fearful. It didn't surprise me due to his lack of care lately.

My life was a mess. It was like I was running a marathon and had to jump hurdles. Only this marathon was never ending, and the hurdles got bigger and bigger, making them harder to jump. The thought crossed my mind that maybe I should just give up.

The sound of my phone ringing makes me groan. I left it in the living room when I came back here, and I didn't want to go out and get it. What if it was a trap; someone calling to lure me out? That was by far the craziest thought I'd had today. But it could happen. Or maybe it was Caleb.

Fear overrides any intentions of grabbing the phone. I'll have to remember to give my home phone number to-the phone on the desk rings cutting off my thoughts. Picking it up, I cautiously say, "Hello."

"Katy." Caleb's voice comes over the receiver. He blows out a breath. "I'm on my way over. Why didn't you answer your cell? Is everything ok?" His concern was flattering.

"Yeah, I'm fine. I didn't want you to leave work early, I was just nervous. But I'm fine, really. You can just come over later like planned."

"I'm coming over now," he says with finality. "I have to stop at home and change, pick up a few things from the store for dinner, and then I'll be over. In the meantime, I've called Mike. He'll be keeping an eye on things until I get there."

"Okay." How can I argue with him? I did feel a little better knowing that he was on his way over in a few. After hanging up, I open my laptop and research some more info on the garden. Knowing that I couldn't do it on my own, I researched landscapers in my area.

A knock on the front door awhile later had me closing my laptop from my landscaping research. It also had my heart hammering in my chest.

Slowly, I rise from the chair and walk across the study. With my hand on the door knob, I was trying to decide whether or not to unlock myself from safety when the desk phone rings again.

Sprinting over, I pick it up on the second ring. "Hello," I say quickly, and slightly out of breath.

"I'm at your door. No one is answering." It's Caleb. His voice is strained, and I think something is up but then he says, "Don't keep me waiting long, I'm holding two bags of groceries, and they are not light. We may end up ordering out tonight if our dinner ends up on the pavement."

"Oh, sorry. I'm coming now." Hanging up the phone, I open the study door quickly, and head for the front door. When I open the door, I back away to let him enter. He walks over to the breakfast bar to set the bags down.

The laughter that bubbles up in me, I just can't contain it. It's loud and painful in my gut, because this is the first time I have ever laughed this hard, I mean ever. "What-what is that?" I ask as tears slip out of my eyes. For the first time they aren't tears of sadness. I bend over with my arm across my stomach, laughing hard.

"What?" he says, clearly unaware of how he looks holding that thing. Holding up the leash he says, "Oh, you mean..." He clears his throat. "Katy. I'd like you to meet Kane." He gestures to Kane.

That just makes me laugh even harder, if that's possible. The picture he is presenting along with the name is too much. A big masculine guy with a little, tiny, pink poodle named Kane. Through bursts of laughter I try to let him know.

"But-he is..." I'm gasping for breath and wiping tears away. "He's a poodle. And he's pink!" The laughing is unstoppable. I think that maybe he will be upset because I am laughing so hard at his choice of pet, but the satisfaction in his eyes is abundantly clear, and the affection. That shuts me up, and it also scares me. I stand up straight and clear my throat.

"Yes, I am aware that poor Kane here is pink." Taking the leash off the dog, he runs over to me. I bend to pet him, but he jumps up knocking me on my butt. "Kane, down," Caleb says in a deep authoritative voice. Kane immediately listens, sitting in front of me wagging his short stubby tail and panting. I run my fingers through his soft pink fur. \

He reminds me of Pixie, the dog my grandma had when we first moved in with her. She was a Shih Tzu, the same size as Kane. She had a cute little pixie cut, and loved to lay in my lap and cuddle. She was old, so three years after we had moved in, Pixie passed away from old age. I remember crying all night long unable to sleep, since Pixie slept with me at night. Grandma did the best she could to soothe me, but I only fell asleep after hours of crying finally exhausted me.

"So, what's Kane's story?" Caleb is taking things out of bags and placing them in drawers, opening one after the other trying to find where everything goes.

"I rescued Kane from a shelter a week ago." Opening the fridge, his next words come out muffled as he puts something inside. "He was a show dog that wasn't making any money." He closes the door and walks over toward me. "The owners dropped him off at the shelter. He's a good dog," he says, petting Kane's head. "I was a little upset that they dyed his hair pink, I mean he's a boy. Huh, buddy?" he says to the dog.

Standing up, he puts his hands in his pockets, watching

as I pet Kane.

"I thought I could leave him here with you for a little while. He's usually pretty jumpy when people are lurking. He barks at the mail man before he even makes it to the mail box. He could be helpful in your situation," he says.

Picking Kane up, I stand and head to the backyard with him; figuring I would let him loose to roam. Setting him down in the back yard, I watch as he runs through the destroyed colorless mess. His pink fur is the only color anywhere. I sag against the door frame trying to push down the feeling of hatred for my mom.

"I have so much work to do back here; it's going to be impossible," I mumble to myself.

"She destroyed everything," Caleb says. "Didn't leave a stone unturned. The gazebo looks like it just needs some paint and a couple of pieces of wood need to be replaced." He walks out into what use to be a beautiful garden. Walking around the gazebo to the small waterfall, he kneels down and starts turning stones over that have been tossed around carelessly.

"What are you doing?" I call clearly confused, wondering why he is even trying to save what is clearly damaged. Looking up at me with his soft blue eyes, his simple words move me.

"Righting a wrong." He continues to turn over stone after stone putting them back in their rightful place.

I feel as though the damage inflicted by my mom was being rewound; like a movie reel at a theatre. But when I pushed play again; I could rewrite what once was.

Walking over, I help him turn stones over as Kane continues to run through the mess and sniff around. A calm blankets over me as we work together to make the waterfall look exactly the way it did a few days ago. Of course, I'll have to replant the flowers, but at the very least the waterfall will be back to its original form.

Caleb untangles the tube that helps the water flow and

places it back in the pump. Luckily it's not damaged. The two lights that were positioned under the water are broken. The bulb and the glass have been smashed into tiny pieces. Once they are replaced, we can fill the pond up with water and turn it on.

Caleb gets up from the ground, brushing dirt off of his nice blue jeans then off his hands.

"We should run to the hardware store and get a glass to replace those."

"Really, you wouldn't mind?" It would be nice to finish it tonight and be able to turn it on. I look at my watch and my shoulders sag. "It's six o'clock. It's really late and we haven't even had dinner yet."

"It's fine. We'll stop off at a little Cafe on the way back and pick something small up. I'll cook when we get back." He grabs my hand, helping me up from the ground, and leads me into the house never letting go. Kane follows us in, sprinting around the house checking everything out.

Caleb grabs a bowl, a few toys, and a small bag of dog food from the counter. Setting the bowl down, he fills one side with water from the tap and the other with food. Kane, hearing the food hit the bowl, comes running up at full speed preparing to dig right in.

When he attempts to stop his paws slide across the hardwood floor, and he bumps into the dish spilling the water all over. Not caring where the water is, he starts to lap it off the floor. I laugh and pat him on the head.

"Thirsty little pup, aren't you?" Caleb brings another cup of water over and a wad of paper towels. I mop up the water as Caleb refills the bowl. It all feels so normal and...domestic. I like it.

"He gets extremely excited, as you can tell. It doesn't bother me, but according to the shelter where I found him, his previous owners would slip ADHD medication in his food to calm him down. I think that's why he stopped performing efficiently for them. They hadn't seen a vet for his issues, they just assumed they knew what his condition was and gave him some of their sons medicine. It's hard to get him to settle down, but I find that if he gets a lot of play time outside he tends to be calmer at night."

"Awe, that's so sad. They must not have cared very much for him." I finish soaking up the rest of the water and give Kane one last pat on the head before tossing the paper in the garbage and following Caleb outside.

I can't help but look around once we are outside, searching for something threatening to pop out at me. But Caleb keeps my hand firmly enclosed by his which gives me some comfort. Opening the passenger side door, I scoot in. He closes it with one last glance and small smile for me, then he walks around and hops into the driver side.

We stop at the hardware store to pick up light bulbs, wood, a glass to cover the light, and paint for the gazebo.

Our next stop is a small Cafe a few blocks from the hardware store. For six thirty, the place is really jumping. Caleb parks the truck and gets out, but I am hesitant to follow him. When Faye took me to the bar it wasn't so bad; there weren't this many people there either. Coming around, he opens my door.

"What is with all the people?" I ask. I clearly hadn't expected this sort of crowd at a Cafe.

"It's open mic night. It's a poetry reading that they do here every Thursday." Helping me out of the truck, we walk toward the door. The smell of coffee and fresh baked goods passes over me as we enter. People are packed into the tiny space shoulder to shoulder. No one even looks our way as we push through the crowd, me sticking close to Caleb as if my life depended on it.

We stop in front of a counter where Caleb starts an order, but I don't pay attention because I am too entranced by the woman on the stage. She is swaying back and forth, her eyes closed, and hands raised to the sky. Her words are pure and beautiful filling me with joy like I have never known before. Whatever she is talking about it's something I want to experience. But just as suddenly as she is speaking of light and love, hope and faith, she speaks of the dark.

Falling deep into a pit where you are burned and broken. The dark will confine you and break you down. Leave you unable to express yourself in a true and pure manner. She closes out by saying three words, 'Destined for eternity'.

I wanted her to continue talking about the light. I didn't mind being destined for the light. Before I knew it, Caleb was grabbing a bag and tugging me out the door. A deep chill went straight through me causing a shiver. Caleb, thinking I am cold, put his arm across my shoulders and pulls me close.

After we are settled in his truck and are heading back to my house, I finally ask, "What was that woman talking about? She sort of freaked me out a little."

"That was Corrin. She goes to my church. Great lady, very poetic." As we come to a stop at a red light he turns and looks at me. "On Thursdays they do a Christian Mic Night. Everything that you hear has to do with the good book. Corrin has a way of describing things; it makes you feel as though you're there. She was speaking of Heaven and Hell tonight." Taking a big gulp, I close my eyes and open them slowly. I swallow the lump in my throat.

"So, Heaven is light and love, and Hell will burn and break you—for eternity."

Taking off again, he says, "Essentially, yes. But I'm not the one you should talk to about this; you should speak with Pastor John. He knows the Bible inside and out." I have a flashback from the day we entered his studio, him sitting on the floor reading a book.

"Do you read the Bible?" I ask.

Nodding his head, he says, "I do." As we turn down my street I ask him one more question.

"Are you ever afraid people will judge you for your

beliefs?"

"Never." He doesn't even hesitate, which leads me to believe that he is very comfortable with all of this. I wasn't so sure, but I did know that I wanted to know more. Did Heaven and Hell exist? Hell did not sound pleasant.

When we get back to the house, Caleb changes the glass and bulb in the waterfall, while I snack on the food from the cafe. We fill the pond with water and walk over to the switch in the sunroom. Caleb grabs my hand as he flips the switch.

The water illuminates with light. It's amazing how it looks as if nothing ever happened. Something unbidden pops into my mind.

"What if she comes back. She could ruin it all over again?" Caleb leads me inside.

"I wanted to talk to you about that. I have this guy who I work with in my security business. He does custom home alarm systems. They can set you up so there is an alarm in the house and around the perimeter." He walks to the fridge and grabs the ingredients he needs for dinner, laying them out on the counter.

"So, if someone tried to get in the backyard..."

"They wouldn't get in the backyard. There would be an invisible trip line set up, and as soon as someone sets foot anywhere inside the fence, the alarm will be triggered. It's very high tech, and no one has been able to breach it."

Thinking about this is a no brainer. I just didn't know why I hadn't thought about this on my own weeks ago. I agree to have the alarm system put in the house and watch as Caleb makes Chicken Primavera while I sit on the couch, petting Kane.

Caleb is very skillful in the kitchen. When I ask him about it, he says that after his mom passed, he was the one who took over cooking for his dad and brother.

Faye came home about an hour later. I was aware of her bad attitude as she stomped inside right past me and walked into her room. I look at Caleb.

"What is up with everyone's attitude around here? I feel like I'm living in an alternate reality." Scrapping his plate off in the garbage he speaks softly.

"All you can do is be there for them. You can't always control another person's behavior, but you can influence them by your actions and way of life." What? How could I possibly be something like that for them? I am too messed up myself to aid someone else with their issues.

"I'm sure that isn't true." I laugh the words out, but Caleb doesn't seem to be joking. "I have issues of my own," I say, laughter aside. Getting up from the breakfast bar, I sit in front of the couch on the floor.

"I am the poster child for issues." He comes over and sits down next to me. "You know about my brother and my mother. What you don't know, is that I was a bad boy."

I gasp, "No!" I put my hand over my mouth more to hide my smile than anything else.

"Sure was. I was into it all; drugs, alcohol, and truancy. You name it, I did it." He shifts so his legs are laying flat and his elbow is on the couch. "After my mother's death, I had a really hard time adjusting. My father did the best he could, but I was a little weasel. All I wanted to do was check out of life. That's when a friend of mine introduced me to a life where I could do exactly that.

"I started to miss a lot of school and never came home at night. I went to rehab twice before I was eighteen. The first time it didn't take because I snuck out on several occasions, and I was only there for two days.

"Mostly, I hated my mom for leaving me and making a choice that was so selfish. I even had my cousin pawn everything that she left me in her will. I didn't want any of it; that's how mad I was at her."

"So you don't have any of her personal effects? What about your father? Does he have anything that was hers?"

"I don't have anything, but my father has some of my

mom's things that belonged to Dillon. My father refuses to give me anything. We don't talk. When he looks at me, he only sees who I use to be." There is sadness in his voice at the mention of his relationship with his father. It breaks my heart to hear that he doesn't have a relationship with him. I grab his hand and squeeze it for reassurance, letting him know that I'm here.

"You have your mom's studio," I say, trying to clear the air that reeks of unhappiness.

"You're right. When my aunt passed, I got that. She is probably the only family that I talked to. Do you want me to go so you can talk to Faye? She seemed pretty upset earlier, and I feel a little more comfortable leaving since she is home."

I don't want him to leave, but he's right. Faye's had enough time to wind down, and I really want to be there for her and whatever she is going through right now. I don't think I can be there for her like Caleb had said, but at least I can listen. Walking him to the door I can't help but laugh.

"What's funny?" he says.

"I'm walking you," I say, jabbing him in the chest, "to the door." He scoops my hand from his chest and brings it up to his mouth; he kisses my knuckles. I'm breathless for a moment as his smile turns from that small smile that I love to the huge grin I adore.

After he leaves, I lean against the closed door, completely baffled by this man. The life that he has been dealt is horrendous, yet he continues to look past those things and be a force for good.

To find out tonight that he has done the very things that I can't stand my mom for, makes me come to one conclusion; maybe it is possible for someone to change. But what does that person have to go through to change everything they are?

Chapter Fourteen

Faye wouldn't talk to me. After I knocked on her door several times, she finally told me that she was fine but never opened the door. She closed me off, and I didn't know why. It hurt, but I let it go, only because I knew she had to spend the whole day with me tomorrow.

When I woke in the morning no one was awake, well, except for Kane, who was panting at the back door wanting to go outside. I let him out and watched as he ran around the yard barking at a butterfly. He was so cute with his bushy little pink tail wagging. I had to talk to Caleb about getting his fur dyed back to its original color.

"What is that?" Faye comes up behind me rubbing her eyes and yawning.

"That's Kane." She bursts out in laughter like I had done.

"Kane, is it even a boy?" She tries to cover up her laughter, unsuccessfully.

"Of course he's a boy."

"But, he's a pink poodle."

"I know he's pink. He didn't ask to be pink. Plus, he's color blind, he'll never know." We walk into the kitchen, and Faye starts making coffee. I get some eggs, ham, and cheese from the refrigerator to make an omelet.

Faye asks, "Where did he come from?"

"Caleb brought him by yesterday," I say, cracking eggs into a bowl. "He rescued him from a shelter. The owners didn't want him anymore. He was a show dog, and apparently, he wasn't performing well, so they took him to the shelter to be put down."

"Man, that's harsh." Walking over to the cutting board, she starts cutting chunks of cheese and slicing the ham for the omelet.

"So, what was up with you last night?" I ask with caution, not wanting to chase her good mood away. But she's my best friend, and I want to make sure she is okay.

Shrugging her shoulders, she looks down as she continues to slice the ham into tiny squares. It takes her too long to answer which has me wondering if she may be trying to think something up. Faye has never lied to me before, that I know of, so I push that thought aside.

"Micah and I had an argument about tuxedos," she finally replies. Putting the knife on the cutting board, she looks up at me. "He wanted a white penguin suit. I wanted to go the more traditional route, black. He argued with me about it," she huffed. "I got mad and asked him why he was suddenly interested in any aspect of the wedding."

Picking the knife back up she continues to slice. "Then he got mad at me and started yelling, talking about how 'I think I should at least get to pick my own tux.' She does her best Micah impression.

She tosses the knife in the sink leaning her hip against it. Blowing out a breath and crossing her arms over her chest, she looks like she's been kicked. "I just want it to be perfect. Is that so bad?" Walking over, I put my arm around her shoulders.

"No, that's not a bad thing." I give her a quick hug and continue to make breakfast. I really hope nothing serious is wrong. The wedding is only a few months away, and there is still a lot to do. I figured the stress of planning a big wedding would cause them to argue. I didn't want to be right. I just wanted my friend to be happy.

Before sitting down to eat breakfast, I decide to see if Collin wants some breakfast, so I knock on his door. When there is no answer, I push it open a little, but there is no one in there. Concerned, I walk into my bedroom and grab my cell so that I can call him. No answer.

"Should I make him an omelet?" Faye yells from the

kitchen. Walking out there, I take my seat at the breakfast bar.

"No, he's not here, and he's not answering his phone either."

"He didn't come home last night?" Faye's voice registers concern.

Picking up my fork, I take a bite of my omelet trying to turn over in my head why he wouldn't come home, but I can't think of anything. He would have told me if he was planning on being out all night. Especially with what has been going on lately, right?

"We talked about this the other night. He said it was about Chelsea, but I thought we had worked it out." I take another bite of my omelet.

"Was he drinking?" Just before I can reply to her question, the front door swings open. We both turn quickly in that direction as Collin comes walking through the front door...let me rephrase that; he comes stumbling through the door.

He pitches forward, falling on his face. He must have tripped over his own feet because there is nothing else in that area for him to trip over. Faye and I jump up and run over to help him hoping that he hasn't hurt himself. When we get to him, he rolls over on his back and starts laughing as if his lack of coordination is the funniest thing he has done.

It stops me dead in my tracks, Faye pulls up beside me. We stand there long enough to smell the alcohol coming off him in waves. It's so strong it smells like he has taken a bath in it. Taking a step back we try to avoid the assault on our senses.

What do I do here? My gut tells me that trying to have a conversation with a drunk person won't go anywhere, but the raging going on in my head takes over and my face starts to heat up. Something starts clawing its way out of me as I explode.

"What the heck, Collin! You think this is funny? We have been sitting here worrying about you. Not knowing if you were okay, while you are out doing who knows what." I'm seething, and his laughter has stopped at the tone of my voice. He sits up, running his hands through his hair.

"What does it matter? I'm fine, see." He gestures up and down his body. "No harm."

I let out a sarcastic laugh; it's either that or scream. Walking over to him, I bend at the waist so that I can be at eye level with him. The need to get away from the stench is overwhelming, but I stand there preparing to give him a piece of my mind. Serious now, I try not to make a face at the smell.

"No harm? How can you say that when you know what it is like to live at the hand of a drunk? How can you say that when you have lived on the other end of someone who has been what you are now? How-" I close my eyes briefly to try and prevent the tears from flowing. "How can you possibly think that—Your. Actions. Do. No. Harm?" My fury is final and he will not be able to forget it.

There is a look in his eyes that says he understands. His lips turn down at the corners and his head lowers in shame. I think I've proven my point as much as it pains me. Standing up straight, I wait for him to make the next move. He clearly has a problem, but I know that he has to make the first move or he'll feel like he is being pushed.

He stands and walks away. That's it, just walks away and into his room. No stumbling, no words. *Just disappointment from me,* I think. Feeling defeated, I slump against the wall that he has vacated. Leaning my head against it, and looking to the ceiling, I slide to the floor. Faye sits next to me but doesn't say anything. She knows I need a minute to think.

Grandma would be so disappointed with him, just like I am. How can he do the same thing that our mom did? The same thing that makes us hate her so much? It makes little sense to me, but who am I to judge him. I don't know what is going through his mind. All I can do is make assumptions based on my past experiences.

Even in my despair, drinking was the furthest thing from my mind. I did retreat into myself and avoid people, but I was working on that. It wasn't easy, and it was a day to day struggle, but I was doing it. I wanted to help Collin avoid anything similar, but I didn't know how or if he even wanted my help.

"Well, this stinks worst then a fat lady after a bath?" Faye's weird statement pulls me away from my thoughts, as

I start to laugh so hard it knocks me over. Rolling on the floor, I think to myself that this is better than being upset. This laughter, it gives me a momentary break from the pain that Collin's actions have caused.

After my laughing session on the living room floor; Faye and I clean up our mess in the kitchen and I let Kane in. He prances through the house until he flops down on the doggie bed in a corner in the dining room.

Faye and I are talking about our spa day, which I don't feel much like doing, when Collin walks into the kitchen showered and changed into fresh clothes. We all stop and stare at each other waiting for someone to talk.

"I'm so sorry you guys." Okay, not what I had expected him to say—at all. He comes over to me and wraps his arms around my shoulders. I hug him back tightly, just glad that he is not acting so distant at the moment.

"Collin, I thought we had talked about this. Did something else happen?" He pulls away and hops up onto the kitchen counter to sit.

"Chelsea is in the hospital." This sounds bad, really bad. Out of instinct, I move closer to him.

Faye follows my direction and is right beside Collin. She grabs his hand and squeezes it; he reciprocates the gesture and looks into her eyes before he stares at his hand in hers.

"She was pregnant, but had an abortion yesterday. They kept her overnight because her blood pressure was high."

"Oh, Collin." I put my hand on his shoulder. I stand there silently with Faye and Collin holding hands. Is that weird? Yes, very, but it's not the time to talk about that. There really are no words for this. None at all, it doesn't excuse him drinking though.

As if he heard my internal thoughts, he looks at me and says, "I know that is no excuse for what I did. Everything you said Katy, is the truth. I knew from the first drink that I was acting like her," he refers to our mother. "But, in the moment, I would do anything to avoid thinking about what Chelsea did. She made a decision that wasn't just hers to make. I feel like she killed my baby. I know that's not rational, considering the circumstances, but I'm not really doing anything rational right now."

"Did she say why she did it?" Faye asks.

"No," Letting go of Faye's hand, Collin hops down from the counter. "I think it's my fault though. If I would have just gone back when she asked, maybe she wouldn't have done this." He closes his eyes tightly and shakes his head as if he can shake the thought away.

"Don't do that," I say sternly. Looking up at me, his brows draw together. "Don't start blaming yourself. That's the easy way out just like drinking is the easy way out, not to mention it's only momentary relief from what's bothering you. It's really not worth it, and I think we know that from experience."

"Yeah, you're right." Looking at me he smiles. "When did you start becoming the voice of reason around here?"

"Hey, someone has to be reasonable. Faye's too aloof and you are too high strung. You're like polar opposites, it only makes sense for me to be the in-between to you two nuts."

"I am not aloof," Faye says in shock.

"Yes," Collin walks over to Faye. Standing in front of her, he taps her nose, "you are. But that's what makes you Faye." It feels like an electrical current of awareness spikes through me at Collin's flirty, playfulness toward Faye. I let it fall away because Faye is with Micah. I keep reminding myself of that.

"Hey." I stop his hasty retreat. "Are you okay then? No more drinking? You know you can talk to me right, and then there are AA meetings."

"Whoa," he puts his hands up in refusal, "I'll talk to you, no meetings. I'm going to call Chelsea right now and..." He stops in thought. "I don't know what I'll say, but it's a start." I nod my head and watch his retreating back.

When I look at Faye she is staring at Collin's retreating back too. Her face is all red. *From embarrassment*, I think.

"Faye?" I call trying to break her from her wide eyed stare.

"Huh? Oh yeah." Smiling she claps her hands together and screams at the top of her lungs, "Spa time, baby!" Her cheerfulness is catching, so I smile as she drags me to the bedroom so that we can get ready.

~~~

The whole thirty minute drive to the Spa, Faye is talking about how fabulous this place is. I tried to listen, but I was having an internal debate about whether or not I should tell her about my mom. By the time we were pulling into the parking lot I had concluded that it was not a good idea. I knew that when she found out, she would be so mad at me. She'd also be two hours away at college, which is where I wanted her to be, so I was willing to risk her wrath.

As we walk into the building, we are greeted by two women who introduced themselves as our hostesses. We are ushered off to a room where we got deep tissue massages, all of my fears of being touched from the last month, gone. It was the most relaxing thing I had ever experienced, and it was well needed.

Faye was lying on the table next to me making noises that sounded highly inappropriate. I snorted in laughter causing the girls who were giving us the massages to giggle.

After our massage, we got manicures and pedicures. This was one of the best days I have had with Faye. There were no pretenses, I wasn't frightened. We talked about everything and nothing at all. I missed girl talk. After hearing Faye's excitement about college, I was satisfied with my decision not to tell her about what was going on.

Our feet were soaking in a tub of warm water as the women who were giving us our pedicures rubbed a gel on our legs that warmed and then cooled. They wrapped both legs in warm towels and told us they would be back in five minutes. My phone beeps with a text message and I reach in my purse and see who it is. It's Collin.

Collin: When were you going to tell me we got a dog?

Oops, I think.

Me: Collin, we got a dog. His name is Kane, and he is very hyper.

Mission accomplished. I hit send and set the phone down on the table next to me.

"I'm sad that you aren't going to be coming with me." Faye turns toward me. If she is sad she doesn't look it, but I think that has more to do with the woman who gave her that deep tissue massage; it sounded like she enjoyed that...a lot.

"Well, you can call me every day, and I'll see you in a few months for Christmas and your wedding. You will call me every day, right?"

"Of course. You won't mind, will you? I'll be having lots of fun while you..." She doesn't finish her sentence, and I know why. She isn't sure what I'll be doing. I'm not sure either. "I'm sorry, I don't want to put a kink in our day," she adds.

"I think you already put kink in it with your noisy

interlude in the massage room."

"I was being expressive," she says defensively.

"Oh, brother."

"No, uh-uh. No brothers here just you and me. Boys are not allowed not even in conversation." Her mention of brothers leads me to my next question.

"You and Collin seem more comfortable with each other lately." I carefully watch her reaction. "I think you even blushed earlier."

At first she doesn't say anything, but I'm not going to let this go. I need to find out, I feel like I am out of the loop here.

"Yeah, we've been talking. He's nice to talk to. I never realized that. Can you believe we have known each other for eleven years, and I knew very little about him?"

"You guys never really got along. He used to pull on your pigtails."

"I know," she exclaims, sitting up quickly, then leaning back again. "There is more to him though. He's not just the pigtail pulling bandit. He's a pretty good guy."

"You do know that you are marrying Micah, right?" I ask astonished and a little uncomfortable with this conversation. But I asked, didn't I?

Pictures started popping in my head of Collin and Faye—as a couple. I shake them out quickly. That would never happen, because for one, she was marrying Micah. That was all I needed, just that one reason.

"Of course. It's not like that. He's just...nice and kind of gets me."

"What? I don't get you?" She gives me that, *are you kidding me,* look.

"You haven't really been available to talk to like a normal human being lately." She's right, "Plus," she continues, "you've been spending a lot of time with Caleb."

"Well, I'm here now. What do you want to talk about? Is everything okay?"

"Yeah, sure. Everything's fine I just...this whole wedding thing has been very stressful."

"And I haven't been much help."

"Understandably so, but Micah's mom, uh! That woman, I swear, we have been together for four years and she hates me."

"She doesn't hate you."

"She wanted me to wear a pink flamingo dress. She said that white was for good girls," she says mockingly.

I was taking a sip of my soda when she said that. It went down the wrong pipe causing me to cough and laugh at the same time.

"Don't laugh, it's not funny. That mean old-"

"Faye!"

"Sorry, I only speak the truth. I had the seal of approval from your grandma." Her bottom lip is sticking out, and she crosses her arms over her chest. "She loved me."

After our pedicures, we head to a restaurant for a late lunch. We choose to sit outside because it is a beautiful day. The birds are singing, and I was with my best friend. I didn't know how I got here after everything, but I was grateful for it.

I couldn't really say that it was a perfect day, but it was very close. I didn't think perfect days existed. Regardless of the day we are having, I felt like something was missing. I just couldn't figure out what. I hope that I can find it someday.

Faye's phone rings just as the waiter delivers our food.

"It's Micah," she says, then flips the phone open and answers it. "Hey." She pauses and sips her water. "Okay, um. Let me call you back. Okay. Love you too." Hanging up, she give me a sad look. "He wanted to talk about our argument. I hate to do this Katy, but I really need to talk to him. It feels wrong, him leaving on such a bad note. Do you mind if we take our food to go?"

What was I going to say? No. I wasn't that selfish. She needed this, I could tell, so I told her it was fine and we packed up our dinner to go and went back to the house.

As soon as we got home, she went straight to her room to call Micah back. I put my dinner, and hers, in the fridge deciding to eat it later.

I find Collin in the garden pulling the dead flowers out from around the waterfall. Kane is running around, bringing some color to the otherwise colorless garden. Collin already had a good pile going, and judging by the sweat that was dripping off him, he had been out here for hours.

"What are you doing?" He looks up from his work and squints against the bright light of the sun.

"I thought I would clean up this mess." Sitting back on his heels he looks around. "It use to be so alive out here. The only place I could come and think clearly when I was young. I know that you and Grandma worked hard on this garden. I wanted to return it to that same beauty."

"That sounds great, Collin. I was actually looking into landscapers yesterday. I didn't find anyone, but I think that has more to do with the fact that I didn't really want some stranger in here messing with things."

"You don't need to hire landscapers. We can do it together. I see you already got started." He points to the waterfall and stands.

"Caleb and I put it back together. He fixed the tubing and the lights." He stands up and brushes his hands off.

"I noticed the wood piled over by the gazebo and figured you had some help. You really like this guy?" I was apprehensive at answering him. Who wanted to talk to their brother about a guy she liked. Oh, I guess I just admitted to myself that I did like him, which made answering Collin much easier.

Smiling, I admit, "Yes, I do. A lot." Here it comes. The big brother talk about how he's not right for me. I can tell it's coming by the look on his face.

"Caleb isn't so bad." *Oh!* "But," okay, I was starting to get worried, "he has a very dark past. His brother..."

"I know," I say with a huff. "I know about his past. I know about his mother, his brother, his time in rehab, and the addiction that he had to overcome. But, he is not that guy anymore. We can't condemn him because of his past." Hesitating for only a moment, I say, "He helped pull me out of this depression that I was in. *He* was there for me." A hurt look crosses Collin's face.

"You've only known him for a couple of weeks."

"I've known him since Grandma died. I met him at Mel's diner the day after the funeral. That was two months ago." He looks momentarily shocked by my admission.

I don't think he expected that. I hadn't told anyone about my afternoon with Caleb at Mel's diner; the day we met and talked for hours. It was the easiest conversation I had in a few days, it was the only conversation I had that I wasn't yelling at someone or checking out of reality.

Collin grabs both of my hands in his and waits until I am looking him directly in the eyes.

"Be careful. I just," looking away, he pauses. He's choked up and needs a minute to collect himself, "don't want to see you hurt again. You've been through enough." Squeezing his hands tightly, I reassure him.

"I'm learning a lot about myself, Collin. Like, I can't let other people determine my happiness. You have nothing to worry about. Caleb is a one-in-a-million type of guy." The look of uncertainty clouds his face, but he doesn't have a choice, it's my decision.

I know he won't fight with me because resignation rings through his voice as he sighs and hugs me, saying, "I love you like a sister." I roll my eyes to no one because he can't see me.

"I *am* your sister." My voice comes out muffled because he is still holding me tight as if I am his life line. And when I think about it, maybe it's not so farfetched. He has lost the same people in his life that I have. He is going through his own struggles. His life is empty like I had thought mine had been. He has me, but who else does he have?

I don't know what makes me say this, but it comes out of my mouth without thinking.

"You should come to church with Caleb and me on Sunday" Pulling away, he kneels and goes back to pulling the dead flowers from around the waterfall. He doesn't say anything, and I'm wondering if he will, when he looks up at me and smiles.

"Maybe I will," he replies.

The relief I feel is immediate. It spreads over every single limb in my body, exposing me to something I haven't felt before; pride in my brother. This is definitely out of his comfort zone.

He absolutely refused to go to church when we were younger. I never understood why, but I remember the bus picking me up alone when I was little.

Kneeling beside him, I help clear the death from the ground so that we can replace it with life once again.

"Oh, I wanted to ask you a question?" He looks up at me as I continue to pull on weeds. "What do you think of meeting the half sibs?"

"Katy, do you really want to give them a complex? I mean, how do you feel about the fact that our mom went out and had three more kids instead of coming and trying to mend a relationship with us? How do you feel about her having other kids, period?"

"Yes, but what if they know about us and think that we don't want to meet them? They might think that we abandoned them like she did." This conversation is making me angry. I take a deep breath and try to rein that anger in. Didn't we just leap one hurdle? Rising, I try not to sound angry, Collin rises too bringing the bucket with him. "I think I want to meet them," I say with finality. He just looks at me for several minutes. I think he is trying to decide whether or not to argue with me some more.

"If that's what you want to do, then I guess I can't stop you. I hope it goes well. I'm going inside. I've got to look for a job before my mind becomes mush from lack of use." He puts a hand on my shoulder. "You good?"

I nod my head, and he turns and walks into the house after dumping his bucket in the wheel barrow. I continue to work in the garden, pulling dead flowers out and turning soil over, for another hour. I think that's enough time for Faye, she should be done talking to Micah. Then we can get back to our girl's day.

We had planned to go out and see a movie tonight. When I knock on her door, I hear shuffling on the other side. She opens it, and I notice she is still on the phone.

She gives me an apologetic look, so I smile half heartedly and wave bye. She smiles back and closes her door. Going into my room, I take a shower and change into something clean and comfortable. When I emerge from my room into the living room, I stand alone in the silence. Even Kane is passed out in his doggie bed. So much for a hyper dog. Looking at my watch, it's six o'clock, so I heat up my lunch from earlier for dinner. Sitting in the sunroom, I eat my lunch while texting Caleb.

Me: Hey, what's up?

A second later a ping announces an incoming text.

Caleb: Heading out right now. Why? Aren't you suppose to be spending the day with Faye?

Me: Yeah, but Micah called and wanted to talk. Apparently they had an argument before he left. He wanted to reconcile, I guess. She left me high and dry, the traitor.

Caleb: Is Collin home?

Me: Yes, he's in his room job hunting.

Caleb: Why don't I come pick you up, and you can hang out with me tonight? I'm helping some kids out, they are great. I'd love for you to meet them.

After a moment of hesitation, I answer.

Me: I'm not really good with kids. Well, actually, I've only ever been around kids my age. How old are we talking here?

Caleb: Six to fifteen year olds. And, if it helps you decide, I think they will love you.

I smile, he really knows the right thing to say, doesn't he?

Me: I don't know about that. You may be a little biased, but I'll go.

Caleb: I'll be there in ten minutes.

My heart quickens and excitement moves through me. I am really looking forward to spending time with Caleb. I hadn't realized how much I had missed him all day until now. I don't know what this means for us, but I do know that I am filled with so much emotion right now I don't know whether to cry, laugh, or thank God. Maybe all three.

Chapter Fifteen

After entering a number into a keypad and passing through a gate, we pull up to Dillon's Light Academy; just as the sun is starting to sink in the sky. Glancing at Caleb, I ask the only question that comes to mind at the moment.

"Dillon?" He pulls into a parking space and turns off the car.

"This place was built two years ago. After my mother passed, I inherited some money. It sat for years in an account collecting interest. It was relinquished to me on my twenty first birthday. I didn't want anything to do with it, being the stubborn child that I was. I was angry at the whole world for something that I couldn't change."

Clearing his throat, he continues. "After Dillon was gone, I decided to do something positive with the tainted money that sat in the bank. I thought that if I did something good with it, it could erase the reason why I got it in the first place." He looks over at me. "It took a long time to consider my mother's exit from life something other than a betrayal. I donated the money to have this place built. They let me name it, so that's where Dillon's Light came in. All of the kids who live here have no one to take care of them." My heart was breaking for these kids that I didn't even know yet.

"That just," I take a deep breath and exhale, "that just makes me so mad. How is it that people can just abandon someone? No one ever asks to be born, yet we are. Then, instead of taking responsibility for the human life that these people have created, they throw it away."

"Hey." Caleb puts a hand on my knee and my anger slowly starts to dissipate. "I've learned that the best thing we can do when there is a bad situation is try to make it better by doing for others, being selfless." I shake my head and take a deep breath as we climb out of the truck.

There are three buildings, each right next to each other on the well manicured grounds. The middle building, which we were heading to, was the largest. It had a huge sign over the entrance that said Harver Hill Administration Building EST. 2009.

"What are the side buildings used for?" My curiosity was exploding. This man had found out so much about me, and I wanted to know more; everything about him.

"The one on the left," he points, "is the girls' dormitory, and the one on the right is the boys. This building holds offices and classrooms," he says, gesturing to the Harver Hill building.

"So the kids live here and go to school here? Are you sure this isn't a prison?" I ask jokingly. He smiles.

"No, most of these kids are excellent. They are trying to overcome so much even though most of them have so little. They are off the grounds almost every day for sports, field trips, that sort of thing. They are not here all the time." Reaching the administration building, Caleb opens the door for me, and I slide in past him.

There is room after room, each one labeled with someone's name, down a long hallway. We walk down the hall and enter a room three doors in on the left.

A boisterous woman sits at a desk, intently writing on a booklet of papers. She looks up when we enter, smiling when she sees us.

"Mr. Mathews!" She beams at Caleb and rises to give him a quick hug. "The kids are all talking about the game today. They are very excited. And who is this young lady?" she says sweetly, looking at me. She comes over giving me a warm, welcoming hug. It's nice.

"Margaret, I'd like you to meet, Katy. She's here to meet the kids." He comes up next to, me placing a hand on my lower back. Margaret doesn't miss it. She gives him a knowing look, the same one a mother would give her child.

"Well, they will be happy to have a new visitor." Walking back to her desk she sits back down and starts rummaging through some papers. "I had a letter for you... Aha! Here it is." She pulls out a brown envelope and hands it to Caleb. He glances at it quickly then folds it in half and sticks it in his back pocket.

"Thanks, Margaret."

"All right," she says, throwing her hands in the air, "go on. Those kids are waiting for you in the recreation center, and you know if you are late they will hassle you." She looks pointedly at Caleb. Grabbing my hand, we step back out into the hallway.

"You know, you have some great ladies in your life. Ms. Jill and Margret, they have that maternal instinct for you. I can see it in their eyes."

"I *do* have some great ladies in my life. Don't I?" He squeezes my hand and gives me a crooked smile. His words bring joy to my fractured heart.

It looks like a long walk to the recreation center, so I use the time to check out the art work and pictures that hang on both sides of the walls. The pictures are of girls and boys, kicking or throwing a ball, laughing and building pyramids with their bodies.

One picture, that I really liked, was a group of kids lying on their backs looking up at the sky. It reminded me of the picture that use to hang in the living room at my house. Our pose was the same. But these kids looked happy and healthy in their picture.

I felt a pang of guilt that I was still upset over something that happened so long ago. I let the burdens of what my mom brought into my life, bring me down. She shouldn't be able to touch me emotionally, because she left a long time ago. But, it was still so very fresh with her recent activities and sightings.

Caleb notices my perusal of the pictures and paintings.

"These pictures are all painted, drawn, or taken by students," he says proudly.

"Amazing. Caleb these are fantastic. They are better than some of the art I've seen in art galleries." I was really amazed by the amount of art work that looked like actual art, and to find out that the kids did it, made it even more amazing. The detail and skill was professional in every way.

"Who teaches the art class here, Picasso?" The shock was clear in my tone, it made him laugh deeply.

"All kids have a gift of some sort; they just need to have the opportunity to cultivate that gift. Most of these kids haven't had that opportunity. Here, they make sure the kids get every opportunity that everyone else does, and then some."

We pass a stairwell and the pictures end. I wish they hadn't, they were fantastic, and I wanted to keep looking.

"Maybe when we leave we can come back down this hallway," I say.

"You're welcome to come back anytime. I actually come here every Friday evening. It would be nice to have someone with me, and I know the kids will enjoy the change."

I can see the recreation center ahead and hear loud voices and a few whoops coming from inside. My anxiety starts to rise as he pushes through the door.

"I'm so nervous," I whisper, as we step through the doorway.

"You'll be great," he replies. Sending confidence my way.

I didn't know what I expected exactly, unorganized chaos maybe, but it wasn't this. If I had to guess, there were probably thirty-five to forty kids, some sitting and some lying on the floor, in the recreation center. They had strategically placed themselves in groups of ten or so and were talking to one another and laughing.

"Hey man, you know that if I could get you anything it would be acting lessons. That way maybe you would have a shot at winning." One of the kids says. He looks about fifteen years old and is lying on his back in front of a chair, his feet lazily thrown over the seat. The kids start laughing at his comment. But the boy he is messing with won't go down without a fight.

"If I could get you something," the boy the joke was made to says, "I'd get you a girl. That way you can stop following Jeanette around like a lost puppy." The girl, who is obviously Jeanette, opens her mouth then quickly snaps it shut crossing her arms over her chest, she shrinks down a little. Her cheeks are red with embarrassment, but everyone takes it as good natured fun and laughs it off, even the boy and the girl who the joke was made on.

A little girl sees us walking in, and the smile that spreads across her face when she sees Caleb makes my heart swell. She bounces up from her group and comes running over to Caleb. Without any pretense, she latches onto him. He quickly lifts her and hugs her tightly. She does the same, and when I don't think she'll let go, she pulls away and he puts her back on the ground.

She looks like she may be about seven with her light brown hair pulled back in a short ponytail, missing front teeth, and smattering of freckles across her cheek bones. All the kids are wearing khaki shorts, pants, or skirts and maroon collared shirts.

"Do you know what I did today?" Her little tiny hands are flying around in front of her as she tells him about the new instrument she started playing.

Caleb gets down on one knee and watches her. He never takes his attention off her, and she loved the fact that he didn't, nodding at all the right moments and smiling as she plays the air violin.

"That's wonderful, Madeline. I want to hear you play. Can you run into Ms. Mackey's room and ask her if you can check the instrument out for tonight?" She nods her head and runs out the same door we just came in.

A few of the other kids walk over. I stand there and watch as the kids welcome him with handshakes, slaps on the back, and hugs. Most of them are shy, but a few offer their hand, and I shake them.

"Hey who's the babe?" Uh oh.

"Blake, where are your manners?" Caleb voices his disapproval.

"Oh, sorry. Hi," Blake says poking his hand out to me, "I'm Blake," he says, smiling big. I smile back and place my hand in his.

"Hi. I'm Katy." His eyes get big momentarily as he slowly looks over at Caleb then back at me.

"You're Katy." It's not a question which leads me to believe that he has heard of me before. "Where have you been the past two months? My man talked about a Katy, but that was almost three months ago? Did you guys have a fight or something?"

Caleb has talked about me? And how old was this kid? He was talking as if he was a grown man, but clearly he was a teenager no older the fifteen.

"Um, I.." I didn't know what to say. He knew something about me, but I didn't know what Caleb had told him.

"Katy has been out of town for a while. But she's back now." Caleb intercedes, rescuing me from an awkward conversation. "Quit making her uncomfortable, and get ready for complete annihilation." Blake turns toward Caleb, our conversation forgotten.

"You won't win this time. We have a plan. It involves deft and precision, it's a fool proof plan. You're going down Mathews."

We walk over to the group and Caleb introduces me. I get some head nods, a few waves, and even a few winks. These boys are crazy. It must be the fifteen-year-old hormones. But they're all really nice and a few very, very shy.

I was shy as a kid. I would usually keep my opinions to myself and would never start or insert myself into conversations. But this type of shy, I have seen it before, and it made my heart turn over in my chest.

These few were withdrawn, avoided eye contact, and sat quietly by themselves; a safe distance away from all social interactions. I was immediately drawn to them. So, when Caleb told me I had to play, I chose to be on their team.

Never having played charades before, I didn't think that I would be any good at it, but it didn't matter. The worse you were at acting things out, the more fun the kids had. They laughed so hard they doubled over grabbing their stomachs. A couple fell off their chairs laughing so hard. When Caleb got up to play, he made a big show of being ridiculously funny.

The time limit was five minutes; the kids were trying desperately to guess what he was doing as he slouched forward and walked like his legs were bowed. One of the boys on his team yelled out 'Hunchback of Notre Dame' very proudly until Caleb shook his head no.

He then opened his arms wide and people started yelling things like 'Earth', 'ball' and, 'big!" He pointed to a girl on his team nodding his head yes at her. She clapped excitedly and watched as he pointed to his foot. That was all they needed to know. 'Big Foot!', they all screamed in unison. They cheered when he pretended to punch a speed bag in the air.

"That's not fair. That one was too easy," someone protested.

I stopped listening to what was going on and focused on the kids I was sitting next to. We had yet to have our turn, but I knew it was coming soon and would probably lose my chance to have any sort of conversation with these kids.

The two girls were probably six and seven, but the boy was older; twelve maybe. The way they flinched and coward back when someone walked by looked so familiar. I knew that something horrible had happened to them.

"Are you guys any good at this? I've never played before." The girls look at me shyly.

"We don't play. We let the big kids play," the one with auburn, pigtail braids says. She has her thumb in her mouth but was way too old to have that habit.

"What are your names?" I was trying to elicit conversation out of them, but the task was much easier as a thought in my head.

The two girls look at each other quickly, and some unspoken approval passes between them so they tell me their names.

"I'm Storm," says the girl with her thumb in her mouth. "This is my sister, Lake." Those were some unusual names.

"Those names are pretty cool. I had a friend once in kindergarten, her name was Mare," I say, looking at them as they watched me talk about my friend.

"Like a horse?" Storm asks around her thumb.

"Yes," I nod my head. "Like a horse. I thought for the longest time that she was named after horses. I thought whoever named her liked horses, a lot. But, when I asked her about it, she said her name was Maria. Her grandma called her Mare for short." Shrugging my shoulders I continue. "Here I was calling this girl 'Mare' thinking it had something to do with a horse; boy did I have it all wrong."

"That's okay." Storm lays one of her small hands on my shoulder and looks deep into my eyes. Her eyes are red rimmed like she had been crying, or maybe like she hadn't slept in awhile. They were turned down at the corners like her eyes were frowning. "She probably never knew. People can't tell what you're thinking." Very insightful, and so very horrible at the same time. I smiled at her and returned my attention to the game.

Catching Caleb's watchful gaze, he was looking at me with wonder on his face. I didn't know what I did to deserve that look, but I like it.

We continue to watch as the kids try to act out whatever they pull out of the hat. Someone got peanut butter, which was an interesting one, because they acted out each syllable.

When it was my turn, I had one goal in mind. I wanted to get Lake and Storm to participate. When I got my paper and it read 'racehorse' I thought it was too perfect. Caleb seemed to be enjoying the show before I even got started. He plastered a goofy smile on his face and leaned back in his chair, getting comfortable. I pushed down the embarrassment that I would have felt, so that I could concentrate on my goal.

How did I act out racehorse? That was the question I asked myself, as I stood there in front of all these kids, who were staring at me, waiting patiently for me to begin.

Deciding I would start easy, I hold up two fingers. 'Two words' everyone on my team says in unison. I nod my head.

Pulling the chair that I was sitting on over, I turn it backwards and straddle it, putting both hands on either side of the chair, like I'm holding the reins. I move my hands up and down. My team just looks at me quizzically. Apparently, my acting skills were nonexistent. Finally, I decide to really get into it, so I lean forward as much as the chair allows and plaster a determined look on my face.

Still nothing. But when I look at Storm, she gets a smile on her face and her eyes widen. She knew exactly what I was doing. Gently, I squeeze my thighs together as if I was trying to move a horse. No one else saw, but Storm did.

She jumped up out of her seat and yelled, "Racehorse!" Everyone turned in her direction. A yelp escaped from my lips and a giant smile that radiated through me and into her. She mirrored my giddiness as did Lake. In this moment, they looked like two little girls; happy and free from their burdens.

When I look at Caleb he only smirks, claps his hands, and bows to me. I curtsy, then gave him a thumbs up. This was a new experience for me. There were classmates in high school who would volunteer to tutor younger kids or babysit for extra money, but that was never something that I had a passion for.

Kids had never crossed my mind, and why would they? I was eighteen. Spending time with these kids did help me realize that I wanted to meet my half sibs, and not out of curiosity; I just wanted to know them. If I seriously based my decision on who their mother was, then wouldn't that make me a hypocrite? After all, we had the same mother.

As much fun as charades was, I was glad it was over. It had been a very long time since I had laughed so much, and my gut was hurting from the force of it all.

Before we left, Madeline played her violin for us. She played Hot Cross Buns, and she played it beautifully. She would go far with this instrument. She had exactly one week of practice and had perfected the song.

On the drive home, I reminisced about my night.

"Thank you," I say to Caleb. He is beating his hands on the steering wheel to the music but stops to let me speak. "That was," I swallow the lump in my throat then continue, "so much fun. Thank you for sharing that with me." The emotion is evident in my voice, but he doesn't say anything about it. He just glances at me with admiration. But he's the one to be admired.

"Do you think I could come back next time? I'd like to visit Lake and Storm again."

"You can come every single time if you want. I think those girls would love to have someone to talk too. They have been very distant since coming to the Academy a year ago. Tonight was the first time I had seen them interact with anyone besides each other. You are amazing, Katy, and you don't even know it. The way you knew what they needed and got them to participate. You have a gift." Shaking his head, he looks like he is at a loss for words.

"Do you mind me asking what happened to them?" I say. I could see him swallow hard before speaking.

"They were physically beaten by their mother for two years. The family knew, but said nothing. That's why they are at the academy; and not with anyone in the family. The academy is an alternative for foster care. We have seen some of them leave with loving family members or get adopted, but most will never leave state care. Instead of moving them around between foster families, they can go to the academy. They only have room for forty children though. I make a point to get to know them and their pasts and insert myself into their lives. They need some stability, and they need friends. That's what I aim to give them."

This man was, by far, the most amazing person I had ever met. His generosity and compassion were both something to admire. He was the type of person who made a difference. Maybe there was something more to his life. Something that gave him this ability to have such compassion and show such care for others. Whatever it was, I definitely wanted to know what and be a part of it too.

"I want to meet my half sibs." I hadn't planned on saying it, but it was the truth, and I was hoping that he would want to go with me. I felt stronger with him.

"I think that's a good idea. What does Collin think about it? Is he going to want to go with you?" Looking down at my hands, anxiety starts to fill me, but I need to talk about this.

"He doesn't want to meet them. He's afraid it will give them a complex, but," this is sort of personal, "I think he is the one with the complex. Our mother treated us so badly, and he remembers it like it was yesterday. When all that happened, he was older than me so he remembers it a little better than I do."

"Give it time, Katy. He'll come around." Nodding my head, I turn to stare out the window. Time always makes things easier. "When did you want to meet them?" he asks.

"I don't know, I hadn't thought that far ahead. As soon as possible though. Maybe in a couple of weeks we can drive up there." I stop, noticing my mistake in assuming that he would go with me. I swing my gaze toward him. I didn't really even know what this was. He had kissed me once, held my hand a lot, spent a lot of time with me, but really, what was going on here? Where was all this leading to? Should I ask? For some reason, I didn't think that my heart could handle rejection.

"I'm sorry. I shouldn't assume that you were going to take me," I say quickly.

Seeing my insecurities, he pulls up to my house and parks, turns toward me, pulling both of my hands into his.

"I'll take you, Katy. And," he moves a little closer, "just in case you don't quite understand what is going on here," he moves even closer and leans in, "let me be clear."

Closing the distance, he brings his hand up to my face, cupping my chin, and planting his lips on mine. The world around me falls away for a few moments, and I take in the quietness his lips on mine brings my heart. I'm not sure what I am ready for, but I do know that I want to be with Caleb too.

Bringing his other hand to my shoulder, he trails it up into my hair and pulls it through his fingers to grip the back of my head, pulling me closer to him. Pulling back he kisses the tip of my nose and the swell of my cheeks.

My eyes slowly flutter open, and I take him in. His beautiful face and dark blonde locks, that small smile from the first time we met plays on his lips.

I don't understand what I did to deserve him. There has been so much bad in my life, but with him, it's different.

Even in the storm I know that there is a way out. *Hope,* that's what he gives me, hope for something good.

"Katy, I want to be with you and be there for you. If you don't want that right now, I completely understand your hesitation. But, you should know that when I am with you, I don't want to be anywhere else. And when I am not with you I want to be anywhere else, as long as you are with me."

I feel a warmth that starts in my chest and spreads throughout my whole body. A swarm of emotion fills me, leaving me dizzy. I let the smile that I feel in my heart show on my face.

"I want to be with you too." I lean in to kiss him, but it quickly turns into something more, and I climb into his lap so that I can be closer to him. Leaning in, I kiss him more eagerly. Maybe this is the turning point in my life. Maybe this is right where I am supposed to be.

This feels right, him here with me, us together. Our lips pressed together and our feelings fully exposed. His hands grip my waist tightly, and it sends a thrill through me.

When he pulls back his breathing is harsh and erratic. He opens his mouth to say something, but then snaps it closed. I can tell he is struggling with what to say. I wait to see if he will say what it is, and when I think he isn't going to, he opens his mouth again.

"There is something you should know about me," he says, breathlessly. His hesitation is slightly unnerving, and it makes me regret my forwardness. I wait for him to say he has an eleventh toe or a giant mole somewhere unseen or that this is a mistake. But what he actually says, isn't really a shock at all. "I'm a Christian." I Laugh. He looks worried, so I tell him why I'm laughing.

"I know you're a Christian. You introduced me to church, remember?"

Smirking he says, "No. I mean, I try to live a Christian life the best I can, Katy."

"Oh, okay." I'm not sure where he is going with this.

"That means that," he looks completely uncomfortable, "I won't have sex until I'm married."

"Oh my gosh, Caleb." I try to get off of him, but he stops me by gripping my waist tighter. "I'm so sorry, I didn't mean to...that's not what I was trying for. I just," I wave in-between me and him insinuating about my previous act. I feel my cheeks heat with embarrassment, but I know that he can't see it in the dark.

"No, stop." He grabs my waving hand. "It's not that." He clears his throat, "You are beautiful, Katy. And, I have the normal male urges, trust me. But, I chose to live my life a certain way. You are making it very hard," he says hoarsely. When I try to look away, he turns my face back toward him. "What?" he asks.

"I don't want to make it hard for you. I like you just as you are. I love everything about you, including your faith." I step over the fact that I just said 'love' and continue. "I wish that I could live more like you. The things in your past, they don't seem to bother you. How is that? How do you do it?" I'm desperate for answers, wanting to know how he can find peace the way he does after everything.

"I have been struggling with the past my whole life." He pushes my hair behind my ear, and shifts so his elbow rests on the back of the seat, getting comfortable. "I always felt angry, unhappy, sad, and closed off. There was so much negative and dark in my world that it seemed impossible to be anything other than those things."

Looking off into space he seems to be remembering something. "Just before Dillon passed, we had an argument. I was self destructing and he was worried. He felt it necessary to tell me, and I flipped out. He started talking about me going to church with him. But, I didn't want to hear it. I passed out in his spare room after a late night drinking binge." He swallows so hard I can see the path it takes down his throat. And I know what he is about to tell me is painful. "I didn't even hear them come in. I didn't even hear the gun shot." Oh no, please no. "But the neighbors fifty feet away did."

I could feel the pain he held for his brother in the tone of his voice. I didn't think it was possible to feel someone else's pain, but at this moment, Caleb's pain was mine.

"Caleb," I whisper. Leaning into him, I throw my arms around his shoulders and press my cheek to his. He wraps me up and puts his face in the crook of my neck. "I'm so sorry you had to go through that." My voice is shaky from the force it's taking me to hold back the tears that want to spill out.

"It took me a long time to stop thinking that I was responsible. I still struggle with it on a daily basis. My brother, he was the good one. The police think that he was shot over old drug money. He never did that, I didn't understand. But when they caught the guy that did it, I knew him. It was someone I had dealt with before when I was using. They were there for me, and because he was my twin, they shot him thinking it was me."

I lean back and look at him, running my hand over his cheek, feeling the light dusting of stubble.

"I've come to terms with it. And in the end, I did go to church. I just walked in one day right after he died, and poured my heart and soul out right in front of the cross; weeping like a baby. In every situation God gives you a road to walk down. You can choose to walk it His way, down a path of self-construction, or continue a path of self-destruction. My brother was a very forgiving person, and he loved me. I vowed to do right by him. But slowly, over time, it became about my own salvation and seeing him again someday."

He really believed in his faith, it was admirable. Me, I didn't believe in anything in particular. I hadn't really thought about it actually, but here lately, I did nothing but think about it.

We said goodbye with a long embrace and a sweet kiss.

When I finally walk inside the house, I find Faye sitting on the floor in the living room reading a magazine with Kane in her lap. She flips through it so quickly, I know she is only looking at the pictures. She doesn't even glance at me she just starts talking.

"Can you believe the number of half-naked women they put in these things?" As she flips to the last page and closes it she says, "Forty-nine!" She would count. I put my keys in the dish noticing that Collin's are missing.

"You're seriously surprised by that?" I say, kicking my shoes off and into the closet. "They wouldn't put those pictures in there if it didn't sell. Which leads me to my next question." Plopping down on the couch, I throw my feet on the table. "Why did you buy that garbage?"

"It was sitting here when I came out of the bedroom. I wanted something to read, so here I am," she says, shrugging her shoulders and throwing the magazine on the table. She tries to hide a smile unsuccessfully.

"What?" I say, confusion lacing my words.

"It took you a really long time to say goodbye." Her sing song voice says she knows something, but really she knows nothing. I feel a pang of guilt at that thought, since I have been keeping this thing with my mom from her.

"Faye, he's not into that stuff." I regret the statement as soon as it's out of my mouth. I just left that open for a whole bunch of questions. I watch as her eyes go wide.

"Is he gay?" she says, seriously.

"What! He's not gay. He's just," I search for the right words, "he's a gentleman."

"Really?" I don't think she believes me, but finally she says, "It's hard to find someone like that. He sounds like a keeper." There is something in her eyes that resembles sorrow. That doesn't seem to fit with where her life is right now. She's getting married in a few months.

"Faye, is everything okay?" Her mouth turns down at

the corners for a moment but then she smiles. It's not her usual goofy smile.

"Yeah, why wouldn't it be? Listen?" she says, She picks Kane up and gets up off the floor. She sits next to me, and puts her feet on the table too. "While I am gone, I expect you to be putting that garden back together. Collin says he will help you, so if he doesn't, let me know, and I will be all over him like white on rice."

"Yes, grand-mom," I say sarcastically.

We spend the rest of the night talking and laughing. She tells me about her anxiety over college, but she's also looking forward to the experience. I'm happy for her, and she really does sound excited.

In the morning, we stand at the bus station, her carry-on bag is thrown over her shoulder. She hugs me tightly, tears start to form in her eyes, and I quickly follow.

"I love you, Katy. Please be safe," she says.

"I will, don't worry. Call me when you get where you're going, okay?" I hug her one last time. She nods her head yes, and I watch as my best friend, the girl I have known for eleven years, the girl who has been attached at my hip for so long, walks away and starts a new chapter in her life.

With one last wave she disappears from my vision. That's when the anxiety starts to set in.

I realize that I had depended on Faye's presence for so long. I depended on her to keep me up, she was my crutch. The fact that I let her walk away even though I knew that one single word from me would make her stay, made me think that this was a big step in my life too. Things were changing. And I needed to make the most of it.

Chapter Sixteen

Two months had passed since Faye left. She called me every chance she got, although *everyday* was not a possibility with her class schedule and work load. It sounded like she was enjoying her college experience; with the exception of a few of the professors who were; and I quote, "Army tyrants set out to destroy my career before it even starts." But, other than that, she had joined a study group, met some new friends, and was getting pretty good grades. She was having the college experience she was suppose to have.

"How's Faye?" Caleb asks.

I had just hung up with her and was watching the long winding country road. It was fall, my favorite time of year. The colors of fall were magnificent browns, reds, and yellows. Leaves littered the grounds and pumpkins could be seen on just about every front porch. Halloween was in a couple of weeks, and I was desperate to skip past the dreaded holiday.

"She's good. At least that's what she says. I'm worried about her. She didn't say anything to me about the wedding; it's three months away; I figured she would have said something, but she hasn't said anything about it since she has been gone. I wonder if something is going on and she isn't telling me." I prop my feet up on the dash, because we still had the whole trip in front of us. Caleb reaches for my hand entangling his fingers with mine. I felt comfort in that one simple move.

"She'll tell you when she is ready," he says. I look over at his handsome face and try to put a name to the emotion that I am feeling, but I can't.

These past two months, we have spent every moment

we could together. I started going to church with him regularly on Sundays. He had introduced me to something that I had never known so closely before. I was trying to figure things out, but when I walked through those doors and was surrounded by people who seemed to genuinely care about me, it was in complete contrast with my wrecked life.

Caleb was still teaching me Aikido, but we were taking it slowly. Practicing Aikido was very relaxing, and I was happy to have someone teach me. Our relationship had grown mentally, and I respected Caleb's choice to wait till marriage. Honestly, it made me more comfortable because it went along with my plan to wait also. After two months at church, I now understood his decision. I was learning so much from his life and his church—my church.

With the feelings that had been brewing inside me, I knew that I was falling in love with this beautiful, compassionate man. Regardless, I was having trouble expressing my thoughts out loud to him. We had known each other for five months; was it too early? Would I run him off? I had told Josh I loved him, but my feelings for Caleb were so much more intense than anything I had ever known. How do you know when you love someone, anyways?

Arriving in Chapelton made my anxiety level rise, and made me forget about my love life. It was a little podunk town on the outskirts of a major city. A month-and-a-half ago I had Caleb look into my half sibs. He found that they lived with their father but were in the process of being fostered. Apparently their father couldn't handle the stress of three kids alone. He started drinking heavily. Then put them into the system and took off. Worse yet, they had no one to take them in.

They had an aunt in Texas, but she didn't even want to see if they were okay. These kids had no one, and like me, they were in a foster home, but I had Grandma to come to my rescue.

Right now they lived with a woman and her husband. They had no kids, but they were able to foster all three of them instead of splitting them up.

It took a month to make arrangements to meet. Their caseworker needed to set up the meeting with the approval of the foster parents. She also had talked to the kid's. If they hadn't known about me before, they did now. I couldn't stop thinking about what must have been going through their minds. Did they think I didn't care? That was the last thing I wanted, so I had Caleb set everything up. Today, I would meet my brother and sisters.

"Here we are," Caleb announced, as we pulled up to a small white house. It was very pretty with an assortment of colors in front. Flowers were spread out neatly under an array of bushes. It reminded me of the garden at home that was starting to get its color back. Cute, little ladybug statues where placed strategically all over the front yard.

I knew from the caseworker that Mr. and Mrs. Falkner were an older couple in their sixties. They had been fostering kid's for thirty-five years but had retired a few years back. The kid's caseworker had contacted them when they had a difficult time getting someone to foster all three kids together. The Falkner's didn't want them to be separated either, so they kindly agreed to take them in temporarily.

Taking a deep breath I hesitate, nervous about meeting my siblings. Wiping my sweaty palms on my jeans, I turn and look at Caleb. He doesn't seem nervous at all, and when I look at him my nerves decrease. He runs his fingers down my cheek in a sweet gesture; leaning into his hand, I close my eyes.

"Are you nervous?" he asks quietly.

"Very," I say, opening my eyes and looking at him.

"Don't be. You have been going with me to the academy every Friday for two months. The kids, they love you. In fact, they told me last week that I'm not allowed to come without you." Sighing heavily, I watch that small smile play on his lips, the one that I love the most.

"That was probably Blake. I think he has a crush on me," I say, trying to make light of a stressful situation.

"I think you're right." Patting my knee he gathers his wallet and pulls the keys out of the ignition. "Ready or not."

I nod my head and step out of the car. Each step I take toward the house, I feel my life changing. These kids will now be a part of my life. Maybe that's what I had been missing.

I haven't seen or heard from my mom in two months, but I don't think that she would give up so easily. I know she is still around. I wonder what she would say to this meeting of her children. Probably something nasty like always. It's sad that I have never heard anything comforting come out of her mouth. I plan to make sure these kids see some positive, because I had no idea what their foster life was like.

After ringing the doorbell, I stand there patiently waiting for someone to answer. Caleb stands right beside me; my ever present support. I hear some shuffling on the other side then the door opens a crack. A petite woman stands there with her glasses pulled down to the tip of her nose. She looks down at me and smiles.

"You must be Katy." Her cheery voice gives me hope. I put my hand in hers and shake.

"Yes ma'am. This is Caleb," I say, freeing my hand from hers and pointing to Caleb. "He's a good friend of mine." She shakes his hand.

"Hello." Opening the door fully, she gestures us inside. "Come on in, it's a little chilly out there." She's right, it was pretty cold. I walk in through the door with Caleb trailing behind me.

Mrs. Falkner walks through the living room and into the dining room. She has an array of finger foods, and a pitcher of sweet tea sitting on the table. We all take a seat and wait, as she pours tea into three glasses.

"My husband took the kids out to get ice cream so that we could talk first," she starts. The fact that she wanted to talk first made me nervous.

"This tea is very good," says Caleb. "My mother use to make some excellent tea. She would put raspberries in it, and refrigerate it overnight. Squeeze a little lemon in it the next day, it was the best tea I have ever had." He takes another sip. "Yours is close. What do you put in it?" Taking another sip, he clicks his tongue a couple of times to get a better taste. "Orange?" Mrs. Falkner smiles.

"Very good. I do put orange in And just like your mom did, I let it sit overnight."

I hadn't heard him talk about his mom in a personal sense. Just the couple of times when he was telling me what happened to her, and that she use to own the dance studio. So I sat there in stunned silence. He glances at me, then takes another sip of his tea.

"Well, I suppose it's best if I just say what is on my mind," Mrs. Falkner says. "I hear from the kid's caseworker that you had no knowledge of these children before a few months ago. Is that correct?"

"Yes ma'am," I say.

"You should know that they have known about you for some time."

"How?" Did I really want to know the answer to that? Probably not, but things were already in motion.

"Madison brought a picture from her house," she says, reaching into her pocket, pulling out a folded up picture. She opens it to show me.

It's a picture of me...when I was ten. I was looking directly at the camera, smiling and wearing a pair of rollerblades. Grandma's house was the backdrop.

I remember the day when Grandma had taken the picture. I had trouble keeping my balance, but she was always there when I fell—catching me. No one had ever spent so much time with me before. We spent hours together trying to get me rolling on those rollerblades. Finally, by the time it was dark outside, I had been able to do it easily.

Taking the picture from Mrs. Falkner, I hold it close wondering how my mom could have gotten it. My grandma must have given it to her.

"She kept this with her?" I ask in disbelief.

"She wouldn't let it go," Mrs. Falkner says, her voice was soft and barely a whisper. It was the saddest thing I had ever seen. But I also knew from experience that these kid's would not want any pity from anyone.

Was it possible that she had found something to hold onto—or someone? Me, maybe she had held onto that sliver of hope that someday she would meet me. Maybe she wanted someone to save her from her situation. All doubt that I was doing the wrong thing by introducing myself to these kid's, vanished from my mind. I made the right choice.

I look up at Caleb's reassuring stare. He knew what I was thinking. I had expressed to him several times the last two months how I thought I was making a mistake.

"The caseworker never once mentioned that the kids knew who I was. I mean, I knew she told them recently, but this..." I trail off.

"No, she wouldn't have because she didn't know. I just recently found this myself," she points to the picture in my hands, "a few days ago. Madison had it hidden under her pillow. Which leads me to believe that she thought it was necessary to do so. I don't think she was suppose to have it."

Handing the picture back to her, I close my eyes momentarily. It's all so surreal; I have two sisters and two brothers. For someone who had lost so many people, adding to my family sounded good.

The front door swings open pulling me from my

thoughts, and in walks an older man. He is carrying a Barbie doll, the image makes me smile. I like this man already. Coming in behind him are Jake, Madison, and Cassy. Cassy, the youngest, runs up to who I assume to be Mr. Falkner and raises her arms. He picks her up, not easily, and holds her tightly, handing the Barbie Doll to her.

Madison walks right up to me and throws her arms around my stomach At eight, her arms are unable to go all the way around me. Without any hesitation, I wrap my arms around her and hold her too. Madison has the same sandy blonde hair and green eyes that I do; she could be my twin.

"I knew you would come," Madison whispers so softly I almost don't hear her.

What do I say to that? It was like she was waiting for me, or waiting for someone to come and rescue her from the hell that she was in. It made me beyond angry at her parents, and it broke my heart into tiny little fragments.

Jake stands at the front door, his back against it, and his arms crossed over his chest. The scowl on his face says he doesn't play but the tapping of his foot says that he is eager to meet me. Either way, I don't make a move. I don't think approaching him is the best thing to do. Instead, I stay where I am with my arms wrapped around his sister—my sister.

"Hi Jake, I'm-"

"I know who you are," he intercedes sharply. I can already tell that this is going to be difficult for him.

"Good. This is my friend, Caleb," I say to the kids. Caleb steps up next to me and lowers himself to the floor so that he is at eye level with Madison. She hasn't let go of me, but when Caleb offers his hand, she releases one of hers from around my waist, smiles, and shakes it.

"Hi there. Madison, right?" His smile is all teeth and his voice is mellow. Madison nods her head. "Madison, do you like to dance?" Her face lights up. "My really good friend, Ms. Jill, runs a dance studio. She has recitals every month, and all the dancers get to show off what they've learned. I have seen so many recitals, it looks really hard."

"I can't get my feet to turn the right way when I dance," she whispers back in her little girl voice, "but I like to pretend."

She is paying rapt attention to him, and I wonder how he knew she liked to dance. Glancing around the room, I see a picture of the three kids. Madison is wearing a pink Tutu standing like a ballerina, Cassy is watching her sister with enjoyment, and Jake is lying on the ground staring in the other direction.

When I turn back toward the door to look at Jake, he is gone. I didn't realize he was missing. Worry starts to take root. Maybe he doesn't like me and will not want anything to do with me. A hand on my shoulder makes me look up, it's Mr. Falkner.

"Don't worry, honey. He is like this with everyone." He winks at me and grabs a glass for tea. "He'll come around," he adds.

Cassy is sitting on the couch in the living room flipping through the channels. When she lands on a show about a princess, she puts the remote down and sits back on the couch. Her little legs are too short to reach the floor, and her thumb is in her mouth.

As we settle into that awkward silence, no one knowing what to say or do in a situation like this, Mrs. Falkner claps her hands and asks, "Who wants to play Monopoly?"

We all sit in the living room, including Jake. After some coaxing, Mr. Falkner was able to get him downstairs. Reluctantly, he played a game of Monopoly with us.

Madison sat so close to me she was a hop away from sitting in my lap. Cassy didn't seem to be impressionable, but I don't think she was old enough to understand much. It was clear that she had been through a lot. It made her quiet and shy, and a little withdrawn; much like Jake.

Jake's withdrawal was the opposite of Cassy's. His was

defiance. He had a permanent scowl on his face. It didn't look good on an adult, so on a kid it looked even worse. Jake would be a tough nut to crack. These kids had been abandoned twice, so it didn't surprise me.

They were fantastic. Even with all they had been through they were still able to laugh and smile. I could tell that Jake was even warming up to us toward the end of the game; especially to Caleb.

"That's not possible," Caleb protests. "You can't possibly have both in that area." Jake had Park Place, Boardwalk, and more money than anyone else which meant he was outdoing Caleb.

"I do, which means that it is possible," Jake informs Caleb. He is looking satisfied, as he picks up his monopoly money and fans it out before setting it down next to him.

Jake is smart. His intelligence needs to be cultivated; just as Caleb had once told me about the kids at the academy. The fact that he won Monopoly against four other adults, with ease, shows his intelligence.

By the time we are done playing it's almost dinner time. Jake tells Caleb he will show him how to make a grilled cheese fit for a man, and they head into the kitchen laughing. They are really getting along, but Jake doesn't talk to me much. I can hear the clinking and clanking of pans and dishes in the kitchen. This day has been an emotional roller coaster.

The ups and downs of what can only be described as an abnormal family. What really would be a description of a normal family anyways? A mom and dad with their kids? That is ideal, but sometimes in life things happen. We don't know why and it's useless to pick apart those reasons. We just roll with the punches the best we can.

These kids are something beautiful that came from a terrible situation. My mother finally did do something great in life; she had Madison, Cassy, and Jake.

If she made a million bad choices for the rest of her

life; this one could make up for them all. The giggling coming from the girls is a gift and it fills me with happiness.

"Where's your mommy?" Cassy's sweet voice breaks me from my thoughts. She is sitting across from me with her legs crossed and tucked under her, waiting for my answer.

Her question takes me off guard. She doesn't know that we have the same mom. Clearing my throat, I try to answer without giving that away because I don't know if it would help her or hurt her.

"Everyone has a mommy," I start. Her little eyebrows draw together as she looks off into space then back at me.

"I don't have a mommy." She doesn't sound sad it was just a fact. She wouldn't remember Julie. She was three when Julie was admitted into the psychiatric hospital.

"You have a mommy. She just..." Oh no, what do I say? Maybe I started that wrong. Maybe I should have just told her that I didn't have a mommy. This is not something I thought I would have to ever explain but here it is, and I am terrified that I will say the wrong thing.

I notice that Madison is waiting for my answer as well. Even the Falkner's are waiting patiently. I thought maybe they would jump in and save the day, but they don't.

I settle on what I would want to hear at such a young age because they wouldn't understand the truth; or it would tear them up even more. It was best to focus on the love and good in life.

"Your mommy loves you guys. She's just sick and needed to leave to get some help." My chest squeezed painfully as I told them that. Because I didn't believe it myself.

"Will she come back?" The hope in Cassy's eyes is almost unbearable. The Falkner's have obviously been doing a great job for the past few months, but these kids need some stability. A few months of it hasn't been enough.

Looking at Madison, she looks doubtful.

"She might come back. But you know what? There are always people all around you who will love you—for you. Sometimes you have to learn to lean on them. They were put in your life for a reason."

I remember my reluctance with Grandma when she came to pick us up from the foster home. How I didn't think she would keep us. Thought that she would get tired of us, but even through all the bad times, she hung on to us and loved us through every single moment in life. That's what they needed, consistency and unconditional love.

Cassy gets up from the floor and comes over to me throwing her tiny arms around my shoulders, hugging me tightly. I lift her into my lap and hug her back.

"Do *you* love me?" she asks, and I can't help the tears that trickle down my cheeks as I choke back a sob. Tears of joy, not pain or heartache. Tears that heal.

"I do love you, Cassy." *And I do.*

I have known them for a few hours, but from the moment they walked in the door I loved them; all three of them. I felt my chest tighten and my throat close up at that first sighting. It was instant love which is something I did not believe in—until now.

"Will you leave me?" Choking out my answer I try to sound normal.

"No, Cassy. I won't leave you."

I look up to see Jake standing at the entrance to the living room with a plate of sandwiches in his hand, looking uncomfortable. He looks away from me after our eyes meet for a moment. I think I see a bit of hope in his eyes too, but he turns so quickly, I can't be sure.

Caleb stands next to him with a look of pure pride on his face. It makes me smile through my tear streaked face. I love it when he looks at me that way.

After Caleb and Jake serve the most delicious grilled cheese sandwiches I have ever had, it's time for us to go. It's the hardest thing I have ever had to do, but I don't live here, and I can't take them with me. I give each of them a hug; including Jake.

"Are you coming back tomorrow?" he asks me. I look at Caleb. It's so hard to have to tell them no, but I don't have to because Caleb nods and smiles.

"Yes." I smile at Jake. "If that's okay with the Falkner's?" I say, looking at them standing in the doorway on their front porch. Mrs. Falkner smiles brightly and looks to Mr. Falkner.

He nods his head, and says, "Of course, dear." Caleb and I make plans with the Falkner's to pick the kids up the next day and take them to the park, dinner, and a movie.

We leave in search of a hotel for the night, finding one just a few blocks from the kids. When we get inside the room, I fall on the bed, exhausted from the drive and the day with the kids. I can hear Caleb outside making a few phone calls and checking on things back home.

Even though I am exhausted from the day, I feel a pulse of energy shoot through me as the door swings open and Caleb comes strolling in. I watch as he takes his watch off and his wallet out of his pocket. Getting up, I walk over to him and wrap my arms around his waist and resting my cheek on his chest. His strong arms wrap around me, and he runs his fingers through my hair.

"What's this for?" I can hear the deep rumble in his chest as he speaks.

"Thank you," I say softly. I am so very thankful that this man has been put in my life. Taking time off and rearranging his life to come with me. Researching the guy that was with my mom. We still hadn't found out much about him. It would be much easier if we could find a record of him somewhere or if he used a credit card, but it was almost impossible with next to no information. But here he was with me, beside me. "For everything," I whisper into his chest.

He squeezes me tighter and lays his cheek on the top of my head. I start to wonder what I have ever given him when he says, "Don't." I look up quickly; maybe I said that out loud.

"Don't what?" I ask quizzically.

"You have given me something, Katy." I guess I did say it out loud. He pulls back, holding my shoulders, bringing his eyes down to meet mine. "You have no idea how much you have given me. Just by being here with me," he closes his eyes and shakes his head, then opens them again, "it's more than enough, and you are more than enough. You don't need to thank me because I want to be here, I want to do this." He pulls me in for another hug.

"I'm so glad you where stubborn that day at Mel's and didn't want to take no for an answer," I say, my voice muffled because my head is in his chest again.

"Hmm, I was always in trouble as a kid because of my stubbornness. I'm glad it comes in handy as an adult. Did I ever tell you that my mother's name was Kate?"

"Really." I can't hide the surprise in my voice. I swing my gaze up to meet his.

"Yes really." I can hear the smile in his voice. "She told me once that I would meet someone who would help me make sense of who I was, because you couldn't make sense of something when you only have half of the puzzle. I remember thinking to myself 'She doesn't make much sense right now'. This was two days before she killed herself. She wasn't always depressed and sad. We had some good days.

"I never found the need to reflect on her statement, in fact, it was forgotten. But today, when I watched you give some excellent advice to a six year old, my heart grew and things did make sense to me. My heart does flips in my chest when I am around you and when we aren't together; I pray that you'll be safe and that you're having a good day."

My heart was doing flips right now. With every word Caleb spoke, I was melting into putty. The words 'I love you' were on the tip of my tongue, but it didn't feel like the right time, so I suppressed them.

"Caleb, I don't know what to do about the kids. I want to stay with them, but it's not realistic. I have a life and a home." We walk over and sit at the little table in the corner. Caleb never lets go of my hands. "But I can't leave them. They have had too much of that already and they're good kids."

"You don't have to leave just because you don't live right next door to them. You can call and visit as often as you want. You're only an hour away." I know he's right, but it still feels wrong.

"What if they are adopted? What if someone moves them states away?" Pulling my hand out of his, I put them on my cheeks and place my elbows on the table. Lost. "The Falkner's are too old to adopt. They're in their late sixties. What happens if they pass? Cassy has twelve years before she is old enough to be on her own."

"Katy, you're asking the wrong person to answer all your questions." I look at him confused. "When I have a tough decision to make, I get down on my knees, and I pray. I ask God, because I have made too many mistakes in my life to make important decisions on my own."

I have never prayed like that before. In church every Sunday, I pray at my seat. I have seen people walk up to the cross in the front, and kneel down before it. Even though I have been to church with Caleb every Sunday for the past three months I'm not sure if I can do it. I'm not sure if I understand it, and uncertainty was not something I liked in my life.

"Do you want to be alone?" he asks me. Is that weird? This whole thing feels weird.

"I guess." He nods his head, gets up, and walks over to me; kneeling on the floor in front of me. Taking my face in both of his hands he kisses me gently, reassuringly.

"Just talk to Him like you are talking to a friend. There

is no right or wrong way. "He smiles and leaves me alone.

Sitting here in this hotel room by myself, I put my head in my hands in front of me. Closing my eyes, I just sit in silence for a few moments.

"Lord, I'm new at this, but I don't think you really care about that. I just, I'm so stuck in my life right now. There are these three little kids who are now a part of it, and I don't know how to deal with that the right way. I can see their little broken hearts on the outside like it was pinned to their shirt. It kills me to know what they have been through. I need some guidance. Please, Lord. What do I do? How do I handle this situation, because it's not about me it's about these little lives and what they need?"

I've never poured my heart out to anyone before. Not even to Caleb or Faye or even my grandma, but here in this noisy hotel room, I gave it all, and let it spill out and overflow. When I felt the tears well up in my eyes and my heart constrict I knew that something was different.

Chapter Seventeen

When I wake up in the morning, I look over at Caleb from across the room, still sleeping. His face is pressed into the pillow, his lips slightly open, and his breathing slow.

After he came back to the room last night, I had already been in bed reading a book. He didn't ask how it went or how I felt. He just got ready for bed, grabbed a book from his bag, and started to read it. I watched him fall asleep slowly. When he finally did, I got out of bed to put his book away and turn out the light. He was reading the Bible; the same book I had seen him reading that day at the studio. How did I get this man in my life? Slowly his eyes open, and he starts to rub the sleep from them.

"Hi, sleepy head," I say happily. He blinks a few times then smiles, sitting up.

"Good morning. You seem like you're in a better mood today." Looking at my cell phone, I see it's eleven in the morning.

"Wow, we really slept in," I say.

Rising, I stretch and yawn then head over to gather my clothes for the day. His eyes follow my every move, and my cheeks start to heat up. Finally, I stop and turn toward him; he is staring at me with a goofy grin on his face.

"What?" I ask, putting my hand on my hips. He shakes his head.

"You are so beautiful, Katy. There is so much about you to admire." I had never heard praise like that before. It makes me very happy.

Walking over, I stand between his legs and pull him into a hug. I enjoy the closeness and comfort that he brings. He hugs me back pulling me in tighter, with his head laying on my stomach. There was a time not too long ago that I didn't think this would be possible.

"All right," I say, pulling away, grabbing his face, and planting a quick kiss on his lips. When I try to move away, he traps my wrists and pulls me down on the bed, pinning me to the mattress. Hovering over me, he looks...nervous. I can see his internal struggle as he leans down and kisses my cheek then further down my jaw line.

Well, this is a surprise. I know his take on things when it comes to sex, but I didn't know what was going on right now, or if he would stop, but my will power to push him away collapsed as he slid a kiss down my neck and all my insides lit up like the Fourth of July.

Opening my mouth to accommodate my breath quickening, I gasp as he nips at my collarbone. What is going on here?

I don't want him to do something that he will regret, so pulling the power from some unknown place, I finally speak, breaking the intensity that was starting to overpower.

"Caleb, I thought..." I say breathlessly. He kisses my neck again and looks at me with heat in his eyes. He closes them for a minute and when he opens them again, the heat is gone.

"It's so tempting, Katy. I wasn't always a man with morals. But when I look at you, I want things that I have not wanted with anyone in four years. You also make it easy to hang on to those morals. That's how special you are to me."

I didn't know what he meant by that. Closing his eyes, he puts his forehead on mine. We stay like that for a while waiting for our breathing to calm down.

"I'm so glad I have you," he whispers, then rises off the bed taking me with him.

We get dressed and head out to the Falkner's house. The whole ride over, I am trying to shake the whole scene out of my head of Caleb kissing me in places that no one had ever kissed, him hovering over me, the heated look in his eyes. A chill runs through my body, and I shiver.

Calling Collin quickly, I tell him that we are going to stay an extra day. He doesn't ask about his brother and sisters just wishes me luck and tells me to stay safe and hangs up.

He's had a real sour attitude about the whole trip. He even argued with Caleb about it; told him not to take me. I didn't know what his problem was with this whole situation because he wouldn't talk to me about it.

I did know that he worked entirely too much. He worked for a local architect who designs houses. It wasn't as good of a job as he had in California, but it had benefits, and he got paid per design and hourly when he was in the office. Last week we had talked about him moving out and getting his own place. It was something that he wanted, but he also didn't want to leave me alone.

Even though we hadn't seen Mom or her friend since the night they tried to break in; Caleb said they were still around living in that same run down motel. The fact that they hadn't attempted anything only added to my worry. It made me feel that they were waiting for something. What they were waiting for, I didn't know.

When we arrived at the Falkner's the kids were sitting outside on the front steps. Madison was wearing jeans and a sweater with a baseball cap, and Cassy was in a pretty blue and black flowered dress with black leggings and a black jacket. Jake sat in between his two sisters and towered over them too. He was throwing a baseball up in the air and catching it. They all looked pretty excited, and I had to admit—I was too.

"Hey guys," I say with excitement. Looking down at Cassy holding her Barbie, I ruffle her neatly combed hair. "And little girls," I say quietly to her. She smiles. Jake throws the ball to Caleb.

Caleb catches it easily and walks over to Jake. "Good hand. Do you play?" he asks, holding the ball in the air.

Jake stands and shakes his head no.

"I really want to though." I stand there for a moment and take in the scene around me. The things that were said and the kids sitting on the steps. I get a sense of déjà vu, but this is only my second visit with the kids.

Then a memory floats through my mind; I have done this before. That's why this scene looks so familiar. Eleven years ago I was that kid sitting on the steps. That was the day that Grandma picked Collin and me up. She took us home and raised us as if we were her own.

That was the day that things had changed for Collin and me. I try not to think about where I would be right now if it hadn't been for Grandma.

But what about Jake, Madison, and Cassy? Where will they be if someone doesn't adopt them? What if the Falkner's pass away before they are old enough to be on their own? Will they get taken away somewhere else? Even if they were adopted they could be split up and separated. These must have been the thoughts going through Grandma's head when she made the decision to adopt Collin and me.

Maybe there was still hope for them to be a family together. I know what these kids need and I know how I can help them. Looking at Caleb, my eyes widen. He knows I have something on my mind, but now is not the time or place to discuss it, so I make a mental note to talk to him later.

We spend two hours at the park before the movie starts. Jake and Caleb play catch. Jake is really good. Collin and Jake would get along really well if Collin wasn't being so stubborn.

Cassy and Madison pull me over to the grass where they had laid out a blanket and some food that they had helped Mrs. Falkner make. The smile on their little faces was one of the best sights I had ever seen.

I sit down and Cassy slides onto my lap. She grabs my

face with her tiny little hands, and says very seriously, "Close your eyes, no peeking."

I wait till her hands are gone to slip a peek, but she is staring at me in disapproval as soon as I dare to open my eyes. I can't help the laugh that bursts through just from seeing such a small child with disapproval on her face.

"Katy, close your eyes." I get reprimanded by her.

"Okay, I'm sorry. They're closed, see." I snap my eyes shut and wait for what I hope is not slimy or gross.

I feel Cassy get up followed by some papers being moved around.

Then Madison says, "No, I want to give it to her."

"Girls? Is everything okay? Should I open my eyes?"

"NO!" They both shout in unison. There is some more rustling around and then pressure on my knees as someone sits down.

"Okay," says Madison from beside me, "open your eyes."

I open them slowly, not wanting to get reprimanded again. There, sitting in Cassy's hand, is a tiny dove made of paper. It's origami. I pick it up and turn the delicate paper over in my hands examining the folds that are precise and clean.

"Did you make this?" I ask Madison. When she doesn't respond, I turn to my left. She is nodding her head rapidly with delight on her face. "It's beautiful. Thank you so much." Leaning over, I hug her.

"My sissy made me one too." Cassy says from my lap. I look at her and watch as her face goes from excitement to confusion. I don't have to wonder long what brought it one, as she asks the question that has her looking like that. "Are you my sissy too?"

Her innocence is sweet and her bluntness is innocent. I love that she can make a grown adult squirm by her questions because that is how kids should be, they keep us on our feet.

"Yes, Cassy; I'm your sister." And proud to be called their sister. This seems to satisfy her curiosity. She picks up a small brush and starts combing her Barbie's hair.

Madison wraps her arms around mine and leans her head against my shoulder. We sit like that for a while watching the boys throw the ball back and forth. Jake keeps throwing it faster and further away. It's a challenge for Caleb, but he gets it; until Jake throws the ball too far and too fast. I watch Caleb make his best efforts to get to the ball but it's useless. When he misses Jake starts whooping and hollering, throwing his fist in the air.

Calmness covers me. And each moment I spend with these kids, I realize just how special they are and how much their mom and dad are missing.

We leave the park after we try our best to eat the snacks Madison and Cassy made with Mrs. Falkner, but it looks like just Cassy and Madison have made them. They're not so bad. I get two of what I think is a cracker with cream cheese and red peppers. Jake absolutely refused to eat any. Caleb had at least four celery sticks that were made up with peanut butter and raisins to resemble ants on a log.

On our way to the movie theatre, I hear a lot of pre-teasers from the kids. They had wanted to see this movie when it came out, but Jake said he didn't feel right asking Mrs. Falkner. Jake had overheard them talking about the money they had gotten from the state to foster them. It apparently was pennies when you compare it to raising three kids. I was happy to take them because it made *them* happy.

The movie was pretty funny anyways, and I enjoyed it. The kids laughed, and Caleb even laughed a few times. He sat next to me and held my hand, while the kids all sat on the other side of me. As funny as the movie was it was even funnier when Cassy eyed my hand in Caleb's and asked 'Is he your boyfriend' really loud.

Caleb and I just chuckled softly, but Madison told her

she shouldn't yell so loud while we are in the movie theatre. Cassy nodded her head and turned her attention back to the screen. Madison was a little mother hen. She was probably forced to grow up early and take care of her younger sister. That's what Collin had to do when my mom went off the deep end. I'm sure Jake had to pick up a lot of the missing pieces in this family when no one else would too.

We had dinner at a little pizza place down the street from the Falkner's. Jake was a frequent customer because he knew everyone inside.

"Do you come here often?" I ask as we slide into a booth and open our menus.

"I use to," Jake replies. Looking down at his menu, he doesn't elaborate, so I wait patiently to see if he will give me more. After a few long moments he adds, "With my dad. We came every Friday just the two of us."

His voice is laced with sadness and it breaks me. My heart aches for him. I would do anything to give him some normalcy in his life. Picking up my menu I open it and huff.

"So, what's good here? Ooh, they have Hawaiian pizza. I love pineapple."

"On your pizza?" Jake asks in disbelief.

"Of course. Pineapple and feta cheese. It's the dinner of champions. You've never tried it, have you?'

"Um, no. It sounds gross. You should try the barbeque chicken pizza," He says delighted.

"Now that is gross." I say clearly disgusted by his choice of pizza. We agree to try each other's. As Caleb and I place our order, the kids go off to the arcade. I watch Cassy jump in Jake's lap as he plays a racing game. The love that these kids have for one another astonished me. They clearly had an abundance of love to give even though they hadn't received the love they needed from others.

"Those are some great kids," Caleb says. I wholly agree with him, and I am glad he sees what I see.

"They are. I hate that they have been through so much

at such a young age. Why would anyone just leave their kids? I mean, I'm having trouble leaving them, and I've only known them for two days."

"Some people are mentally ill. People like that will irrational choices; especially when there is alcohol involved." He puts his arm around my shoulders and pulls me in tighter and planting a quick kiss on my head. I relax in the comfort he provides. "Have you ever thought that their dad might have given them up because he knew that his problem would, in the end, just hurt his kids?"

"I thought of that. I don't understand it though. His choices should not have included; stay and do harm or leave and do harm. It should have been to stay and sober up, be a father to them." Sighing, I lean my head on his shoulder.

"I agree. There should only be one option when it comes to loving your kids. Just remember that the decisions that seem easy for us to make are going to be more difficult for someone who has an addiction. He has to go away to sober up. It's not easy to do. He will always be labeled an alcoholic and will have to attend AA meetings for life."

"Do you go to meetings?" I ask him quietly.

"I do" Some new information about him.

"You know, you amaze me, and you are doing really well with all of this. Those kids are lucky to have a big sister like you," he says, finishing the conversation.

We drop the kids off at the Falkner's with lots of hugs and a few tears. I tell them that I will see them soon, but they don't look very optimistic. Pulling away from that house was hard but Caleb and I had to get back home. He had a business to run, and I was just trying to decide what I wanted to do with my life. College had always been my dream. Faye and I were supposed to go together, but that didn't work out the way we had planned. I'm glad that she at least was able to follow through on that.

I just didn't know if I wanted to leave my home, Grandma's home. And now, there were Madison, Cassy, and Jake to think about. If I went with my original plan that would be hours in the opposite direction even further away from them. I knew for sure that I didn't want to do that.

Not completely throwing college out of the window, I start to think about other possibilities. I can start taking classes, here, next fall, maybe work with kids. I decided that I had time to let the answers come to me from up above.

"What are you thinking about?" The sun had sunk and the night was ominous and dark. It didn't help that most of our drive involved the back roads and the country. I was thankful for his question because the quietness and dark was a bit eerie.

"College," I say. Caleb clears his throat

"College where Faye is?" he asks, hesitating.

"That was the original plan but so much has happened. I don't think I can go with my original plan."

"Then you need a new plan." It sounds simple, but I know it never is.

"Well, I wanted to talk to you about something. Possibly get your help. I had an idea."

"I thought you might." He smiles. "You always get this look on your face when you have an idea. Your eyes get really big, then you get this tight lipped smile; because you're trying not to smile. It's very cute."

"Geez, thank you. You're such a sweet talker." I use my sweetest voice. I'm not sure how he will react when I tell him what I want to do. There is only one way to find out though. "I was thinking, maybe I could foster the kids or even adopt them." His expression is blank, so I continue. "They have no family, and the Falkner's are really nice, but I wish they were twenty years younger. They are too old to take care of them for very long."

"Katy, it's not that easy. There is a legal process, not to mention you are eighteen and not really a responsible adult yet."

"What?" Anger seeps through my bones deep, and I can't help the next words that come out of my mouth that are fueled by that anger. "What were you doing at eighteen? Because I have a house with no payment, plenty of money to raise three kids, and I don't exactly go out anywhere. What did you have?" He flinches from my anger, and I feel a little regretful at the tone in my voice. How dare he tell me I'm not mature enough to take care of my brother and sisters. They need me.

Shaking his head, he says softly, "That's not what I meant. The courts won't let an eighteen year old foster or adopt three kids. If they did, it would be under severe circumstances. They won't care how much money you have or how many character witnesses you have. The bottom line is, you're eighteen. And yes, you're their sister, but you have only known about that for two months and only have known them for two days. The odds aren't with you on this one. But, you should pray about it."

There is complete silence in the car for what seems like too long. Sighing, Caleb grabs my hand and kisses it.

"I'm not trying to sound negative, but I don't want to go through all of this without the facts. It's very rare for a court to let someone so young become a foster parent. They may even require you to be a certain age. It's something I can check into of course."

When the anger starts to replace itself with worry and regret because of what I said to him, random thoughts take over. These kids need someone, and I want to be that *someone* for them.

The Falkner's, I know, would love to keep them, but they are getting old and even they don't feel they are up to the task. I hate it most of all that they are being shuffled around and that it will continue the longer they are in foster care. I would do anything to take that heartache from them. A heartache that I've known before. A heartache that I still am trying to overcome, even now.

"I'm sorry for lashing out at you," I apologize.

He doesn't say anything. The rest of our car ride home is silent. I turn thoughts over in my head, and I come up with one final thought that makes me realize that Caleb is right. The likelihood that I would ever be able to foster the kids is slim. Do I try anyways? And then there is college, the kids will have school; maybe this *wasn't* the right way to help them. Then what was? I didn't know, but I would pray about it.

When we pull up to my house it's late. I am surprised to see Collin sitting outside on the front porch with a man I have never seen before. I turn to Caleb. He looks worried as he parks the car and turns toward me too.

"That's undercover." He points to a black car about two houses down. "He came in an unmarked car and street clothes. He doesn't want anyone to know he's here. Something is up."

The kids; that's my first thought, but the Falkner's have my number and would definitely call me if something happened.

"Do you think something happened to the kids?" I ask anyways. He shakes his head looking off into the distance.

"No. I think it's about your mom." He opens the door and climbs out then comes around and opens my door. I climb out trying to prepare myself for whatever it is that I am going to be told. The worst thoughts come to mind as I approach Collin and the officer.

"Ms. Laudin," the officer says, facing me and offering his hand, "I'm Officer Sommer." He doesn't look like an officer. He is wearing a blue torn baseball hat, blue jeans and a black t-shirt. His hair is neatly combed to the side and his mustache is perfectly groomed. But I think that is the purpose when you are undercover. He doesn't want to be known as an officer. He looks completely comfortable and at home like he is a friend.

I shake his hand wishing he could skip the

introductions and get right to what he's doing here.

"What's going on?" I ask.

"Your brother told me that your mother came back into town." Officer Sommer crosses his arms over his chest and leans against the porch railing.

"Yes, but I haven't seen or heard from her in two months." Caleb comes up behind me putting a hand on my shoulder. Letting me know that he is there if I need him.

"She's been laying low because of the man she is with. We have been trying to catch him for three months; of course Julie has been helping him flee the authorities the entire time."

He reaches into his back pocket and pulls out a folded up photo. Opening it, he shows it to me. It's the same man that my mom was with that night she tried to break into the house. It's sort of blurry, but I can see that it's him.

"I've seen him with her once." The same man that struck so much fear into me was staring at me from the photograph. His big burly arms full of tattoos, his beard unkempt, and his steely gaze like nothing and no one mattered. A chill ran down my spine making me shiver and cross my arms over my stomach. I felt like I knew him from somewhere, but before I could take a closer look, Officer Sommer folds the picture and shoves it into his back pocket.

"Can you tell me where you have seen him?"

"He was here, with my mom. She attempted to break in, but Caleb and I walked up before they could do anything," I say, turning my gaze toward Caleb.

"You didn't think to report the crime?" Now I just felt stupid. The accusation rang in his voice, and I thought that I couldn't get any smaller.

"I'm sorry, sir. I don't think we have met. I'm Caleb." The officer looks at Caleb's outstretched hand and reluctantly shakes it once. "I did attempt to report the crime, but according to the officer at the station if there was no evidence then there was nothing they could do. I gave a full description, but didn't argue with the man out of respect. The suspect and Katy's mom were just standing at the window." Caleb points to the side of the house behind the officer. "I advised Katy to let me keep an eye on her mom. I own a reputable private security business, and I have had one of my men following her mother non-stop for the past two months." The officer stands up straight.

"So I should be talking to you? Have you seen the man with her recently?" He is excited about this break in his case as he starts asking Caleb a ton of questions.

"Yes, she has been with him every day. I can tell you where they are. I have a man out there now." Caleb is interrupted by his phone, the beep sounding like a cannon going off in my ear. The beep that indicates he has a message He pulls it out and opens it reading the message. Turning back to the officer he says, "Julie and your criminal just fled the hotel in a rush. I've got my guy following them." He types out a quick message. "Let me get you that information."

They step off to the side as Caleb gives the information that he knows. I take the time to walk up to Collin.

"Hey, how are you doing with all of this?" Sitting back on the swing he puts his left ankle over his knee.

"I'm fine, I'm not surprised that she is with a criminal and brings him around here. She has complete and total disregard for anyone or anything." He huffs. I sit next to him on the swing. Using my toes, I kick off to start swinging.

"What do you think this man did?"

"He beat someone, nearly to death, Katy." That was blunt. I stop swinging and look at him. He looks frustrated.

"Hey, what's wrong?" I put my arm over his shoulders trying to give him some comfort because something is clearly bothering him.

"That night he was here with Julie; I was drunk, passed out on the couch. If Caleb hadn't been with you, anything could have happened. You've been through so much, I don't want to put you through more."

"That's in the past, Collin. You haven't been drunk since then, have you?"

"No," he says shaking his head. "No, I just- I messed up, and it could have ended differently."

"There is no use in living in the mistakes you made in the past. All we can do is try to remember our mistakes and not repeat them. I'm fine, everything turned out fine."

"I know it did, but this man bludgeoned another man till he was barely breathing all because of a woman." I didn't want to think about that word bludgeoned because it insinuates that he used something to assist in the beating.

"Did the man do something to the woman?" Staring off out over the yard he shakes his head no.

"He has a rap sheet a mile long. But this particular time, he beat him because the woman told him to. She said that the man stole her money and groped her. So he beat the man, and the woman stole *his* money and anything valuable that he had on him. Do you know who the woman was, Katy?"

"Mom," I whisper. The thought that I was born from this woman makes my stomach hurt. "How can she be like this? What makes a person so cold and distant, so heartless?" Collin shrugs.

"I don't know; maybe the drugs." He clears his throat, leans his head against the swing, and closes his eyes. "How was your visit?" Surprised by his question, I stumble over my words.

"The kids- they are- you mean the kids, right?" Collin nods his head. "They are great, Collin. You have a lot in common with Jake. He loves baseball and is very hardheaded. Cassy is the sweetest little girl and very smart for six. She is curious about everything. Madison, she is so loving. She looks a lot like I did at eight. I can't believe they have so much to give at such a young age and after what happened to them." When I look at him he is staring at me, paying rapt attention.

"I haven't seen you this excited about something in a long time," he says.

"They are great, Collin. You should consider meeting them. They are nothing like Mom if that's what you think. And, they did know about us. Madison had a picture of me."

"How did she have a picture of you?"

"I don't know. Mom probably. But she must have gotten it from Grandma. It's the only thing that makes sense because I was looking at the camera."

"Huh." After a long moment, he says, "Do you think Grandma knew about Julie's other kids?"

The thought never occurred to me. Nothing over the years ever suggested that she had, but Grandma knew everything. I could never get away with anything without her knowing exactly what I did.

Finally, I say, "It's possible I guess." We sit there in silence as Caleb is talking to the officer. He turns around and heads back as the officer leaves. His worry has turned to stress, and I immediately stand at attention.

"What is it?" I ask.

"It's Mike, the guy I had following your mother. He followed them to the edge of town, the man, his name is Claude, stopped the vehicle, so Mike stopped behind him. He got out and walked up to Mike's car. Claude punched right through the glass and broke Mike's nose. Then got back in his car and took off. He must have cut up his arm pretty badly. So Officer Sommer is checking the hospitals." He didn't look convinced by this.

"You don't think he went to the hospital?" I ask

"No, he seems too smart to go to the hospital. His priors where robbery, breaking and entering, assault, and an attempted rape. They wouldn't give me much more information than that. I'm going to see if we can talk to someone about getting more information on him because officer Sommer doesn't seem to know what he can give away." My heart sinks, and I shiver. How could she be with this man? Caleb starts rubbing my arms, attempting to rub the cold away.

"The hospitals will be the first place they'll look for him and he knows that. Listen," he steps in closer, putting his hands on my shoulders. "I have to go check on this. Mike is heading to the hospital, and I need to make sure he is okay."

"Absolutely." I say completely understanding. Caleb had close relationships with all of his employees, but Mike and Caleb were like brothers,

"I'm going to look for him and follow up on some leads. I gave all the information I had to the officer, but I have an idea that he didn't want to listen to. I'm going to check it out. I want you to go inside, lock the doors, and turn on the alarm system. Do not answer the door for anyone."

"Do you think she'll come here?" I squeak.

"I don't know, but I don't want to take any chances. Just go inside and stay there. I'll call when I know something. He pulls me in for a quick hug and kisses my head. When he releases me and starts to walk away, I grab his hand.

"Wait!" Pulling him back to me, I wrap my arms around his waist and hug him tightly. There is no way I am letting him go that easily when there is something ominous lurking around us.

I hold on to him as long as I can, feeling his grip just as tightly around me. I don't want him to go but telling him that, I know won't make a difference, so I just hang on.

"Please be careful," I whisper into his shoulder.

"I will. Don't worry, okay?" The softness of his voice makes my heart clench, and I know in this moment that I love him.

I love him for the man he is and the man he wants to be. I love him for his morals and his personality but most of all, I love him for what he is about to do. Because I know that he is doing it for me. Out of all the things in life he could have chosen to do, he is a protector.

As he releases me and hands me over to Collin; I miss the opportunity to tell him how much I love him. Silenced by such an enormous revelation.

Chapter Eighteen

Waiting for something, anything, to happen is stressful. I bite my nails down to nothing and bounce my leg so many times it feels overworked; like I ran a marathon with just this one leg.

It's been two hours, and there hasn't been a call from Caleb. So when my phone rings, I jump and answer it without looking at who it is.

"Hello." My voice is rushed and hopeful.

"Well hello to you too." It's Faye. I sigh not thinking it through. "Oh, I'm sorry to disappoint you. Where you expecting someone else? Like the Queen of England."

"No, I mean yes—no! I wasn't expecting the Queen, just Caleb. What's up with you?" Sitting back on the couch, I finally push some of the nervousness to the back of my mind because I don't want Faye to catch on. She doesn't need this with her classes and studying.

I look over at Collin who is giving me a questioning look so I mouth 'Faye' while pointing to the phone. He nods and continues flipping through the television stations.

"Awe, how sweet. Are you guys holding hands yet because I believe in taking it slow, but the rate you guys are going your more like moving backwards." I roll my eyes, even though she can't see me, and listen.

"So... in two weeks I'm taking a road trip to surprise Micah," she continues, " and do some wedding stuff. I thought maybe you and Caleb could meet us there, make it a sort of couples retreat?"

With everything going on right now, I just couldn't think about a trip, but I was trying to sound like I wasn't worried, so I entertained the idea.

"Yeah, that sounds like fun. I'll see if he can get away

for the weekend. So how are things going up there?"

"Without sounding like the worst best friend in the world; I love college; with the exception of that one professor. When you have a question, he answers it condescendingly it makes me feel stupid. Okay, so he's smarter than me. He has been on this earth since the dark ages, he should be, but he doesn't need to rub it in everyone's face. After two months the man still won't give me a decent grade. It's public speaking! I love talking, it shouldn't be this hard to get an A."

"Are you inventing your own dictionary of words again? Because in that case, I can see why he is giving you a low grade."

"I'm so going to publish my very own dictionary then he'll have to revisit and revise my grade."

"You go, girl. I love your ambition."

"How's the garden coming along? Finished yet? Is Collin helping?" she asks. Collin and I had been working on it adamantly on the weekends. Caleb would help occasionally so it was just about finished.

"It's good. I planted yellow calla lilies last weekend. Collin and Caleb have been helping."

"Good! I would hate to have to stop by there and beat the living crap out of your brother for going off the deep end again. You don't need that, Katy." Looking at Collin he is still flipping through channels starring straight at the television, but his smirk shows that he heard Faye.

I smile too, then it quickly disappears as I think about what is going on in my life that Faye doesn't know about.

"You know, I wanted to talk to you-" I start, but my phone beeps, signaling another call, and it has me sitting straight up in my seat. "Faye, let me call you back." I don't even wait for her answer; I hit the switch button on my phone and answer the other line.

"Hello?" There is some rustling in the background and for a minute no one says anything. Then he talks and the relief is immediate as my body comes down from being strung so tight.

"Hey, I'm on my way back to you." The best words I have ever heard.

"How's Mike?" I ask.

"He has a broken nose and several cuts from the shattered glass. It's not the first time Mike has had a broken nose. He'll be fine. Can you call the Falkner's and tell them what's going on?"

"Do you think she will go that way?"

"No, but I don't want to take the chance. Just let them know so they are aware. I'll be there in fifteen minutes."

"Okay. See you then." We disconnect and I call the Falkner's, relaying the message to them.

Walking into the kitchen, I grab the fixings for a late night omelet. I don't notice that Collin has followed me until he starts pulling out a pan.

"You want one?" I ask.

"Here," he takes the ingredients from me, "I'll make *you* an omelet." Sitting at the breakfast bar, I throw my elbows on the counter, and put my chin in my hands.

"What did you do?" I ask.

"What?" He turns to me with a smile on his face. "I didn't do anything. I just thought it would be nice to make my sister an omelet." He breaks two eggs into a bowl and starts to whisk them. "But-"

"I knew it. You are learning some bad habits from Faye!" I exclaim.

"What? No. I'm not learning anything from Faye," he's flustered. What is this all about? "I wanted to talk to you about me moving out after all this mess has died down." I knew this would be coming, that he was staying because of the unknown threat that hung like a dark cloud over us. It wasn't the first time we had talked about it.

"Do you have a place in mind? Wait, are you staying in town?" For a minute there is nothing. I don't want him to leave town, but I wouldn't keep him from doing what he wants.

"I've been looking for a new job. I'm not entirely happy working for someone else. I want a partner like I had in Cali."

When he left for college he had ambition. Grandma and I knew that he would go where he was happy with his job; even if that did take him to California.

"So you may leave town again?" I ask, trying to clarify and get him to answer my initial question.

"I've been looking at jobs out of town, yes. But, none are that far away. Maybe a few hours at most. I may take a few classes too."

"What about Chelsea? Have you talked to her lately?" I knew he probably didn't want to talk about her, but he was my brother and I loved him. Keeping your feelings locked tight was never a good thing, and men; they just tended to push their feelings to the back and leave them stuffed there; right next to picking up after themselves and not peeing on the seat.

"No, and I don't want to." His voice is low and holds so much malice it creeps me out a little. His last conversation with her must not have been a good one. It's not for me to pick apart so I leave it alone.

"So, do you think I should be afraid with Mom out there running around?"

"I think we shouldn't underestimate Julie. We know that she has a problem with you and that man she is with he seems a little disturbed and brutal."

"You don't think she will try to bother the kids, do you?" I was still worried that she would. If she felt she needed to make my life miserable, why not theirs? They would be easier to pick on anyways.

"I don't know. Like I said, she is unpredictable." Scooping the omelet onto a plate he sets it in front of me.

Caleb comes in the door before I can even take a bite of

my omelet.

I walk up to him, a little too eager, and wrap myself in him. He holds me tightly. Taking off his coat he hangs it in the small closet by the door.

"They put an APB out on the vehicle," he starts. "Not even ten minutes after that, they found it abandoned by the expressway. They have been searching the area but have yet to find them." He starts rubbing his hands together in an effort to warm them up.

"Do you want some coffee? I have decaf." I ask him.

"Yes that would be great." I turn and head off to the kitchen. "Thanks, honey." It's the first time he has called me anything like that. I smile but no one sees.

For some reason, I don't want him to see how much that one word has affected me. A lot of bad words and negativity have been thrown my way so those words of endearment are more than just words to me, they are a bandage for my heart.

Pouring a cup of coffee for Collin, Caleb, and myself too, we sit at the dining room table just talking about nothing in particular. It felt normal; which considering how my life has been going, normal could have been me standing on my head singing the alphabet song.

I didn't forget about the looming threat that hung over us or the kids. I hadn't forgotten that Faye knew nothing, and I hadn't forgotten the feelings that I had, as Caleb left to chase my mom and her murderous boyfriend. Fear was present in boat loads, and trying to push it down was not easy. Surprisingly, I was able to though.

I was afraid to say the words 'I love you' to Caleb. I had told a boy I loved him before but now I knew that I hadn't meant it. When you are in love there is no doubt in your mind you just know. The question 'would I rush into it' hung heavily over me, but the urge was so strong. The mistake I had made in the past had me holding my words in.

As Collin and I headed to bed and Caleb made a bed on

the couch, I figured we could talk about it in the morning. He would be here and he would be safe.

~~~

When I woke in the morning, I didn't feel ready for anything. But regardless, I dress for church, grab my grandma's necklace, and head out to where the smell of cinnamon and vanilla was.

"Something smells good," I say, trying to hook the clasp on the necklace. It didn't matter that I had done this so many times before; it was being difficult today. Caleb was standing by the stove stirring what looked like oatmeal, already dressed for church.

He glances up and does a double take noticing that I am struggling with the necklace. After laying the spoon down he walks over to me.

"You look nice. Here," he moves behind me and grabs each end of the necklace, "let me help." He hooks the clasp but doesn't move. Instead his fingers slide to my shoulders. I feel warmth and contentment fill my body. How- with what's going on- can one touch from him elicit that feeling? Closing my eyes, I lean back into him resting my head on his chest, letting the feelings devour me. *So right.*

"Thank You," I tell him.

"Where did you get this necklace?" He wanted a story?

"When I was six my grandma gave it to me."

"Did she happen to tell you where she got it from?"

"Uh, I'm not sure. I think she said she got it from a pawn shop. I'll never forget what she said to me when she put it in my hands." I grab the tiny sapphire teardrop and rotate it in between my finger. "She said that it looked like a teardrop had been caught. Then she told me that she would be there to catch mine for as long as God saw fit. I didn't understand it then, but I do now. Why do you ask?" I shift back to look at him.

"Curiosity." He kisses my cheek and pulls me in tighter

resting his chin on my shoulder. "It's very beautiful. She chose wisely and it looks magnificent on you. I'm glad she found that." There is more too it then that; I can tell, but I can't ask about it because Collin walks in.

"Stop it. You guys are making me feel mushy, and slightly uncomfortable might I add." Collin says, rubbing his eyes. Surprisingly, he is dressed too.

"What are you doing dressed? Going somewhere?"

"Yup." He swipes a bottle of water from the fridge and twists the top off. "Church."

I glance quickly at Caleb, but when I register shock on his face, that I am sure mirrors mine, I turn back to Collin and watch as he takes a swig of his water and reveals a goofy smile.

"Really," is all I can manage to say.

"Yes," he says drawing the word out, "really."

I have asked him every Sunday for the past two months to go with Caleb and me, but every single time he turned me down. This was a miracle. Collin didn't do religion, and he definitely didn't talk about God.

"Well, okay," Caleb says. "Collin if you want to grab the berries I'll serve up the oatmeal. We can eat and head out in about thirty minutes."

~~~

The church was packed today. It was usually pretty full, but today there wasn't a pew open. We ended up having to sit in the back in the same seats that I first sat in with Caleb over two months ago. It didn't seem like it had been that long. This time I wasn't looking around waiting for someone to jump out; and I was guarded by my two favorite men.

I shook hands and said hello to people, and had full conversations with some that I have gotten to know.

A group of kids from the academy where here, so I introduced Collin to every single one. We missed our usual visit on Friday because of our trip to Chapleton.

When the service started, I stood but didn't feel comfortable singing and swaying like others did. I was use to Caleb singing in a low voice next to me, but Collin wasn't. He looked at me a few times and smiled. Ignoring him was difficult.

I was quickly learning to be comfortable here, and, as always, I felt better somehow and more knowledgeable when the pastor was finished with his sermon.

As people filed out during communion, I had a sudden urge to go out too. I had never done this before, always too nervous and shy to do it. But there was a pull that was beyond me.

I walked out of the pew and toward the front with countless others. I didn't look to see if Caleb had followed. I had seen him do this a few times before.

As I got closer to the front, I saw people dropping to their knees in front of the cross. The cross meant something different to me now that I knew a man had hung and bled till he took his last breathe. A man who gave his life so that I could be free to live a life of peace when I left this world; a place I knew I would meet my grandma again.

The thought filled me with so much joy, that it pushed all of that dark that was still lingering—out of my life. I knew I had so much to learn, but that was the greatest thing about God. He was a forgiving and merciful God, and He would be patient with me as I found my way.

When my knees hit the floor, tears started to roll down my cheeks. I knew that I had found something great.

There was nothing that had ever felt like this in the whole world. The emotions that flooded my body felt real and raw. I welcomed them.

I confessed to God that I knew I was a sinner, that I knew I needed Him, and asked Him to come into my life and fill me up with His spirit. I prayed for everything and everyone. I prayed for my brothers and sisters; all four of them. I prayed for some guidance in my relationship with Caleb and my relationship with my siblings. I prayed for Faye, and asked God to be with her. My heart flipped wildly inside of my chest.

Whatever was missing from my life, I had found it. I had a long way to go, but I would embrace every single step I took in this direction.

This moment was a defining moment in my life. I knew that it would be something that I would talk about with my children someday. And I knew that I would tell anyone who listened how my heart and mind had been set free in a tiny church amongst strangers in the midst of a rapidly declining time in my life.

And when I stood and walked back to my seat, those things that had felt heavy on my shoulders, they didn't seem so heavy anymore. They weren't gone, but they were in His hands now.

Caleb's gorgeous smile made me realize what I had in him. A friend and a confidant, but I also realized that there was no reason to rush anything when it came to our relationship. I had a feeling that we would be together forever. God had sent him to me in a moment of pure despair. *He was sent to me.* I felt so loved by my creator that he would give me such a gift.

On the drive home from church, I couldn't stop the smile that stayed plastered on my face. Collin had taken his own car to church so that he could go into work afterwards. So it was just Caleb and me.

"I feel different, lighter somehow. It's weird, but in a good way." I wasn't really speaking to anyone, but I wanted to say it out loud. Caleb grabs my hand and holds it tightly but has to release it when his phone rings.

"Hello." I tune him out not wanting to intrude on his phone call. It doesn't take long for him to end it though, and when I look at him he seems worried.

"What is it Caleb?" He grips the steering wheel tighter

making his knuckles turn white.

"They searched the hotel were Julie and her boyfriend were staying." He swallows hard. "They found some pictures; mostly of you. They were all recent from the last few months."

"What does that mean?" I ask him.

"That's not all, Katy. Some of the pictures were of you in New York."

"What? How is that possible?" I whisper as chills run down my spine and end in my toes prickling every single natural alarm system my body holds. This isn't right. I can only come to one conclusion and I don't like it. "Do you think my mom was in New York?"

"I don't know. That's what they are trying to figure out. I hope it was her because the alternative is making me extremely angry, and that's not a feeling I have been familiar with for a very long time." His jaw twitches from how tightly closed his mouth is.

This is definitely a side of Caleb that I haven't seen. Attempting to cool him down, I rest my hand on the back of his neck and start drawing slow circles. His grip on the steering wheel loosens making me feel slightly better, but I know the alternative that he is talking about.

"You think the boyfriend has been following me?"

"I want to say no. Maybe your mom *was* in New York? I told Officer Sommer that we would meet him at the station. He wants to speak with you." We sit in silence the rest of the way to the station with my hand tightly wrapped in Caleb's.

The station is busy. People are rushing in and out as the loud rumble of the police scanner goes off every few seconds alerting to another crime. I notice Mike standing at the front desk and start to ask why but Caleb answers me before I even ask the question.

"I asked Mike to meet us here. We did the research on

your mom together. I think he has some new information that the police don't have." He's holding a manila envelope stuffed under his jacket covered arm.

"Hi Katy." He greets me. His eyes look a little sad beneath the black and blue from his run in with Claude.

"How are you feeling?" I ask Mike. He nods his head once.

"I'm fine. It only hurts a little. Looks worse than it is though."

I turn and watch as Officer Sommer is making his way to us from the hallway. I close my eyes and pray to God that whatever he has to say, it will be good news. But when he leads us to an interrogation room and Hank, my doorman from New York, is sitting at the table my stomach drops.

Seeing Hank takes me back to that night in the stairwell in New York. Shock overrides my ability to walk forward so I stop and stare for a moment. Hank doesn't even look up at me. Some of those old feelings that I endured as I thought I was going to lose my innocence, or even my life, tried to push their way to the surface. But there is a force in me that quickly pushes it away. Instead, I walk over and sit across from Hank who is still avoiding eye contact with me.

Caleb pulls up a chair next to me and Officer Sommer sits at the end of the table while Mike stands at the door revealing his private security side. There are books scattered on the table with pictures of mug shots. Caleb hands over the manila envelope to Officer Sommer. He opens it and pulls out a stack of papers and starts skimming through them.

Caleb clears his throat, becoming impatient. Officer Sommer looks up at Caleb with annoyance, but then his attention drifts to me.

"Katy. We've apprehended your mom." I sit up straight in my chair waiting as my mouth hangs open. "She returned to the hotel where she was staying with Claude. She had been badly beaten." I tense and Caleb starts rubbing my back soothingly. It didn't matter what she had done, I didn't want her hurt.

"They took her to the hospital for her injuries but have her heavily gaurded. Now, with that out of the way," He says it like it doesn't matter that someone has been beaten. I want to know more about it but he continues. "I need for you to verify something for me about the events that happened three months ago while you were visiting New York. I have asked Mr. Dressler," he says pointing to Hank, "if he would be willing to come down here to help us out. Would you like for me to ask anyone to leave the room before I continue?"

"I'm not so comfortable discussing this in front of everyone. Obviously Hank already knows and you do as well, but it's not something that I want others to know about."

I hear the door open and close, so my attention turns in that direction. Mike has left the room. But I was referring to the two sided glass.

"Do you want me to leave?" Caleb asks. Yes is right on the tip of my tongue, because I don't want him to know these dirty details. When I think about it I feel sick. But I have to remember that I have moved on from this. I can't let my past control me. Caleb already knows what happened.

"No, don't leave," I tell Caleb. Looking at Officer Sommer, I say, "Is there anyone on the other side of the glass?"

"No. We are not interrogating anyone so no one needs to be there," he says. I feel relieved as I turn back to Caleb and he gives me a reassuring smile.

There are a lot of things that I want with Caleb, and trust is one of them. Not only that, but I feel like even if he knew all of the details it won't change the way he feels.

I can tell that it feels like a small triumph when he puts

his arm around my shoulders and pulls me in for a quick kiss.

"Don't worry. I'm not going anywhere," he whispers.

I turn my gaze back to Officer Sommer.

"What do you need to know?" He clears his throat then begins.

"Did you know that the man who had been accused of your attempted rape was let go on bail?" I gasp as the implication of his words knocks the wind out of me.

"No. I thought they had to keep me informed of all that? No one has gotten in touch with me. How? Why? It-"

"There was an error, and he was given bail. He didn't return for his court date, and fled the state. The officer in New York had been looking for him for a while without any luck. He came across a video surveillance tape from a gas station where a man had been attacked by someone who fit his description. We thought that he was still in New York until he resurfaced here."

I felt sick as I put my head on the table and take in deep breaths. I don't let panic take over. Instead—I pray.

"This can't be happening, it just can't be."

Looking up at the officer, he places two pictures in front of me. One is of my attacker, and the other is Claude. They are two very clear pictures, side by side, and I can see that my attacker and Claude...are one in the same. I shake my head.

"He didn't look the same when I saw him with my mom. He had facial hair, but in New York he didn't have that."

"Claude is wearing a disguise. The beard he has is not real," Officer Sommer says to me.

"Someone made a stupid mistake." I hear Caleb say. He is beyond mad.

"Mr. Mathews, I can assure you that it is being handled. The people involved are being reprimanded accordingly. Obviously, he was not supposed to be released due to the nature of his crime."

"In the meantime, Katy is a sitting duck," Caleb sighs his anger dissipating a little.

"We brought Mr. Dressler in to identify when necessary. Mr. Dressler confirmed that it was the same man and now you have too, so there is no mistaking his identity at this point. Mr. Dressler has asked to speak with you, Katy."

I remember Hank coming to visit me in the hospital. But I was too embarrassed, and yes, a little upset that he had left his post. The anger I felt then didn't rear its ugly head today.

"I'm so sorry, Katy. I'm so sorry." For the first time Hank looks at me and my heart twists. How long had he been tormented by this? His eyes were swollen from...crying. He had been sitting here silently crying while we were talking. I wanted to take that tortured look off this aged man's face.

Getting up from my seat, I walk around to him and wrap my arms around his shoulders. Giving him what he needs—forgiveness. I felt like I was releasing something. Maybe the forgiveness wasn't just for Hank. Maybe it was for me too.

"I'm fine, Hank. I'm fine. I'm sorry that I didn't tell you that sooner. It wasn't your fault." His body shakes almost uncontrollably and a sob breaks from his lips as he tries to talk.

"My wife, she's dying. She called me because she thought someone was in the house." Sobs are ripping through him making it hard for me to understand. "She's bedridden. I left for forty-five minutes to check it out for her." He looks into my eyes pleading with me. "Forty-five minutes Katy, I was gone for forty-five minutes. I heard you as I was doing my checks. I opened the stairwell door, and I heard the scuffle. Oh, I'm so sorry," he sobs. "It took too long to get to you. My old legs, they just don't work they way they use to." He didn't know what he did for me. I had to tell him.

"Hank, you saved me that night. If you hadn't shown up when you did-" I close my eyes trying hard not to think about what may have happened if Hank hadn't shown up. "You saved me," I whisper gently.

We sit there for a long time waiting for Hank to come to the realization that I have forgiven him.

I invite him to get some coffee with me in the morning, but he declines so he can get back to his wife. He hugs me and says goodbye. Tells me not to be a stranger, that I should come back to New York sometime. I wish him luck and tell him that I will pray for him and his wife.

Something I heard in church this morning comes back to me, as I watch Hank walk away. The pastor was preaching and he said, "There is something redeeming about forgiveness. Christ forgave all of us of our sins. When He did; it gave us new life and new hope for the future. How do you feel about being forgiven for everything that you have done in the past?" I remember feeling free to move on in my relationship with Christ now that my past was no longer holding me back. "Forgiveness is not only for you." The pastor continued. "It can be redemption for the person you have forgiven. Hasn't God called us to disciple for Him? Should we sit on the sidelines and hold onto our pride? Or should we face our fears and step forward in our relationship with Christ...while bringing someone with us."

That was when I walked up to the cross and dropped to my knees. I asked God to come into my life because I was a sinner and I knew it. One person's forgiveness can help another person find redemption in Christ.

After Hank left, Officer Sommer pulls out another file. I was still reeling from the news that the guy who had tried to rape me was released on bail, fled the state, then showed up where I live hundreds of miles away with my mother. He was here, and it had to be because of me. What he wanted from me, I didn't know; but it probably wasn't anything that I wanted to find out.

Thumbing through the stack, Officer Sommer pulls out a sheet and hands it to me.

"Your mother was in New York when you were there. She's not talking, but that seems to be where Claude and your mother met. This is an invoice from a stolen credit card she charged. Do any of the highlighted places look familiar to you?" As I studied the statement I could see that there were several places that I was familiar with.

There was a charge for the musical I went to see, a restaurant I ate at, the coffee shop down the street from where I was staying- the one that I met Amber at every morning.

None of this made sense to me. I wish that I could get in her head and figure out what she was thinking when she made the choice to be an alcoholic and drug addict instead of love her kids. I wish I knew why she chose to say nasty things to me, and why she decided that she would ruin Grandma's garden. But I also understood that I wouldn't always understand everything in life. I have to trust that what happens, happens for a reason.

"Why would she follow me?" It's just a thought in my head that I say out loud. I don't expect to be answered but Caleb speaks up.

"She's not herself half the time, and most of what she does isn't going to make sense because of her mental instability, but from what you've told me she probably has an unhealthy obsession with you."

"But why?"

"You have things that she didn't. Your grandma, her house, all of her things, money, a life Katy. You have a life. A good one, and for someone who is mentally unstable it could seem to them that you have it all, and she may even think that you took that from her." Sitting back in his chair a look of realization passes over his face. "Jake, Madison, and

Cassy are in your life too. I'm sure she found some way to blame you for her inability to love her kids."

I can see how she may have thought these things, but she made those choices and they ultimately led her to where she is now. She was never a good mother, and all these years I thought she didn't want me or disliked me so much that she would choose my safety and my company as the last thing.

The same question that I had been asking myself for years perks up; why was I unlovable? But I wasn't unlovable; she was just unable to love. I think I have to accept that.

"So you think she is jealous?" I ask Caleb.

"Could be, but there is no use trying to get inside someone's head, especially if it's as disturbed as these files say she is." Stacking the papers up, he slides them back into the manila envelope. "I'll take you home. We'll hang out there tonight so I can keep an eye on you and we'll let the police handle the rest." He leans forward and grabs my face. "He can't be far. They will get him."

The drive home is short, and I notice Caleb constantly looking in the rear view mirror. It's starting to make me nervous. Every time he looks I want to ask him if he sees anything. I don't, because I think he is trying to be subtle. I turn and face out the window leaning my head against the cold glass until Caleb clears his throat. Looking at him, I wait.

"I asked Mike to research the kid's father today." I sit up and lean in.

"You did?" I can feel the slow smile expand across my face it seems out of place for the situation that is surrounding us. My smile dims a little when I think about Caleb and his father. Every time he has tried to call his father he doesn't answer or hangs up on him when he does answer. And every time I can see the hurt in his eyes. I've only been witnessing it for four months; he's had to deal with that for years. "Maybe you should write him a letter?" I say quietly.

Taking a quick glance at me, Caleb nods his head knowing exactly what I am talking about.

"That's a good idea. I think I'll do that." The smile returns as I slip my arms around his right arm and hug it. He is such a good man. His father should know that.

I am so happy to be home.

As Caleb taps the numbers into the alarm system, I yawn. It's gotten late. All the lights are out in the house which means that Collin is working late. The sun is starting to drop behind the horizon as night falls. We spent eight hours at the station and I am so exhausted even though the clock in the kitchen only reads seven. I hang my purse and jacket in the closet. Caleb starts to take his off but his phone rings.

"It's Mike. I'm just going to step right out on the front porch. Okay?"

"Okay," I say through another yawn. I put my hand over my mouth to hide the yawn. He gives my hand a quick kiss through my yawn and steps out, closing the door behind him.

I head to my bedroom to shower and change. I haven't heard from Faye yet, so I take my phone out and step into my room, flipping on the lights. I start to dial but remember that she told me she'd be with her study group till nine so I forget the phone call to check my voicemail instead.

I have one message from Faye. I listen to the message as I enter my closet and head straight to the back forgetting the light. I've done this a million times. I know right where my pajamas are.

Faye is sobbing into the phone. "I can't believe he did this to me, Katy. Call me I need to talk to you." I delete the message and use the glow from my phone to grab a pair of pajamas at the back of the closet.

What is going on with her? Faye never cries so her

distraught is mine as I can think about nothing but calling her back.

As I reach down to grab a pair of socks out of the bottom drawer, I hear a noise by the closet door. And that's when I realize that Kane didn't greet us when we came in. Where was he?

When I was little this closet used to scare me because it was so big. As I got older, I also got over that fear. But the sound I hear coupled with the smell, made my blood run cold. I could hear heavy breathing, and the pungent smell of alcohol came rushing over me. Standing at the back of my closet I can't see anything but the glow from my room at the entrance, so I hold the phone out in front of me to light up the area around where I am, my hand shaking uncontrollably.

There is no way someone got in, the alarm was set. Maybe I'm hearing things. To rectify that thought, I turn the phone toward the noise that has disappeared. Maybe it's Collin. I hope he hasn't gotten drunk again. But when I shine the light in the direction of the noise, I freeze as Claude's face is illuminated.

Before I can do anything, he lunges forward covering my mouth with his big sweaty hand. I thrash my arms, my legs, everything just so I can try to get away, but he is stronger, he is always stronger.

"You think you're real smart," he seethes. The fumes from the liquor he must have been drinking is so strong, it almost knocks me unconscious. "I'm going to make you wish I had killed you in New York," he says. It sends a chill down my spine.

I continue to thrash and move due to the insurmountable fear I feel. As he leans forward putting his nose on my collar bone and inhales, bile rises up into my throat and into my mouth. The squealing noises I am making sound weak even to me, but it's the only sound I can make, and something is better than nothing.

When he pushes a knife to my throat, I stop and close

my eyes. Stop squealing for mercy, stop thrashing around, and wait for him to slice into me.

I close my eyes and pray to God and thank him for the life he has given me. For bringing such beautiful people into it to teach me and guide me; Collin, Grandma, Faye, Caleb. *I love him*, I think.

He must still be outside talking on the phone because my closet is on the other side of the living room wall. He would have heard the struggle. Thinking about Caleb, all the moments we have spent together play through my mind, but one stands out more than any of the others.

We were in his studio and he was laughing because I couldn't successfully knock the weapon out of his hand as he held it to my throat. He was trying to teach me to disable someone in this exact situation. After at least ten tries, I finally put the right amount of pressure on his hand and twisted it in the right direction to disarm him. I was so excited to have been able to do it that I threw myself into his arms. My eyes fly open as I remember the movements, the pressure point in his wrist, and the direction of the twist.

I quickly bring my knee up, and with a loud grunt, I stomp as hard as I can on his foot. Then I pull my left arm back and elbow him in his gut. When he loosens his grip on my neck I grab his wrist and turn right gliding easily under his arm as I bring his wrist palm up toward the ceiling causing him to drop the knife. At the same time, I thrust my knee him as hard as I can into his groin. He doubles over in pain as I stand up defensively putting my arms out in front of me, waiting for another attack.

I start yelling Caleb's name. I don't turn my back on him, and I can't get out of there because he is standing in front of the closet door. He gains his ground back much quicker than I had anticipated.

"You ain't getting off that easy," he says grunting. "You're coming with me, and when I get you-" I don't let him finish as he tries to reach for me again with his right hand.

I move back to avoid him, and push his elbow as hard as I can toward the ground causing him to spin out of my closet and into my room. I'm guessing the alcohol set his balance off as he crashes to the floor. He groans and gets up on a knee. He just won't stay down. I prepare for another attack as I move into my room when Caleb bursts through the door looking panicked.

I take my eyes off Claude for a second, but that's all he needs as he grabs my ankles and I fall on my back, the force of it knocking the wind out of me as my head slams into the floor. The ache in my head is almost unbearable as I lose sight of what is happening.

The last thing I remember is hearing a scuffle, and then Caleb's voice as I groan and try to get back up.

"Moving is not a good idea right now, but I won't leave your side. Don't worry, it's just you and me," he says. I feel the pressure of his lips on my forehead.

I want to rejoice in the fact that this is finally over, but it's not and that's life. There will always be a battle whether it is in your head or in your physical life. The dark is always there to take you on, but you have to find a light in the dark to be able to pull yourself out. Without the light there is no hope, there is no redemption, and there is no mercy. Luckily, I have found the light.

Spots blind me as history repeats itself and the dark takes me, but I'm not scared.

Epilogue

Caleb
Two Weeks Later

"What are you doing?" The most beautiful smile flits over her face, and lights up the entire room causing my heart to beat erratically. She's been doing that since the moment I saw her in that diner five-and-a-half months ago. The moment I saw her sitting across the room crying with an emotionless expression on her face. I don't know what pulled me, but I assume it was a power much bigger than anything I had ever known.

It was when I got closer that I saw she wore my mother's necklace. The necklace that I had pawned at twelve because I had been so furious with her for leaving me the way she did. My father had not been too thrilled about that, and nothing between us had ever been the same.

After writing him a letter; surprisingly he called me. Katy and I went over to visit him last week. After a few very tense moments and conversation, he was still being stubborn. How many times did I have to say I'm sorry? He didn't hate me, but he couldn't forgive me for how I acted after Mom died. He felt that forgiving me was condoning it.

Katy brought us together again as she showed my dad that love was forgiving. Forgiving me didn't mean that he was okay with it, it just meant that he wouldn't let it determine our relationship. She was blunt, but it was what he needed to hear. I was a lost boy that needed some guidance after my mother had taken her own life. We still had a ways to go, but talking was a start.

I thank God for the moment I met Katy that day in Mel's diner. I had felt like the air had been knocked out of me as my whole body got swept away in her beautiful green eyes that glistened with tears. I learned years ago, after my brother's murder, that what is already written for our lives, will be if the path you are traveling down is the right one. So I didn't second guess myself, as I sat down in that booth across from her even though she hadn't wanted me to. That moment brought us to where we are today.

"I thought I would just check on her again," Katy says. That's what I love so much about her; she has come so far from that broken, lifeless girl I met that day. I knew I would meet her again because our lives were destined to intertwine. Wrapping my arms around her, the feel of her warm body against mine, relaxes me.

"You are supposed to be taking it easy. I don't think that traveling every day is taking it easy." Kissing her cheek she leans into me and looks up into my eyes.

"I've got you to hold me up. I won't fall." She is right about that, I will never let her fall.

As we stand here leaning against the door frame to her mother's room, I am in awe of her. Her grace, her beauty, and her heart. It was once obscured, tainted, and fractured, but we know that it can be healed over time through God's mercy.

Spending a week in the hospital with her going in and out of consciousness made me realize that I needed to say out loud what was on my mind. Who was I to stand in the way of what was already written in the stars? Kissing her lips so gently, she sighs in contentment.

"Katy," I start, "you are the missing piece to the puzzle that is my life. There is nothing I wouldn't do for you even if it is throwing myself in front of danger to make sure that you are okay." Reaching up, I put my hand gently on her beautiful, soft skin, and look into eyes that are filled with hope and love. "I love you," I say to her. The words hang in the air for only a moment, as she closes her eyes like she has been waiting to hear me say those words for far too long. When she opens them she looks right through me and shatters my world with her reply.

"Love is not a grand enough word for what we have, but there is absolutely nothing in this world that can describe how I feel for you. So for now, while we are here, I will say that I love you, and I will mean it every single day; until forever."

I hug her tightly and let her go, let her do what it is that I know she is meant to do. She is not meant for love; she *is* love. It radiates from her like a beacon. Anyone who is lucky enough to know her, will be touched by it.

Without hesitation, she walks out of my arms and into her mother's room. I trail behind her wanting to be her support, but also wanting to be there if she needs me. Her mother doesn't even look toward her she just stares at the ceiling with a blank expression on her face.

Katy puts her hand over her mothers and pulls up a chair next to her bed. Julie doesn't move, but her eyes are open, and the nurse said that she is now taking her medicine again. So I know that she understands every word Katy says.

"Hi Mom." Katy grabs the tube of balm from the side table and rubs some into the back of Julie's hand while she talks to her about the weather. Julie never moves, never responds in anyway, and Katy never talks about anything personal.

Katy's mom has been in shock from the blood loss she endured. She had been hit so forcefully in the head that there was a hole. When she saw the wound she passed out and woke up like she is now. Even though the doctors say she should be responsive she hasn't done much of anything but blink. I'm beginning to think that being mute is voluntary.

Katy has visited every day for the last week trying to get her out of this shocked state. The doctor said that it was the best thing for her to have family of some sort talking to her.

Jake, Cassy, and Madison didn't want to come up and see Julie. It would take time for them to heal their relationship with their mother; if that was in the plan.

They were at the Academy temporarily. Mike found their father in a rehabilitation facility. He hadn't wanted to give his kids up, but he was an alcoholic and thought about their safety only when he turned them over to the state. He was doing well, and visited the kids often at the Academy. He wasn't ready to get them back yet, but one day he would be. I had hope.

As Katy sit's here with her mother, tending to her needs, even after what she has done, that hope rises in me again. Today is different though. I can see it in Katy's eyes.

She leans down and whispers three simple words that are so hard to say, because I have been on the giving and the receiving end of them. Three simple words that could be Julie's redemption. *I forgive you.*

~~~

Acknowledgements

There is no way to know in advance what journey lies ahead of you. So when I decided to write my very first novel, and publish it for the whole world to read, my first thought was, *I'm on my own*. That was not the case at all. Because, for one, God is with me. He is always with me, and I could never get anywhere in life without His grace and mercy. There were many nights and days that I spent working on this book. My husband, Doug, was amazing as I would lock myself in the office and tap out the words on my laptop. I love that man dearly. My kids, Christopher and Matthew, they make the world go around. There are so many people that God has placed in my life that have helped me along the way. Not just with this novel, but also with life in general. My grandma. She was truly a blessing in my life and taught me some great things while she raised me. I love that woman dearly and miss her, but she is at peace and that puts my mind at ease. Aunt Barb; your encouragement gives me the power to continue on in many things. I love you for that. My family; I love you guys no matter what. Makaela Hall for being a willing participant in the making of this beautiful cover. Pam Bell for taking such amazing pictures of Makaela and making me realize how precious all of God's gift are, through picture. Mia from Serenity for doing an amazing job with hair and make-up. Heather Holland Hall, Lynda Holland, Tara Moore Ocepek, Sandy Lewallen; all of these people were essential in the writing and publishing of this book in some way. Whether it was reading an unfinished copy or encouraging me. I also want to thank you—the reader. You are amazing, you are loved. Thank you...thank you...thank you.

God bless.

Follow Faye and Collin's journey in book two of
The Redemption Series

Reckless Heart
Coming in 2014

www.ingramcontent.com/pod-product-compliance
Lightning Source LLC
Chambersburg PA
CBHW020345180626
46812CB00001B/347